The Weaver's Allotment

by

Lyn Dyson

Cover Image: A Chartist cottage

This style of bungalow was the model for the Chartist Land Movement estates, and although this illustration is of a different property at Snig's End, the cottages at Lowbands were all built to this specification.

The illustration has been reproduced from an original, printed in the Illustrated London News c1850, and is from the author's personal collection.

Acknowledgements

With thanks to Keira Michelle Telford for setting up the book for publication, to Gaile Bishop for proofreading, to Mark Crail for permission to reproduce his article on Feargus O'Connor, and to University of Nottingham Manuscripts and Special Collections for permission to use their photograph of Feargus O'Connor.

Author's Note

Lowbands was one of five locations involved in the Chartist Land Scheme. The scheme was the brainchild of Feargus O'Connor, and its aim was to resettle factory workers on the land and reduce unemployment in the industrial areas.

The Chartist Co-operative Land Society was founded in 1845. Workers bought shares in the Society and were then eligible to take part in the ballot for allotments. The first estate purchased by the Society was at Heronsgate, near Watford, in 1846. This was closely followed by Lowbands and Snigs End, near Gloucester, Charterville near Minster Lovell, and Great Dodford near Bromsgrove in 1848. Plans to purchase a further estate at Mathon, near Malvern, fell through because of the financial and legal difficulties the Company was in by 1848.

The Society changed its name to the National Co-operative Land Company in December 1846, but the new company could still not satisfy the requirements of either the Joint Stock Companies Act 1844, or the Benefit Societies Act. The Company was declared illegal following an enquiry by the Parliamentary Select Committee.

The Company was finally wound up by Act of Parliament in 1851 and management of the estates was handled by the Court of Chancery.

The allottees were given the opportunity to continue to rent their allotments, but failure to pay the required rent for a year would result in repossession. Allottees wishing to relinquish their land could do so and claim compensation for any losses incurred.

The Lowbands estate was finally sold at public auction in 1858. The tenants' rights were protected in perpetuity.

The cottages are still standing, extended and modernised; the allotments are for the most part still intact. They serve as a monument to one man's vision of a better world.

That man, Feargus O'Connor emerged from the collapsed Land Movement, a broken man. By 1852 he was living in neglect and poverty, his mental health suffering. Allottees and former members of the Movement set up a fund to ensure that he was not in absolute poverty. However he was admitted to a hospital for the insane in Chiswick in June of that year.

He died 30th August 1854.

On 10th September 1854 his funeral at Kensal Green Cemetery was attended by between 30,000 and 40,000 working people. In heavy rain they formed a long procession behind his coffin, carrying banners inscribed, "He died for us."

Lyn Dyson
April 2021

Prologue

August 1847

"No, ROB. I CANNOT COME WITH YOU."

Elizabeth Berrow sat, back straight and lips compressed, her heart beating rapidly as she waited for her husband's reaction.

He stared at her dumbly, feeling certain that he must have misheard her. A frown formed upon his brow and he pulled his hands through his hair.

"What do you mean?" he whispered at last.

Elizabeth sighed. "What more can I say, Rob? I have thought about nothing else these past few months and I cannot come with you."

"But why not?"

She shrugged her shoulders. "I don't know. I just don't feel that it would be the right thing to do, I suppose. It seems the height of folly to pack up all our belongings, leave our own home, our friends, and everything that has been our life up until now. It is too much to ask of me, Rob. I will not do it. And neither do I think it would be the best thing for Jenny."

"I don't believe this!" Rob cried out. "You can't know what you are talking about! What good can we do Jenny here? What sort of life can she expect? It is partly for her that I contemplated this venture in the first place. She is five years old now, and already she is working six hours a day. Before long she will be working as long as you and I."

"No, she will not! I won't permit it. Besides many children her age work much more than she does. Jenny is lucky she does not have to do more. When I was her age I was already working ten hours a day threading bobbins. She doesn't do so badly."

"So, because you had to do it, it is all right for our daughter to be brought up as a slave to the factory masters, is it?"

"I have just said that I will see to it that she is not!"

Rob grunted in disbelief.

"In any event," continued Elizabeth, "I fail to see how by uprooting ourselves to go to work on the land things will be any better. How do you know you will not merely be exchanging one form of slavery for another? What do you know about farming, anyway?"

Rob sat down, temporarily defeated.

"Not much. I had thought that I could learn. It can't be that difficult to plant a few seeds and watch them grow. And it would be a much healthier life for all of us. Poor Jenny has little enough opportunity to play out in the sun. Most of her short life has been spent cooped up in this room; listening to the clatter of my loom and winding bobbins until she almost falls asleep over them. How can you suggest that life in the country will not have more to offer her than that?"

"I expect she would have to work there too. How can it be any better?"

"It will be a different kind of work, Liz. Can you not see that? Here we all slave all the hours God sends for a mere eight shillings a week. There we will be working to put food on the table. We'll eat our own crops, have our own hens to provide eggs, and a cow for milk. And the work will be so much healthier! Haven't you understood what it is all about?"

Liz shook her head. She hadn't understood at all why two shillings of their hard-earned wage had been paid every week to the Chartists for the past two years. She had begrudged the loss of that money each week; money which could have brought a little cheer into their bleak existence, and she had felt a burning hatred for the Chartist Land company and its leader Feargus O'Connor. As Rob's investment increased so too did her hatred, festering like an open wound within her, dragging her further and further apart from her husband until there seemed to be nothing but a deep void between them.

"I'll have nothing to do with it. If you want to go, then go you must. Jenny and I will stay here."

"You can't do that! You know it is not possible. How would you live? This is nonsense! If you do not come with me, then how can I go?"

Rob paced restlessly about the room, every muscle in his too thin body taut with nervous energy. He smashed his fist against the wall until the sampler, sewn by Liz in happier times, rattled against the bricks.

He was conscious of an overwhelming despair. It was as if all the hopes and dreams of a lifetime had been shattered in an instant. The exhilaration he had felt upon reading in the "Northern Star" in March that he had been a winner in the ballot for an allotment at Lowbands, the second colony to be set up by the Chartist movement's National Co-operative Land Company, had carried him through the succeeding months and remained with him until this very moment. Now all his hopes had been dashed because Liz would not go with him.

Desperately, he tried to calm the anger rising against her. For a moment his hands even itched to attach themselves to her neck and wring the life from her. Instead, he clenched his fists and thumped the wall again.

Finally he managed some semblance of calm.

"Why didn't you tell me before?" he asked at last, turning to her.

9

"Would it have made any difference?"

"Yes it would!" he shouted. "All the difference in the world! I would not have spent the past six months making plans; dreaming of how it will be! It is an opportunity I never really thought would come to me! A chance to escape from the fight against poverty! A chance of a better life, free from oppression. A chance to be my own man!" His voice dropped to little more than a whisper. "It is a chance for us, Liz," he added, kneeling beside her and taking her hands in his own.

"I know I have not always been a good husband to you, and recently we have drifted further apart. Do you not think we could use this as a means to start over again?"

Liz stared at her husband, momentarily tempted by his obvious sincerity; but deep within her she knew that it was too late. Early in their marriage she would have welcomed the chance to embark upon a new life with Rob, but whatever feelings she had for him then had died when he had turned his attentions to the Chartist cause. She could pinpoint the exact moment when the rift had begun. It had been early in the year of 1842 when he had stopped and listened to "The General" addressing his followers one Sunday evening. He had come home bright eyed and excited; almost feverish in his enthusiasm. She had been heavily awaiting the birth of Jenny, and had been too weary to share in his excitement. Rob failed to notice her discomfort and as the days passed, Liz became more withdrawn until Rob was totally immersed in the Shakespearean Brigade of Leicester Chartists. All his non- working time, which was little enough, was spent in attending meetings, learning to read and write, and attending lectures given by Thomas Cooper, "The General". There had been no time for her and scant attention had been paid to their daughter when she finally arrived in the spring of 1842.

She withdrew her hands from his and stood up, staring out of the large window of the cottage, to the narrow street outside, gloomy now in the gathering dusk.

"You don't really want to start over again, Rob. I know when I am beaten. You have not wanted me for a long time now. I know that I take second place to "The General". I'm tired of it. I don't think we could ever bring back what we once had. It is gone for ever, and time we both realised it."

Rob frowned. "This is nonsense, Liz. I know there has not been much time recently. But my work has been more important than us. I thought you understood that!"

She shook her head. "No, Rob. I never understood it at all. What possible difference could it make whether you have the right to vote? No-one will ever take any notice of us! All this education and learning long words that mean nothing to me won't make any difference. They'll find some way to see to that. The rich will always be powerful and the working man will still have to slave all day for a pittance. It is the way it has always been, and nothing you can do will change that, Rob. You are wasting your time, and you have sacrificed too much to it. I will not be the sacrificial lamb any longer. I want no more of it."

"I cannot give it up, Liz. I have worked too hard in the Movement to give it up. Someone has to fight, and there are thousands of us up and down the country seeking reform. There has to be more to life than this. What kind of existence is it for us and for our children?"

"It would have been a better existence for me and Jenny if you had spent more time at home with us, rather than gallivanting back and forth to your meetings and getting so much learning that I hardly recognise you. You don't even speak the way you used to. Sometimes I think that you and the man I married are totally different people! And if you had not spent so much time with your books, and your new friends, maybe you would have been able to work a little harder and bring home more of a wage than we have seen. It wouldn't have been so bad if you had kept what you had earned. That would have made a difference! Just how much have you paid to this wretched land company?"

11

Rob stared at his wife, aware for the first time how strongly she felt against the Movement which had formed the centre of his existence for the past five years. Never before had she voiced her opposition to him. Instead, he realised, she had bottled up her frustration behind a wall of silence until all communication between them had virtually gone.

"Why did you not tell me before that you felt this way?" he whispered at last.

Liz sighed. "Nothing would have changed."

Rob sat down on the chair Liz had recently vacated and stared in front of him.

"What are we to do?" he asked quietly, the enormity of the gulf between them apparent to him for the first time.

Liz shrugged. "I don't know. I only know that I have given up enough for your cause and I don't intend to give up anything else. How much has it cost us, this cottage in the country?"

"Ten pounds."

"Do you own it?"

Rob shook his head. "I shall have to pay rent to the Land Company. So far as I understand it I shall be a tenant of the Company."

"So what is the difference between that and what we have now? You have paid ten pounds for nothing as far as I can see."

"No, Liz. I have paid ten pounds for a new way of life. It is like paying ten pounds for my freedom. You still don't see it, do you?"

"No. I don't think I ever would, Rob."

"Do you want me to sell my interest?" he asked dully, feeling his dreams slip away from him.

Liz turned and stared at him thoughtfully.

"Would you?" she asked quietly. "Would you do that?"

"You do not leave me with much choice, do you?"

"Oh, I see. You will give it up for me, but spend the rest of your life blaming me for your lost opportunity. No, Rob, I don't think I could bear that either."

"What other choice is there? You will not come with me, yet you do not want me to stay. I warn you, Liz, there is no way that I can afford to keep you here if I go."

"Well maybe there is no need for you to keep me. Let's face it we have nothing to offer each other, have we? You want to buy your freedom for ten pounds. Well, why don't you buy mine too?"

"I don't understand. What do you mean?" Rob asked, frowning.

"Oh, Rob, you ever were the innocent! I can make my own way as well as you. You give me half of what we have and I will make no further claim upon you. Doesn't that sound like a reasonable bargain?"

"No it does not! How long do you think it would last you? How would you pay the rent? Don't be silly, Liz. I never heard of anything so ridiculous! You are my wife! I can't just leave you to fend for yourself. Whether we like it or not, I am responsible for you and Jenny. I can't just walk out on you."

"Has it never occurred to you that I might not want to be your responsibility? There are things that I want to do with my life, Rob. I have my dreams too, you know."

"But what are they? You talk of pursuing dreams, but you don't say how you can do it, or what those dreams are. Come on, Liz! I need to know."

Liz eyed him thoughtfully, wondering how much to tell and how much to leave out. Was it fair to burden him with the consequences of his own neglect of her? Did she want to send him away with the loss of his idealism, or did she owe him something?

She sighed. They had after all felt something for each other once, and Rob had always meant well.

"No. It must be a clean break, Rob. No questions; no explanations. Suffice it to say that I can be happy without you and this is what I want. Well, is it a bargain?"

"No!" cried Rob. "This is madness, Liz. There must be some other way!"

"Believe me I have thought of nothing else this past six months, Rob; and there is no other way."

He put his head in his hands wearily, realising for the first time how much he had failed as a husband. He supposed that he had loved her once, when they were young. Or had they ever been young and carefree? What had happened to them to bring them to this? Surely there had been something between them in the beginning. Had it been love? If so, where had it gone?

If he were honest he knew that it had gone very soon after their marriage. It was true that he had devoted all his energies to Chartism, but that was only because he had found some void in his life which needed filling. Not that he blamed Liz. She, after all, had not changed suddenly when they had wed. Neither did he blame Jenny who had put in her appearance some seven months after the wedding, so big and bonny that no-one could be deceived into believing that she was a seven month baby. No, he realised that if anyone had changed it had been him. Maybe he had not been ready for the responsibilities of marriage and a family. Maybe he and Liz had not known each other well enough to embark upon a lifetime of matrimonial harmony. One quick urgent coming together was not much of a base on which to build a marriage.

No, he knew that he did not love Liz; maybe had never done so. She had been the object of a fleeting desire, soon regretted; and although he had done his best, it had not been enough for him; or for her, apparently.

He stared ahead thoughtfully. Liz was offering a way out for both of them. Could he accept it and walk out to a new life? What did his future hold if he did not?

He stood up.

"What about Jenny?" It was a token resistance.

"What about her? She will stay with me, of course."

"How will you support her?"

"I told you, Rob. No questions! Jenny will be fine with me. You have never taken much notice of her anyway."

It was true. Maybe his daughter had been the visual reminder of a moment's folly. He did love her, but in a passive uncommitted way.

"Are you sure everything will be all right?"

Liz nodded. "Of course it will. It will be for the best, Rob; believe me."

He sighed. "Very well; if that is what you want."

As soon as the words were spoken it was as if a great weight had been lifted from them. Liz turned to her husband and smiled. Dimly he realised how long it had been since she had looked happy. He smiled ruefully, and held out his hand to her, to seal the bargain.

"If you should change your mind, you know where to find me," he said in a final magnanimous gesture.

She nodded. "Yes, I know; but I shall not be needing you now, Rob. You can go to your Lowbands without a care in the world. I do wish you good fortune. I hope that it brings you all you want."

He shrugged his shoulders. "Maybe I am clutching at straws. But it's something I feel I must do."

"I know. When do you leave?"

"So anxious to get rid of me?" he enquired with a wry grin.

"No," she responded unable to prevent a note of uncertainty. "It is just that now that we have made the decision I can't help thinking that we should act upon it before we change our minds."

"Yes, but I cannot go without saying good-bye to Jenny."

"No, of course not. But I don't know how we are going to explain it all to her. She won't be able to understand; and I don't know why it should be, but she does seem to idolise you. Maybe it would be best to tell her you are going away for a while and will be back sometime. Children have short memories, and she will soon forget you, so little has she seen of you."

Rob sighed, but could not argue with her. It was a sad reflection upon his life that his daughter would so easily forget that she had ever had a father.

15

"I may as well go tomorrow, then. I need to be at Lowbands by the sixteenth of this month for the settlement. I had intended to go by train, but I could save the fare and walk."

Liz nodded, her eyes unusually bright now that the final moment had come. On an impulse she put her arms about his neck and kissed his cheek. For a moment their eyes held, and something from the past stirred them.

"Are you sure it has to be this way?" he whispered.

Liz nodded. "Absolutely sure, Rob."

He put his hand to her cheeks, and stared at her.

"I'm sorry, Liz, that I have been such a poor husband and father."

Liz smiled. "I suppose it wasn't all your fault and if we are being honest, I have to admit that I've not been much of a wife either. It was all a big mistake, and far better that we put it behind us once and for all."

Rob nodded.

"If I just take my clothes and leave everything here for you, do you think it would amount to ten pounds?"

Liz looked around the sparsely furnished room, dominated by Rob's loom, and sighed. What she could have done with that two shillings a week.

"I suppose so. It would be pointless for me to argue anyway, wouldn't it? There is nothing else."

Rob shook his head.

"Do you want me to help you to pack?"

"Thank you, but no; I think I can manage that for myself. It's not as if I have a vast wardrobe is it?"

Rob kissed her cool cheek and turned to climb the stairs. He looked in on Jenny, who slept peacefully; seeming even smaller and more vulnerable as she slept, her skin pale, made more so by the mass of dark curls upon the pillow.

He felt his heart lurch within his chest at the sight of his daughter, and he regretted that he hadn't spent more time with her, getting to know her better. Maybe deep down he had always known that this day would come, and he had been mentally preparing both of them for the inevitable parting.

He leaned down and kissed her cheek. The child sighed and stirred but didn't wake. Rob blinked quickly and stood up, surprised to find his cheek damp, and unable to recall any other occasion when he had been moved to tears.

He took one more look at his daughter and drew in a deep breath, turning to the bedroom he shared with Liz. The room was dominated by the large bed in which they had slept together, close but rarely joining. Liz's clothes were scattered about the bed and the one straight chair. The top of the dresser was filled with Liz's things; bottles of rose water and lavender water, brushes and combs, hair pins and ribbons. As he looked about the room he was surprised that there was so little evidence of his own presence. It was almost as if he had never belonged there.

He opened the cupboard and pulled out his Sunday best clothes. He folded the trousers carefully and wrapped them inside the frock-coat with his two shirts and a change of linen.

It took him but a minute to prepare for the long journey to Gloucestershire.

Chapter 1

JOHANNA SHIFTED EASILY IN THE SADDLE AND STOOD UP IN the stirrups to gain a better view. Although it was still quite early in the day, and promising to be wet, a substantial crowd had gathered already in the normally peaceful Gloucestershire countryside, for the inauguration of the second colony of the National Co-operative Land Company.

Johanna, along with the rest of the local population had known little about the Chartist land movement before Feargus O'Connor had bought the Lowbands estate at public auction. His sudden arrival within the community had caused quite a stir and when the extent of his scheme became known, local landowners had mounted a campaign of opposition. Undeterred, Feargus O'Connor had pursued his plans relentlessly, quickly becoming a familiar, if unwelcome, figure as he organised and supervised his workforce.

Now, all about her Johanna could see the results of those labours. The land had been divided into neat plots, some as small as two acres, others as large as four. On each plot there stood a small three roomed cottage; each with its central gable, identical to that of its neighbour.

A gate stood at each property with a path leading to the front door. The land on either side of each gate had been prepared, and neat rows of potatoes, turnips and swedes were already well established.

"Do you think we might take a look inside one of the cottages?" Johanna asked her companion at last. "I can't help but be intrigued by all this, having watched it appear almost from nothing."

Miles Woodthorpe looked about him and noted that all the activity seemed to be confined to the field at the opposite end of the estate. The cottages gave no sign of habitation.

"I don't see why not," he replied, dismounting and looping the horse's bridle to the gate post. He turned to Johanna and held out his arms to help her down. She jumped into them with ease, and turned quickly, knowing from recent experience that he would grasp the opportunity to hold her for longer than was strictly necessary.

Impatiently she pushed him from her and led the way down the garden path. He caught up with her and placed his arm about her shoulder in the easy confident manner which resulted from a longstanding relationship.

The front door opened easily and they found themselves in a good sized kitchen. There was a sink with a pump, and a black leaded stove, as yet unlit. A dresser stood against the wall, and a table with two chairs had been placed in the middle of the room. The red tiled floor was spotless.

"What a charming little kitchen!" Johanna couldn't resist saying. "It's far better than anything in my father's cottages."

Miles nodded. "Yes. Even the most radical landowners I know don't provide anything as pleasant as this for their tenants. I wonder what is through here?" He crossed the room and opened a door to his right. "Ah," he nodded with some satisfaction.

Johanna joined him and followed him through to the bedroom. It contained a generously sized bed with feather mattress and a small chest.

19

"Not bad at all," Miles commented as he sat upon the edge of the bed.

Johanna sat beside him, and bounced tentatively on the soft mattress.

"Yes, I could be quite comfortable here," she agreed, and before she could make any further comment, she found herself imprisoned in Miles' arms, his breath warm upon her cheek as his lips, soft and moist, searched for her mouth.

She gave herself up willingly to his kiss, which was at first gentle, but which grew gradually in intensity until it bore no resemblance to the chaste kisses they had been used to sharing when no-one was looking.

Johanna responded eagerly to Miles' probing tongue, but as the kiss deepened, a dart of fear fluttered within her, and she began to doubt that she would be able to keep Miles under control.

A part of her wanted to respond to the new sensations being thrust upon her. As Miles pushed her back upon the bed and eased himself on top of her, she could feel the impatient hardness of him, and she was uncertain how to deal with the sudden passion that had been aroused.

His ardour should not have come as a complete surprise to Jo. As close neighbours they had grown up together, and it was generally assumed that one day they would marry. However whilst their relationship had always been on a basis of friendly familiarity, it was only recently that Miles had begun to demand more.

She could feel her own resistance weakening, but as he raised his head from hers to transfer his attentions to her throat while his fingers moved to the buttons of her bodice, she managed to murmur a reluctant "No."

Her protest sounded feeble even to her own ears and when his mouth sought her breast she knew a momentary hesitation. Such a delicious sensation ran through her that she almost weakened. But as he fumbled with his breeches, reality returned and with it the knowledge that this was not what she wanted.

"No, Miles," she repeated more forcefully, trying to push him from her.

"It's no good, Johanna. It's too late to change your mind. You know that this is what I've wanted for a long time. You do too. You cannot deny it."

His lips moved enticingly across her breast, and Johanna groaned.

"Please, Miles. This must stop."

"Don't keep blowing hot and cold Johanna. There is nothing to worry about, believe me. I'm not going to hurt you," he murmured.

"No, Miles!" cried Johanna in growing alarm as he grasped her wrists and pinioned her to the bed, transferring his grip quickly to one hand, whilst the other searched urgently for the hem of her skirt.

Any doubts that Johanna had felt, either that she could control Miles' passion, or that she didn't want to control him were now banished. She knew without any shadow of doubt that she did not want him in this way. She screamed loudly, struggling furiously against him, knowing all the time that she could never match his strength.

Suddenly, when she thought that all was lost, she became aware of a new voice.

"I think, sir, that the lady is unwilling." It was a calm unruffled voice, with a hint of an accent, denoting that its owner was not a native of Gloucestershire.

Miles heard it too and immediately looked up, ceasing his attentions on Johanna, who quickly seized the opportunity to roll from beneath him on to the floor.

"Who the hell are you?" demanded Miles, aware that with his breeches about his knees he was somewhat awkwardly placed.

Rob Berrow eased himself from the door jamb on which he had been leaning, arms folded, and surveyed Miles coolly.

"This happens to be my house, and I don't recall inviting you in."

He glanced at the girl, her face flushed and her dark eyes flashing with relief at her narrow escape from some

21

unmentionable fate. She seemed unaware that her bodice still gaped wide open to reveal generous breasts. Quickly he returned his attention to the man, who was hastily pulling up his breeches.

Johanna watched Miles curiously, her attention focussed upon that part of his anatomy which he was at pains to keep hidden, and then she gave way to an irrepressible desire to laugh. It was too much to see the normally staid, sometimes even pompous Miles, in such an ignominious position.

"Oh, Miles, you do look funny!" she cried between giggles.

"Really Johanna! I don't see what there is to laugh about. This is a very awkward situation, and now that we have been caught out, so to speak, I don't think there is any solution but for us to name the date for our wedding as soon as possible."

Johanna's laughter immediately subsided. "What do you mean?" she whispered. "What are you talking about?"

Miles sighed heavily as if he were addressing a child with little understanding. "I am talking about our marriage, Johanna. We must make sure we arrange it at once, before word of this episode leaks out. If it did, both our reputations would be in shreds."

"Well I don't care!" she responded mutinously, her bottom lip pushed out. "I have no intention of getting married, Miles; not yet anyway. And I'm not at all sure that I want to marry you."

"Of course you do, Jo. You know that we deal well enough together. You can hardly blame me for getting a bit carried away. You know that I want you, and I don't think you were as unwilling as you pretend to be."

Johanna bit her lip, honest enough to admit that there had been some moments when she had been tempted.

"Well, so what? That doesn't mean I have to marry you! And I won't!"

Rob, whose presence had been overlooked during this discourse, decided to step in.

"If you fear that I shall say anything, then you may rest easy. Both of your reputations will be safe with me."

Johanna and Miles both stared at him, as if seeing him for the first time. Johanna nodded and flashed him a smile that set her dark curls dancing about her face. She got to her feet and blushed as she realised that her breasts were revealed to the admiring gaze of both of these men. Hastily she pulled her bodice together, only to find that several buttons were missing.

"Now what am I to do? This is all your fault Miles Woodthorpe. I can't possibly ride home like this."

Miles, his own clothing now set to rights, groped in the mattress and found the buttons, handing them to her with an apologetic smile.

"Thank you very much! But how am I to sew them on?" She turned to Rob hopefully. "I don't suppose that you have a needle and thread, do you?"

Rob shook his head with a grin. "It was not something high on my list of priorities. As you see I am not fully settled yet."

"Oh well. You will just have to lend me your coat, Miles. We shall have to think of some story on the way back to satisfy my father's curiosity."

"Do you intend to ride back with him?" Rob asked, surprised that having been so recently the victim of what appeared to be an attempted rape, she was happy to remain in the company of her attacker.

Johanna smiled confidently. "I'm sure Miles won't try that again just yet, will you? Besides it's raining quite heavily now and I doubt whether my attractions are sufficient for Miles to want to roll in the mud with me.

"What do you say, Miles? Do you give me your word that you will not molest me on the way home?"

"Of course I do, Johanna," he replied impatiently. "This must have been a momentary aberration, and I am unlikely to repeat the performance. That is, of course, unless I should once more find you in my arms on a soft feather mattress."

"I shall certainly try to ensure that you do not, Miles. Come on, we have taken up enough of this gentleman's time."

Johanna turned to Rob and beamed at him. "I am sorry that we trespassed on your property. It was my fault. I was curious to see what these little cottages were like inside. I had no idea that anyone had yet moved in."

Rob nodded in acknowledgement of the apology, a lock of fair hair falling across his face as he did so. He brushed it back with his hand.

"If you wish, you are welcome to look around. Today is by way of an open day and all of the cottages are open for inspection and admiration. As you have apparently confined your explorations to the bedroom, I shall willingly escort you over the remainder. As you see, I have not yet fully established myself here; I arrived only yesterday and I do still need some furniture. However it will have to wait until I receive my aid money."

"Aid money?" queried Miles.

"Yes. It's a sort of grant to enable us to set up home and buy seed and tools and household implements."

"How much do you get?"

"It varies, depending upon the size of the allotment. This is a four acre plot and so I shall get thirty pounds aid money."

Miles whistled. "That's quite a lot. Who pays it?"

Rob shrugged his shoulders. "The Company pays it out of subscriptions, I suppose."

"Do you have to pay it back, then?"

"No. No-one has said that it has to be repaid."

"So how much are the subscriptions?" enquired Miles, intrigued by the novel financial transactions involved.

Rob shrugged his shoulders again. "You have to buy shares. They are two pounds ten shillings each."

"How many shares do you have?"

"Four."

"So for an investment of ten pounds you get all this and thirty pounds?"

Rob nodded.

"It sounds like a good return to me. Where's the catch?"

Rob frowned. "I don't know. I don't think there is one, unless I am just one of the lucky ones. I suppose there must be a lot of investors who haven't yet been successful in the ballot."

"Ballot?" asked Miles. "What ballot is that?"

"It's a bit like a lottery. All the names of the subscribers are put in a box and the names of the winners of the allotments are drawn out."

"Ah, I begin to see the catch," commented Miles thoughtfully. "There is presumably no guarantee that every investor will receive an allotment?"

Rob shook his head. "No, you are way off mark there. Every investor will receive an allotment. The ballot merely determines the order of it. Feargus has said that every subscriber will receive an allotment within five years."

Miles raised an eyebrow doubtfully. "I should like to know how your Feargus O'Connor can do that."

Rob nodded in agreement. "I confess that I'm somewhat curious about it too. I'm hoping that I'll understand it better after the conference. Feargus himself will be speaking late this afternoon."

"That should be interesting. I wonder if I would be able to get in to hear him. Or is it for subscribers only?"

"There are so many people around today I shouldn't think that anyone will stop you."

Johanna who had been feeling rather left out of the conversation, but who had nevertheless been taking it all in, turned to Miles eagerly."

"Oh, please let's go. I have never met Mr O'Connor even though I have seen him on a number of occasions. I should like to hear what he has to say. After all, we are almost neighbours, and everyone should take an interest in their neighbours shouldn't they?"

"But what would your father say? He has always been somewhat dismissive of the Chartists, and he may not want you to come. No, I believe it would be better if I came alone."

"Oh, Miles; please!" pleaded Johanna, her large brown eyes raised soulfully to those of her companion.

Miles appeared to hesitate for a moment, before his face split into a wide grin. "Well, I suppose it will do no harm for you to come, but you will have to change your clothes first. Come, let's get you home and decent again."

Rob stared at the two thoughtfully, intrigued by the nature of their relationship. It seemed strange to him that not ten minutes earlier he had been witness to an attempted rape, and now they were exchanging fraternal banter as if it had never happened; completely at ease with each other once more.

He shrugged his shoulders slightly. "Did you want to look over the house?" he enquired again, for although they had moved from the bedroom to the kitchen, their progress had been halted by their conversation about the financial affairs of the Land Company.

"Yes please," said Johanna. "May I have a look in there?" She pointed to a door on the opposite side of the kitchen.

"I should prefer to look outside, if I may. The yard seems to be well set out," said Miles who had been looking out of the window.

"Be my guest," replied Rob, moving to open the door to the sitting room for Johanna. The room was empty save for cupboards built into the alcoves on either side of the fireplace. The floor was again of red quarry tiles.

"I've not yet managed to furnish it. I hope to buy some chairs out of my aid money."

"It's a lovely room; light and airy. You should be well pleased, Mr ..."

"Berrow; Rob Berrow."

Johanna held out her hand. "My name is Johanna Martin. My father has a small farm over by Redmarley. It's not far from here."

Rob nodded. Her hand felt warm and soft in his firm grasp. He moved toward the window and looked out at the pouring rain.

"Are you sure you will be safe going home with him?" he asked at last.

Johanna grinned and nodded. "Oh, yes. As I said, Miles will not try anything again. He just got carried away, and in truth it was not entirely his fault. I could and should have stopped him earlier, but just for a moment, I ..." Johanna blushed and turned away from him.

Rob waited, understanding now that she had not been an entirely unwilling recipient of Miles' attentions.

"I should not be talking to you like this. Whatever must you think of me?"

"Few women would be so honest under the circumstances."

"Yes, well I'm afraid I have always been painfully honest. I have this awful tendency to say what I think or feel without restraint. My mother used to despair of me. I don't know what she would have said about this morning's adventure. Most likely she would have blamed me."

"Johanna! Jo! Come and see this!" called Miles from the yard.

Rob led Johanna out through the kitchen to the yard. To the right there was a small wash house with a large stone sink and a copper for heating water. Past that there was a dairy, complete with marble slab. Beyond the dairy was a wood store, full to the top with neatly piled logs. A chicken run, as yet empty, lay at the end of the yard and opposite that there were two pigsties, complete with inhabitants. A privy, stalls for a cow and a pony, and last of all, outside the kitchen a covered area for a cart completed the collection of out-buildings. It was to this latter area that Rob led Johanna to Miles.

"I'm impressed," said Miles. "You have everything you could need within this confined space. I might be able to get some good laying hens for you at a reasonable price."

"Thank you. I would appreciate that. I have never owned a hen in my life and could hardly tell the difference between a good laying hen and a cockerel."

Miles laughed. "Well I don't know how you will go on then. It seems to me that you could do with an adviser."

"What a good idea, Miles. Why don't you become his adviser? I doubt if anyone is better placed than you to give advice on agricultural matters," said Johanna.

She didn't know why she had put him in the position of being unable to refuse. She gazed at Rob, a slight frown on her brow as she tried to understand why she felt this sudden urge to help him. He was clearly the oldest of the three, Johanna guessed that he was somewhere near thirty years of age, but in terms of agricultural experience, he was an absolute novice. She knew that Miles was right and that without someone to advise him he would have little chance of making a living on his small holding.

"There's no need to put yourself to any trouble, Sir, interjected Rob. "Feargus is always available for advice."

"What does he know of farming?"

"I don't exactly know whether he's had much experience himself, but he seems to be very knowledgeable."

"I had understood him to be a lawyer," remarked Miles.

Rob nodded. "Yes, he is. But he has edited and owned several newspapers."

"Well I've yet to hear of anyone being able to learn all they need to know from newspapers. Yes, I will be happy to be your adviser, if you would like me to be."

"How do I know that your advice will be any more sound than that of Feargus?"

Miles laughed. "Well, I suppose you don't. But ask anyone hereabouts where is the best managed farm this side of Gloucester, and they will tell you that it is that of Miles Woodthorpe."

"It is true, Mr Berrow. If I were you I would accept Miles' offer at once. You will not get a better one."

Rob smiled ruefully. "Yes, I know; and I am not ungrateful. It is just that I do not wish to be beholden to anyone. All my life I have been at the mercy of factory owners, and I have come here to put an end to that. If I make mistakes, then so be it. Hopefully I shall learn from them."

"But if you make mistakes here you will starve," argued Johanna. "Surely you want to succeed in this venture."

"Of course I do."

"Then you must accept Miles' offer. You need not feel beholden to him. Accept it as recompense for the trouble we have put you to today. I'm sure that Miles will be happier if we find some means of repaying you. It will thus ensure your silence on certain actions which are best forgotten."

"Well I wouldn't put it quite like that, Jo, but I should be happy to give you the benefit of my experience whenever I am out riding this way. What do you say? Is it a bargain? I can see that Johanna will not give me any peace if you decline," Miles added with a grin.

Rob glanced at the eager faces of the young couple before him and knew that he could only benefit from the help they offered.

He held out his hand to Miles with a resigned grin, and the bargain was struck.

As Miles and Johanna rode away in the rain, with promises to meet again later in the afternoon, Rob found himself somewhat bemused by the encounter. Indeed, he was almost convinced that he had imagined it, until he went into his bedroom and saw his bedclothes in a crumpled heap.

He tried to cast from his mind the picture of Johanna in a state of disarray, but as he folded the blankets neatly, the image refused to be banished. He shrugged his shoulders with a reluctant grin, beginning to feel a little envious of Miles.

Chapter 2

JOHANNA MANAGED TO REACH HER BEDROOM WITHOUT being seen by either her father or their one old maidservant, Emily. She sighed heavily as she removed her soaking riding habit, and wondered, not for the first time, what she should do about Miles.

They had grown up together; her father's farm adjoining the much larger estate of Miles' family. They knew all there was to know about each other, and they loved each other dearly. But just recently a new element had crept into their relationship and whilst Johanna, ever honest with herself, could not deny that Miles' attentions were pleasant and comfortable, she was not at all sure that she wanted to marry him.

There could be no doubting that she and Miles could live together in amicable contentment, but was that enough? Sometimes she yearned for something a little more exciting, something a little less predictable.

She buttoned her gown, combed her hair, and settled down to sew on the buttons that had been torn from her discarded riding habit. The garment was wet and it was not easy to draw the needle through the thick fabric, but when the task was done she felt much better, and she was quite her usual optimistic self when she eventually made her way to the kitchen for luncheon. Vaguely she wondered what Rob Berrow would be eating as she and her father tucked into cold roast lamb and peas.

"Did you enjoy your ride this morning?" Peter Martin asked his daughter as he watched her help herself to a generous portion of apple pie and custard.

"Yes. We went to Lowbands."

"They've got an open day there today, haven't they?"

"Yes. There are thousands of people there."

"It's a pity about the rain."

Johanna nodded, gazing out of the window at the still pouring rain.

"It doesn't seem to have dampened their enthusiasm too much," she said between mouthfuls. "Miles and I are going there again this afternoon. Feargus O'Connor is speaking and we'd both like to see him. Why don't you come too?"

Peter shook his head. "I don't want to get involved with them. It's not that I have anything against them, but I think it's a mistake to bring so many strangers into the community, where they might well end up a drain on the Parish."

"We met one of the settlers this morning, and looked around his allotment. It's all very well laid out, you know. Miles was quite impressed. He thinks that if they are given enough reliable advice, they might succeed."

"I don't see how. We hardly make much of a living on our two hundred acres. How can they expect to survive on two?"

"Mr Berrow has four."

"Mmm...That's not much better," muttered Peter thoughtfully as he started on his apple pie.

The meal was hardly over when Miles rode into the yard and Johanna rushed out to help him saddle her mare. In no time they were headed for Lowbands, and although it was still raining, it was no longer a consistent downpour, but more of a light drizzle.

They decided to leave their horses at Rob Berrow's house, not knowing what arrangements had been made for their accommodation at the conference. Rob was nowhere to be seen, so they led the horses to the stalls behind the kitchen, unsaddled them, and gave them a quick rub down.

Arm in arm they headed towards the field where all activity seemed to be centred. The narrow roads of the estate were by now crowded with sightseers, marching bands, and groups of allottees eager to take possession of their new homes.

"We shall never find Rob amongst all these people," murmured Johanna.

"Rob, is it? What happened to Mr Berrow?"

Johanna felt herself blushing. "You're right. It should be Mr Berrow; but somehow I can only think of him as Rob; it's almost as if we have known him for a long time."

Miles nodded. "I know what you mean. It must have something to do with the circumstances of our meeting. It's difficult to remain on terms of formality with someone who has caught you with your trousers down, so to speak. I must say he behaved admirably about the whole thing."

"Oh, don't remind me, Miles. I dread to think what sort of opinion he has formed of me."

"I don't think you need concern yourself, Johanna. No blame can attach to you; you were after all fighting for your honour quite vigorously, as I recall." Miles rubbed his chin ruefully, and turned her to face him. "I really am sorry about this morning, Jo. You need have no fear that such a thing will happen again. I am truly ashamed that I could so easily forget that I was brought up a gentleman."

Jo reached up and kissed his drizzle damp cheek

"Let's forget it, Miles. I don't hold you entirely to blame. I'm sure everything will work out for the best in the end."

"But you still don't want to marry me, do you?"

"I love you very much, Miles. I just need a little more time, that's all."

Miles squeezed her shoulders. "I know. But don't make me wait too long, will you, Jo?" His voice was hoarse with remembered passion, and Johanna found it difficult to meet his meaningful gaze.

She smiled weakly. "I promise I'll give you my answer as soon as I can, Miles. Now come on, or the conference will be over before we get there."

As they walked through the narrow lanes, Miles took a close look at some of the crops planted on the allotments. He was impressed with the turnips and parsnips, and surprised to see potatoes flourishing in trenches. Cabbages were also thriving on each allotment.

Miles sighed thoughtfully.

"What's wrong?" asked Johanna.

"I don't know. It just seems such a lot to ask of these people, to be able to survive on two acres. It might just be possible on four, with good husbandry, but two is little more than a garden."

"That's what Father said at lunch time."

"Sometimes I can't help thinking that this Feargus O'Connor must be some kind of misguided fool. I only hope it doesn't all end in disaster."

Johanna echoed that hope.

They were now quite close to the conference field where the loud hubbub of thousands of voices threatened to extinguish the brass band.

A large marquee had been erected at one end of the field, and hustings were in the process of being built at the other. The thousands of people milling around seemed happy, excited even, in spite of the never ceasing rain. They were assembled in groups, behind banners and flags to show where they had come from. It was a bright and colourful sight on such a grey day.

A loud spontaneous cheer arose from the crowds as a watery shaft of sunshine fell upon them.

Johanna glanced up at Miles and found herself smiling brightly at him; the natural optimism of the people was infectious.

Miles smiled back. "Do you think we might get some ale in that marquee? I confess I feel quite thirsty."

"Let's go and see."

They made their way to the marquee which had been full to bursting most of the afternoon, but now that the rain had apparently stopped it emptied a little, and Miles soon found himself at the counter.

"A pint of ale and a glass of lemonade, please," he asked the assistant.

She smiled. "You won't find any ale here, sir, I'm afraid. Coffee or tea are the only beverages we have."

Miles frowned. "I didn't know that Chartists were teetotallers."

The woman laughed. "No, and I don't suppose they do, either! The fact is that Mr O'Connor decreed that there should be no intoxicating beverages available. It's even said that he has promised personally to duck any drunk who dares to put in an appearance here!"

Miles grinned. "Well, I am hardly a drunk, but if you have nothing stronger then I shall have to be content with coffee. What about you, Jo? Will you have coffee or tea?"

Johanna opted for coffee and with cups warming their hands they made their way to an empty table.

"I don't think we shall find Mr Berrow, do you?" asked Johanna, as she sipped the hot brew.

Miles shook his head. "It will be like looking for a needle in a haystack. I think you may as well forget that, Jo."

Johanna nodded. "What do you think of it?"

"What? The estate?"

"Mm."

"I reserve judgement," replied Miles. "I'm looking forward to hearing this Feargus O'Connor speak. Even if I think the whole thing is a mistake, I can't help but admire a man who can manage to put so radical an idea into action. It takes a man of vision and courage to do that."

Johanna nodded. "I can't explain why, but I find the whole thing rather exciting."

"Intriguing, certainly," agreed Miles.

They had almost finished their coffee when the assistant who had served them came up to them.

"I'm sorry to push you out in such a hurry, but it is nearly five o'clock, and Mr O'Connor is due to speak then.

We are shutting up shop for a while so that we can listen to him."

Miles smiled. "Thank you. We'll not hold you up. We too are anxious not to miss Mr O'Connor. It is after all what we came for."

Once outside the tent, Miles and Johanna followed the crowd towards the hustings.

An air of expectancy seemed to run through the assembly, and loud cheers erupted as Feargus O'Connor walked on to the platform.

Johanna recognised him at once. He stood over six feet tall, broad shouldered and well girthed; a mop of red hair framing his round ruddy face.

His voice reached out to all the assembled company as he told them how he had very nearly missed the auction for Lowbands. He had been out looking at farms near Worcester and had arrived at the inn, wet to the knees, after the sale had begun. He had called out to the innkeeper to hold his horse while he rushed into the sale room to join the bidding. He had raised the last bid by one hundred pounds and the hammer went down at £8000.

Feargus' round face beamed upon his gathering, and Johanna's heart warmed to him. His red hair and powerful voice may have been an indication of a hot and fiery personality, but the overriding impression that Johanna had, was that he truly cared for 'his people'.

Once the cheering died down, Feargus turned to more serious issues.

"We are building these home colonies to obtain a legitimate influence, by achievement of the franchise!" he said to loud cheers. He went on to say that in his capacity as MP for Nottingham he would proclaim the Chartist principles.

"The Whigs said you were too ignorant to be given the vote; but when did the Whigs build schools like the one you have here, to teach you and your children?"

Johanna realised that she had not yet seen the school room and she whispered to Miles that they must have a look at it.

Feargus then raised a general laugh by reminding all the allottees that the rain that had dampened them all day would be swelling their potatoes.

Finally he told them that he would not be with them for much longer as it was time for him to move on to develop another estate.

Cries of dismay were heard, but Feargus reminded them that he would continue to be a frequent visitor.

The crowds began to disperse soon after Feargus had finished speaking. The allottees to their own houses, along with some of the hundred and forty official delegates to the conference. It promised to be an uncomfortable night for most of them, but at least they would have a roof over their heads.

The thousands of other visitors, subscribers and sightseers, made their way back whence they had come, their hearts and spirits raised by what they had seen.

The roads were packed once more with vehicles of all descriptions and people carrying folded banners. Johanna and Miles eased their way through the crowds back to Rob Berrow's house.

They met up with Rob almost at the garden gate. He was walking purposefully in the opposite direction.

He grinned widely when he saw Miles and Jo. "You made it then. What did you think of Feargus?"

Miles frowned thoughtfully. "I don't know what to make of him. I'm sure he means well, but I really am not convinced that he knows too much about farming."

Rob sighed. "I think you may be right. Well, doubtless we'll learn one way or another. You must forgive me if I leave you now. All of the allottees are to assemble in the schoolroom to collect their aid money. I don't want to be late in case it all goes before I get there!"

Miles nodded. "I'll come over tomorrow and take a look at your crops. If I'm going to advise you I'll need to see what you have got."

Rob smiled. "Thank you. I do appreciate your help." He waved cheerfully and carried on his way, leaving Miles and Jo to saddle their horses.

"May I come with you tomorrow?" Jo asked as they rode slowly through the crowds.

"What for? We will only be inspecting and talking about Rob's crops. It would be very boring for you."

Jo's lips curved thoughtfully. "I don't know," she whispered, wondering why all of a sudden the prospect sounded appealing. "But I would like to go."

Miles shrugged. "Well, all right then. I'll call for you at about ten o' clock."

They rode home, each deep in thought as they tried to put some order to the confusion of ideas they had been faced with during the day.

Jo in particular found herself thinking of Rob Berrow, a delicious sense of anticipation filling her as she thought of seeing him again the next day. She was puzzled as to why he should so occupy her brain when she had only met him that morning, but she could find no answer to that problem. She didn't think it could be merely that he was handsome, in a lean and hungry sort of way. Maybe it was just because of the way his deep blue eyes crinkled when he smiled. She shrugged her shoulders. In the end it didn't matter why she felt as she did; she only knew that she wanted to get to know him better.

Meanwhile Rob Berrow joined the other allottees in the school room to collect his aid money. Names were called out by Feargus, who gave each of them the cash payment agreed.

The allottees drank tea together and discussed what they intended to do with their land. There was some confusion when it was found that one person had arrived all the way from Hull, with his belongings piled high upon a cart, only to discover that he had made a mistake and his name was not upon the list of allottees, but on a reserve list.

There was silence in the school room as everyone waited to see what Feargus would do.

"Look, I'm sorry, Mr Graham," he said. "But all the allotments have been allocated here. I'll give you five pounds which you can repay out of your aid money when you are allotted a property. This should be enough to get you and your belongings back to Hull. I will see that if any of these properties become vacant, you are offered the first one. It is the best I can do, I'm afraid."

Mr Graham nodded weakly, his disappointment evident as he swallowed a lump in his throat.

Rob took him a cup of tea. "What will you do for tonight?" he asked.

The man shook his head, dazed. "I don't know."

"Well you had best come to my cottage. I can't offer much in the way of comfort, but it will be better than sleeping under a hedge. It is an unfortunate business."

Mr Graham nodded and gulped down the hot tea.

"I thought I had won!" he whispered. "I don't know how it could have happened."

"You'll be all right. Will you be able to get your job back?"

Mr Graham nodded. "There should be no difficulty. It's a good thing I didn't bring my wife with me. She and the children were staying with her mother until I could get the house sorted out. She will be even more disappointed than I am. What am I to say to her?"

"You will have to tell her the truth. I'm sure you can rely on Mr O'Connor to find a solution as soon as he can."

Mr Graham nodded. "I knew it was too good to be true."

"We all feel for you. I don't think any of us can believe our good fortune yet."

Mr Graham drained his cup.

"Come then," said Rob. "let's get you settled for the night, and hope that before long you will be back again on a more permanent basis."

It was dusk as they approached the cottage in Mr Graham's loaded cart. Far and wide lamps were lit in the cottage windows, as Feargus had decreed that the properties should be illuminated on this, the first night of the inauguration.

Rob climbed wearily into his bed, after settling Mr Graham on a mattress on the parlour floor. His last thought before falling asleep was the memory of Johanna

Martin as she had stood defiantly in front of Miles, her ample charms delectably exposed, refusing to be coerced into marriage.

****

The next day Johanna awoke to find the sun streaming brightly through her window. She jumped out of bed, and washed herself in the cold water from the jug on her washstand.

She looked into the mirror as she brushed her long curls until they shone. She was aware that whilst hers was not a beautiful face, it was an attractive one, and this was at least partly due to a lively animation which she found difficult to contain. Her father had always told her that he could read all her emotions in her face. She wondered what he would find there now.

Peter Martin didn't fail to notice his daughter's agitation at breakfast, but whatever else he read in her face, he thought it wise to make no comment.

She was ready and waiting for Miles at ten o' clock, in a state of almost fevered excitement. She couldn't tell why she should suddenly feel like a child at Christmas, and gave up trying to answer that question.

When Miles had failed to show up by half past ten, Jo stormed into the kitchen and put together a basket of food. There was still some cold roast lamb left and she carefully carved a few slices from the joint. She took also some bread, a pot of butter, some of her own chutney, and the remains of the apple pie.

When the basket was prepared she went to the stable and saddled her mare. She had been looking forward to the morning so much that she was not going to be disappointed merely because Miles had changed his mind and gone without her.

As she rode out of the farmyard, she hoped fervently that her father had not seen her. She had been used to riding about the countryside unaccompanied for several years, but recently, with the advent of the Chartists, he had tried to instil in her a greater awareness of the dangers. There were after all a lot of strangers in the district, and who could tell what they were like? They might well take the view, and who could blame them, that a young girl who rode about unaccompanied was no better than she should be.

Jo grinned to herself. Life was too short to always behave with the decorum which her father would have liked. She knew that if her mother were alive she wouldn't be able to get away with so much; but her mother had been dead this ten years past, and Jo had long since become accustomed to life without her.

When she arrived at Rob's cottage, she was surprised to find no sign of Miles' horse in the stable.

Rob walked into the yard from his plot and was startled to find Johanna alone.

"Where's Mr Woodthorpe?" he asked, a heavy frown upon his brow.

"I don't know. Isn't he here?"

"No. Didn't he come with you?"

Jo shook her head. "I thought he had come without me."

"You mean you came here alone?" Rob demanded.

Jo frowned at the suppressed anger in his tone.

"Yes," she whispered.

"What on earth do you think you're doing, girl? Don't you know any better than to go visiting a man without an escort? Have things changed so much since I was a young man that this sort of behaviour is allowed these days?"

Jo giggled. "What do you mean, since you were a young man?" she smiled. "You're hardly in your dotage!"

"Don't try to divert me, child!" said Rob, feeling an overwhelming urge to laugh himself. "You shouldn't have come here, and well you know it!"

Jo pressed her lips together. "I'm sorry. I suppose you're right, and now my reputation will be beyond even your redemption."

Rob's lips twitched uncontrollably. "You're a shameless hussy, and one of these days you will get what you deserve," he said, giving up his attempt at wrathful indignation. "The best you can hope for is that no-one round here will know who you are, and so will be unable to carry the tale back to your family. Whatever would they think if they knew that you had ridden here alone?"

Jo stared at the ground, her boot making idle patterns in the dust.

"Why did you come here, anyway?"

Jo shrugged her shoulders. "I told you, I thought Miles was here," she replied lamely.

Rob felt his heart go out to the girl before him. She was after all little more than an impetuous child, he tried to tell himself, in spite of his earlier, more robust visions of her. "You really shouldn't have come here, you know," he continued in a more gentle tone.

"Yes, I know. I don't know why I did, really. Miles had said that he would fetch me and I was very angry when I thought that he had come here without me."

Rob moved a step forward, unable to resist the childlike simplicity of her words. But the memory of their meeting the previous day came unbidden to his mind, and he knew that this was no child. The realisation brought him to a halt. He stood close in front of her, within reaching distance, fighting the urge to put out his hand to her.

Johanna looked up then, her brown eyes large and velvety, filled with confusion and something else he must not try to define. Suddenly he felt so old and he wished it were not so. As he gazed into the depths of her soul, he wished that he could have back his youth and his freedom. For a moment he felt as if he were drowning. He even held his breath as if by doing so he could survive the sudden surge of emotion that hit him like a tidal wave.

He sighed heavily and raggedly, turning his gaze from her whilst he was still capable of withdrawing.

"It won't do, you know," he whispered regretfully, his eyes studying the pattern made in the dust by her boot.

Johanna realised that she had been holding her breath for what seemed to be an eternity. She breathed out slowly, in an effort to calm her trembling nerves.

"What won't do?" she asked at last.

"This won't. You must go now, before any damage is done."

"Has it not been done already?" she whispered.

He looked up at her, a smile breaking upon her lips. It would be so easy to take advantage of her youth and innocence. He knew that he must tread carefully to avoid hurting or disappointing her. The child was on the verge of womanhood, and had little idea how to handle her own sensuality. He was surprised to find that he was experiencing similar problems himself.

He groaned. "I fear you may be right. But let's not tempt providence by making matters worse for both of us."

"I can't just go. I need to understand what is happening to me."

"I don't know what's happening to you!" Rob cried. "I don't know what's happening to myself. I don't think I know anything at all!"

"It is the same for you then? It isn't just me being foolish?"

Rob sighed. "I think we are both being foolish. We hardly know each other. There can be nothing between us. Go away, girl. I have enough problems of my own, without you adding to them. There is nothing to understand; there can be nothing. We are just suffering from over active imaginations."

"Both of us?"

"Yes, both of us," he admitted.

"I suppose it would have been better if I hadn't come here," she whispered.

"Yes. Now will you please go, Miss Martin?"

Jo grinned. "That's better. I thought you must have forgotten my name. But you can call me Johanna if you like; Jo, if you prefer."

"I don't think I should be calling you anything at all. Don't you know that every minute you stay here you are endangering your reputation even further?"

"But I brought us some lunch. Can we not eat it?"

"Lunch?" Rob stared blankly.

"Yes; food. I suppose that you do eat? Although perhaps not a lot, judging by the look of you. Have you always been so thin?"

Rob glanced down at his spare frame. " I never thought of myself as thin; slim maybe; lean would be better. Am I too thin?"

Jo laughed. "Only to the extent that I have this overwhelming urge to fatten you up!"

Rob grinned. "You will have to do something about your overwhelming urges, Miss Martin. Before you land us both into trouble."

"Jo. Please, it's Jo."

Rob sighed. "Very well. I know when I'm beaten. Did you say something about food, Jo?"

"Good," Jo whispered. "Do you think we can be friends?"

Rob shook his head. "No, I don't. But I'm willing to give it a try."

"Well, what more can a girl ask for?" asked Jo with a smile as she picked up the basket of food and headed for the kitchen.

"Not in there," said Rob urgently. "I think that you'll be safer out here. We'll have a picnic by the cabbage patch. We can't get into much trouble in the cabbage patch, can we?" he asked, taking the basket from her hand.

Jo had to agree, and she followed Rob across his land towards the cabbage patch, where they settled themselves on a narrow band of grass which served as a path.

The meal passed pleasantly enough. Each of the participants anxious to avoid bringing to the fore the emotional tensions which they both knew hovered just below the surface of their conversation.

As soon as he was decently able to, after finishing eating the food she had brought, Rob instructed Jo to return to the bosom of her family.

"I shall not be held responsible for my actions if you stay here any longer. You may have assuaged my hunger, but I do have other appetites which have not been so appeased, and I don't want you to outstay your welcome." Rob packed away the remains of the lunch in the basket as he spoke.

"Am I welcome?" Jo whispered.

Rob held the basket out to her.

"I don't think you should come here again, Jo. It is too risky."

"Why?"

"You know why, Jo. Now heed an old man, and take my advice and go."

"You're not that old, are you?"

"Too old for you, Jo."

"How old?"

"Nearly thirty."

"Well, that's not old at all. Mature, perhaps; but certainly not old."

"It's too old for a child of your age."

"I'm not a child!" cried Jo indignantly.

Rob grinned. "No, I guess you're not, at that," he said cheekily as his eyes roamed the curves of her body. "Now, go, Jo. Thank you for the meal; but I should be grateful if you would let me get on with my work now. I do have my land to till you know!"

"Yes. I'm going! But don't think you have seen the last of me! I'll be back, you know!"

She grinned as she made her way back to the stable and she was still grinning when she arrived home.

Chapter 3

JOHANNA STARED INTO THE MIRROR, HER ARM ACHING from brushing her hair, which now cascaded about her shoulders, reaching almost to her waist. She sighed, lay the brush upon the table, and rested her chin in her hands.

She had slept little that night, and she searched anxiously for evidence of her restlessness upon her face; but her skin was cool and clear as usual, and her eyes had their normal sparkling brightness. No, perhaps there would have to be more than one night's unrest before she started to look hagged; and she didn't intend to pass another such night.

In the broad sunshine of early morning it was difficult to remember why she had been unable to sleep. Her meeting with Rob Berrow had disturbed and excited her, leaving her confused; but she didn't consider that there was any reason for her sleep to suffer. The incident with Miles was over and done with and gave her no more than a momentary concern. She certainly didn't feel that there was any need to lose any sleep over that either.

She wondered what she should do about Miles. Her fingers stroked the bristles of her hairbrush as she pondered upon her feelings for him. She was very fond of him, that much could not be denied; but did she want to spend the rest of her life with him? Was she in love with him?

She shrugged her shoulders. How was she to know? She recalled the delicious sense of excitement she had felt when Miles' urgent desire had made itself known to her. For a moment she had been carried along with him and she had been tempted to succumb. She could not avoid a certain amount of curiosity and she wondered what it would have been like if Rob Berrow had not intervened.

But Rob Berrow had intervened, and she recalled with a blush, his lazy grin as he leaned against the door frame. What a picture they must have presented; Miles with his trousers down and she, legs and breasts exposed. If she had thought about it, she would never have been able to face him again.

Well, it was a good thing she hadn't thought about it, for then she would have missed seeing him yesterday afternoon. She smiled wistfully to herself as she recalled those few minutes when the world had seemed to stand still for her. He had said that it had been the same for him, and she knew that it was so. It was a shared moment, a significant moment, maybe one to remember all their lives.

She sighed. Now she really was suffering from romantic delusions. Maybe Rob Berrow had been right when he had said that it wouldn't do. What after all could she have to do with one of the tenants of the Chartist land company? Her father owned and farmed two hundred acres of prime arable land: that was almost as much as the whole land colony had, and there were getting on for forty families dependent upon their few acres.

Miles was right; it wasn't going to be easy for the smallholders to scratch a living. She couldn't help wondering what had made someone like Rob Berrow give up one way of life to pursue an agricultural dream. He hadn't seemed to be physically cut out for heavy land work. He was very tall, but thin and pale, as if he had spent little of his time out of doors, and neither had he spent much time in hard physical labour.

Her father had said that most of the colonists were factory workers; weavers and spinners from the cotton mills of the north of England.

Johanna nodded her head. Yes, she could picture Rob in some vast factory working long hours at some dreadful noisy machine. If that were the case then maybe she could see why he would exchange such a life for a different existence, breathing the clean fresh air, and being warmed by the summer sun.

"Miss Johanna! Miss Johanna!" called Emily from the foot of the stairs.

Johanna sighed and went to the door. She would have to see about another maid to help Emily. It was not really acceptable to have her shouting about the house in this way, but she couldn't be expected to climb the stairs now that she was suffering so badly with arthritis. Johanna had several times suggested that it was time for Emily to retire to a quiet cottage, but the old maidservant would have none of it, and Johanna had not the heart to insist upon it. No, a younger maid would be the answer. She must put her mind to it without too much delay.

Johanna ran lightly down the stairs.

"What is it, Emily?" she asked with a bright smile.

"Master Miles is here, Miss Johanna. Again."

Johanna grinned. "What's the matter, Emily? Do you think I am seeing too much of him?"

"That's not for me to say, Miss; and well you know it," replied Emily in the disapproving tones permitted to an old and loved family servant.

"But you will, nevertheless," responded Johanna.

"Well, if you insist. I think it is high time you put that young man out of his misery and either agree to marry him or send him packing."

Johanna sighed. "I can't send him packing, Emily. He is my dearest friend. What would I do without him?"

Emily hobbled away, muttering under her breath about young girls who kept young men dangling.

47

Johanna stared after her thoughtfully. She knew there was some justice in Emily's remarks, but she didn't know what to do. If only her mother were still alive, maybe she could have helped her out of her dilemma. As it was there was no-one to whom she could turn for advice.

She straightened her back and walked down the hall to the parlour where Miles was seated in the comfortable armchair reading an old copy of the Times.

"Miles, how nice to see you. But I had expected you yesterday. What happened to you?"

Miles stood up, grinning, and taking both Johanna's hands he bent and kissed her cheek.

"I'm sorry about yesterday. I was tied up with my agent. You look ravishing as usual, Jo," he greeted her.

"Perhaps I had better do something about that," replied Johanna with a wicked smile. "I don't wish to be ravished again today."

Miles' face sobered instantly. "About the other day, Jo; I feel I must ..."

Johanna cut him short by putting her fingers to his lips.

"Let's say no more about it, Miles."

"That's all very well, but I can't forget that it happened. I'm not made of steel, you know."

Johanna giggled. "Yes, I know. I think I have a better idea of what you are made of than I had before."

Miles grinned and made to box her ears. "You cheeky minx!" he laughed, and then once more he became serious. "But we can't go on like this, Jo. I think we should marry, and soon. Please say you will, Jo."

"I don't know, Miles. It is such a big step to take."

He moved closer to her and raised her chin so that her eyes met his. "What's the matter, Jo? Why do you hesitate? You do love me, don't you?"

"I don't know, Miles. What is love anyway? I feel so confused. Emily thinks I should either marry you or send you packing, and to be honest, I don't want to do either at the moment. I don't think I'm ready to be married yet. If I were I wouldn't have these doubts, would I? And I don't want to send you packing because I love you too well for that. I like to see you and to be with you. I want us to stay as we are. Why can't we do that?"

Miles sighed and stroked her hair which still hung in dark tresses to frame her face.

"Because I don't know how long I can go on like that, Jo. The other day I lost control, and if Rob Berrow had not turned up when he did, we both know what would have happened. I love you, and I don't want to hurt you, and yet I nearly did just that. It would be better all round if you were to marry me now. Then neither of us would have to resist the temptation to do what we both want to do."

"I know, Miles; and I understand. But I do need more time to think about it. It's too big a step to take just because once we nearly got carried away. I am only eighteen years of age. I don't feel any overwhelming desire to be married, with a handful of children at my feet.

"Can you give me more time? Let me think about it; get used to the idea, and then maybe I shall find that marrying you is what I want above everything."

"I don't have much choice, do I? I can hardly force you down the aisle, even if I wanted to; which I don't. I don't want you to feel forced to marry me. I want you to want to marry me. That's a different matter altogether, isn't it?"

Johanna nodded. "I'm glad you feel that way, because that means you must understand why I need more time. Please say you understand, Miles."

He gazed down at her tense eager features and felt immediately so old. She would probably never understand the depth of his feeling for her. He hardly understood it himself. He was twenty-five years of age, and whilst there had, of necessity, been some other women, he had not felt drawn to any of them, as he did to Johanna. In his past relationships he had been driven solely by a physical need. With Jo he knew that it was different. He loved her; he wanted to protect her and care for her; maybe he wanted to protect her innocence, but he couldn't see how he could do that whilst at the same time wanting to possess her.

"Yes, I think I understand, Jo," he whispered, not understanding at all. He bent and put his lips to hers in what was intended as a chaste kiss. Immediately he felt her respond to him, placing her arms about his neck and drawing him closer to her.

He groaned and with difficulty wrenched himself away from her. "Watch it, Jo; or I'm likely to get carried away again. You are too much temptation for any man to withstand when you kiss me like that. I don't think you know what it does to me."

Johanna giggled again. "Oh, yes I do," she replied.

"Well that's enough!" reprimanded Miles. "If you do that again I shall give you your just deserts!"

Johanna laughed. "I promise to be good for the rest of the day. Will you promise as well?"

Miles relaxed and grinned at her. "Yes. Now what shall we do?"

"Shall we go for a ride? We could go again to Lowbands to see what they are up to today."

"I understand that their conference is to last all week. Maybe I should advise Rob Berrow how to spend his aid money. I thought we could get him some laying hens from old Jake Comberton. I'm sure he'd let me have some at a good price."

"Let's go then. Will you saddle my horse whilst I go and make myself look respectable?" Johanna put her hand to her loose curls.

Miles grinned. "Yes, you'd better not go looking like that. You would never be able to convince Rob Berrow that you are a respectable young lady. You look as if you have just been doing something you ought not to have been."

Jo blushed and pushed him away playfully, departing quickly to her bedroom where she hastily tied back her hair.

They set off at a brisk pace ten minutes later to Jake Comberton's cottage in the village of Redmarley.

After a glass each of homemade cider, bargaining for half a dozen laying hens was successfully concluded, and Miles and Johanna set off rather more sedately, the result of their negotiations protesting noisily in a crate in front of Miles.

As they reached Lowbands, it was clear that there was still a lot of activity about the estate. The mass of visitors of the preceding day had departed, but the allottees were busily settling themselves into their new homes. Outside many of the cottages there stood carts containing the furniture and personal belongings of the new residents. They seemed to be unloading systematically, all helping each other, amid much joyful laughter and joking,

At some cottages the unpacking had been done, and whole families were already working vigorously on the land.

They found Rob Berrow busily digging at his plot with a fork. Sweat poured from his brow and he mopped it off with the back of his hand, straightening his aching back as he saw his visitors approaching.

"That looks like hard work," commented Miles.

"Yes, it is; but it's better than sitting inside at a loom all day."

"You were a weaver, then?" asked Johanna.

Rob nodded. "And glad to be out of it. There's nothing wrong with honest toil, but I'm sure that this will be healthier work than that."

Johanna nodded. "Did you work in a factory?"

"No. It was not quite that bad. I had my own cottage and my own loom."

"Did you bring your loom with you?"

"No. Well, it wasn't mine to bring. I didn't own it; I rented it from the factory owner."

"Oh, I see," said Johanna vaguely.

"We've brought you some hens," said Miles, holding the crate out to Rob, who eyed the squawking contents apprehensively.

"Shall we put them into the pen?" asked Miles.

51

Rob smiled. "Yes. Please do. What do I feed them on?"

"You can give them corn or maize, and they will eat any household scraps. They shouldn't cost much to keep, and they will provide you with beautiful brown eggs which you can either eat or sell at market."

"How much do I owe you?"

Miles shook his head. "Regard them as a gift. A sort of 'welcome to your new life' gift, if you like."

"That's very kind of you, but there is no need. I can pay my way, you know."

"I'm sure you can. However I owe you something for our intrusion the other day."

"You don't need to buy my silence. I said that I will tell no-one, and I keep my word." Rob said stiffly.

Miles grinned and held out a hand. "You are a bit touchy, Rob Berrow; but can you not see that this is a gift between friends? There is really no need to get on your high horse about it. Come on; let's shake hands to our continued friendship."

Rob relaxed and grinned at last, extending his hand to Miles. "All right. I confess that I shall be glad of a friend, and I'm probably in sore need of some advice."

"Well, for a start, what is that instrument you're using?" asked Miles, staring in amazement at the fork with tines over a foot long, with which Rob had been turning the soil. "You surely don't intend to turn over all your land with that? You'll break your back before you're finished."

Rob grinned. "This is what Feargus O'Connor recommends. What would you use?"

"I'd use a plough. It would be much quicker and easier and leave you more time for other tasks. You're wasting your time and energy using that."

"Feargus says it does the job better than any plough."

"To what purpose? The plough turns the soil sufficiently to yield good crops. I should doubt very much whether turning it your way would improve on yield, so why bother?"

Rob shrugged. "Well it makes no difference. I haven't got a plough, and I can't afford one. I have got a fork and I am available to dig the soil. Apart from which, don't you need a horse for a plough? I don't have a horse."

"Didn't I see horses on Fortey Green?" asked Johanna, referring to a patch of common land close by.

"Yes, very likely. But they belong to the Company and are used for pulling heavy loads and carts. They are not plough horses."

"Well I don't see why I shouldn't lend you a horse with a plough. I agree that one is not much good without the other. But this is not the right time of year to be ploughing. It is too late to plant the land for summer crops and too soon to plant for winter. You would be best advised to leave the grass to grow and let the cattle graze on it. You will need to fence off this part from your other crops or the cattle will eat those too. However that shouldn't be too difficult. We are never short of fencing stakes around here. Shall I have a look at your crops whilst I am here?"

Rob nodded and led the way to his half acre of potatoes. Miles dug up one of the plants and seemed quite impressed with the tubers lying beneath.

"I have never seen potatoes grown in trenches before, but I cannot fault the results. Is it the Irish way of doing things?"

"I've no idea, but it seems likely. I guess it was Feargus who ordered the planting this way."

Miles nodded. "You should have a good crop here in two or three weeks time. Have you planted any beetroot? That should be ready by now, if you have."

Rob smiled and led Miles to another area of his smallholding on which a fine crop of beetroot was evident.

Miles pulled up a root. "It's certainly ready for harvesting. I should do it without delay if I were you. If you leave them too long they will become coarse and you'll not get a good price for them at market." Miles cast his eye about the allotment. "Is that cauliflower over there?"

Rob looked to where his companion pointed. "Yes. They're very good. I had one for my supper last night."

Miles headed towards them. "If you bend a leaf over them, like this," he demonstrated," You will be able to keep them looking clean and get a better price for them. They should be harvested immediately otherwise they'll bolt and do no-one any good. If I were you I would do that tomorrow if the weather is fine. You can then hang them upside down in one of your outbuildings for a day or so if you cannot get to market the next day. Where will you take them?"

"I had thought Gloucester."

"A wise choice. If you want to go with me on Friday, I'll show you the ropes, then you will know what to do in the future."

"That is very kind of you. I haven't often been to market so am unfamiliar, even from a customer viewpoint.."

"Where did you get your food from, then?" asked Johanna, interested in this domestic detail.

"My ... sister ... used to do all that for me."

Rob gazed into the honest open features of the young girl before him, and wondered why he had felt it necessary to lie.

"Will she be joining you here?" enquired Johanna.

Rob shook his head. "No. She has wed now and I am alone." This last was at least true.

"Are you a good cook?" asked Johanna.

"I confess that I've done little. My sister used to do all that."

"You must miss her."

"No," replied Rob, surprised by his own response. "No, I don't miss her as much as I thought I would. We have not communicated much in recent years. She was against my joining the Chartists."

"Why was that? Doesn't she agree with the Chartist demands?" enquired Miles.

Rob shrugged. "I don't think she necessarily disagreed with them, but neither did she agree with them. She was completely antipathetic towards them, and resented the amount of time and money I put into the cause. She felt somewhat neglected, I think."

"So now you have no-one to look after you."

Rob stared at Johanna. "That's true. But I don't feel an overwhelming need to be looked after. I shall manage well enough."

"What have you eaten since you arrived here?"

"I cooked the cauliflower last night, and I did bring a little bread with me. And I ate quite well yesterday lunch time," Rob said with a grin, wondering whether Jo had mentioned her earlier visit to Miles.

Jo blushed and silently shook her head at him, relieved when she saw his answering nod of reassurance.

"That's not enough to feed yourself when you are doing physical work. It may have sufficed when you were weaving, but you are not weaving now. Do you have any flour?"

"Yes, I have a sack of wheat flour. It was one of the items of provisions we were given."

"May I take a look in your kitchen?"

"Feel free; but it really isn't necessary. I can look after myself, you know."

Johanna ran back through the allotment to the house and once there she started to rummage through the drawers. She found some salt and the sack of flour in a cupboard, and she quickly mixed up a dough which she began to knead vigorously. There being no yeast, she shaped the dough into buns and put them in the oven. She was relieved to find that the stove had been lit. Whilst the bread baked, she made a shopping list of the provisions needed.

When she had finished the list, she took it out to Rob, who was now helping Miles to get the rebellious hens installed in the hen pen.

"You'll need to keep them penned in for a little while, but you shouldn't leave them confined for too long. These hens are used to roaming free and may decide not to lay if they are not happy with their new quarters. Tomorrow I should give them the freedom of the yard, and you can leave some corn scattered about for them to scratch at. Don't leave them out at night, though. There are usually foxes roaming about and they appreciate a chicken dinner as often as they can get one."

Rob sighed. "If it's as difficult to round them up at night as it has been now, then I might be quite relieved if a fox were to get them. They seem a bit fierce with their beaks!"

Johanna laughed. "Believe me, they won't hurt you, Rob. They can't bite very hard; they don't have any teeth."

"Don't they?" remarked Rob dubiously, as he rubbed a finger which had been pecked quite ferociously. "Well next time I shall see about getting some gloves!"

"Talking about getting things, I've made a list of provisions you will need."

Rob took the list from her, and glanced down it, whistling beneath his breath as he saw how long it was.

"I don't really need all this, do I?" he asked at last. "What do I need with tea? I drink either water or ale when I can get it."

"You need tea to offer your visitors," said Johanna briefly.

Rob looked up at her and smiled. "Yes. Thank you for reminding me."

"If you think you can't afford it, then I'll bring some from home."

Rob's smile vanished as quickly as it had appeared. "That will not be necessary. I should like to provide for my visitors myself. I don't want to frighten them away with my lack of hospitality, do I?"

"No. I should think not," responded Johanna, meeting his eyes thoughtfully. "But I will save you the expense of a teapot, as I am sure we have one or two old ones at home that we no longer use."

Johanna took the list from Rob and went back into the house to check that her bread was baking satisfactorily.

Before long the little cottage and yard were overwhelmed by the inviting aroma of baking bread. Rob came in and grinned..

"That smells good," he remarked.

"No, it doesn't. It smells delicious," said Johanna, grinning. "There are some things I am not very good at, but baking bread is not one of them."

"I'm sure it will be wonderful. I've just realised I'm starving!"

"I can't find anything to go with it."

"It will be a meal in itself."

"Well at home we usually have cold meat or a pie or something, or even some cheese, but you don't seem to have anything yet."

"Give me time. I have only been here three days. I can't have everything at once. And I only got my aid money the day before yesterday. I've had no chance to spend it yet. Miles has said that he will be going to Ledbury tomorrow, and he has invited me to ride with him. I am beginning to feel quite glad that his baser instincts got the better of him, and I was able to rescue you both from what would undoubtedly have been a great moment of folly."

Johanna turned from taking her bread out of the oven, and stared at Rob indignantly.

"Surely it is not so great a folly where two people love each other."

"No-o; not when they love each other. But you don't love him, do you?"

"What makes you say that?"

"Do you?"

Johanna hesitated. "I'm not sure. I don't know how I'm supposed to tell."

"Believe me, Johanna; if you loved him, you would know."

"How would I know?"

"You just would."

"But I think I must love him because I enjoy his kisses and I didn't really want him to stop that day."

"Then why did you stop him?"

57

"I was under the impression that you did that."

Rob shook his head. "If I had thought that you didn't want to stop him, I might well have walked away and saved us all from some embarrassment."

"Would you have done that?"

"I don't know. I might have done. Do you wish that I had?"

Johanna shook her head.

"Why did you stop him, then?" Rob repeated.

She shrugged. "I don't know. Somehow it didn't seem right."

"It would have done if you had loved him."

"How do you know so much, anyway? Have you ever been in love?"

Rob bit his lip and pushed his hands through his hair. "No, I don't think I have ever been in love. But I have been attracted to women. That is not necessarily the same thing."

"Do women feel that too? That attraction to a man without being in love with him?"

"I suppose so," replied Rob, wondering how he had got himself into the position of mentor to a young girl.

"Well that's good," sighed Johanna. "I was beginning to think that there must be something wrong with me."

"Why?"

"Because I don't think I'm in love with Miles, but I can nevertheless enjoy his attentions."

Rob threw back his head and laughed. "Believe me, Johanna; there is nothing wrong with you. You are a healthy woman and probably have a healthy appetite which the right man will be privileged to satisfy."

Johanna stared at him. "I don't think it is anything to laugh at!"

Rob stopped laughing and gazed at her, his deep blue eyes boring into Johanna's large dark ones.

He suddenly seemed unable to breathe, and he couldn't take his eyes away from her.

"No. I'm sorry," he whispered hoarsely at last. "I wasn't laughing at you, believe me. It's just that I'm not the best person to be giving this kind of advice to an innocent young girl. God knows I've made enough mistakes in my life to last an eternity. I wouldn't wish to see you do the same."

"I suppose that we must all make our own mistakes," Johanna whispered, feeling herself to be on the edge of something she couldn't comprehend. She gazed into his eyes, and slowly moved closer to him.

He held out a hand as if he would touch her hair, but he withdrew it without ever carrying out his intention.

"Don't let me be yours," he replied with a sigh. "I can be no good for you, Jo. You know that, don't you?"

Jo nodded weakly. "I think so. But I feel so strange when I'm with you. I don't understand what it means."

"It means nothing, Jo. It's merely an attraction between two people; like magnets are drawn to each other. But don't ever mistake it for something else."

He needed to convince himself as well as Jo; he knew that he hadn't succeeded. He was in danger of falling in love for the first time in his life. It was folly, but he seemed helpless to control it.

His hand reached out to her once more. Jo had not taken her eyes from his, and she wanted nothing more than to feel the touch of his hand upon her cheek. She took a step closer.

"Jo, do I smell bread?" enquired Miles, entering the kitchen noisily and disturbing the current which seemed to have sprung between them.

"Yes," said Johanna, shaking her head, momentarily bewildered by her sharp return to reality. "But I didn't make it for you. It's for Rob's lunch and supper. If you start eating it there will be nothing left for him."

"Not even a crust?" pleaded Miles.

"Oh very well, then. But only a small crust. Rob needs building up and you don't."

Rob broke off a piece of crust and handed it to Miles. He gave another to Johanna, before breaking one for himself.

"It tastes as good as it smells," murmured Rob, speaking with his mouth full.

"Johanna is an exceedingly good cook," commented Miles. "You must ask her to cook you a proper meal one day. You wouldn't get a better one anywhere."

"I'll bear that in mind, when I have something more interesting to cook than cauliflower and beetroot."

"I dare say I could come up with something. For the moment, however I must get back home. I promised Father that I would call on Mrs Tucker this afternoon, and if I don't go now it will be too late."

"Who is Mrs Tucker?" enquired Rob.

"She is a very dear old lady who used to look after my father when he was a little boy. He has always been very fond of her and he likes me to visit her every week with some little treat. She lives in one of the farm cottages."

"Quite the lady of the Manor, aren't you?" murmured Rob.

Johanna blushed. "Hardly that; but we do like to care for those who have been dependent upon us for their livelihood. What's wrong with that?"

"Nothing; nothing at all," replied Rob, sorry that he had let his tongue run away with him. He didn't like to admit that the realisation that he and Johanna were from totally different worlds had hit him hard, almost as if he had been slapped in the face.

"I suppose that benevolent employers are not something with which I have much experience. I did not intend to demean your endeavours. I'm sure that Mrs Tucker must look forward eagerly to your weekly visits."

"Well, she says that she does," replied Johanna seriously. "I wouldn't do it if I thought that she looked upon them as acts of condescending charity. Mrs Tucker is too much a friend and a loved one for that."

Miles put his arm about Johanna's shoulder. "Well, come on, Jo. We had best make a move. I have a lot to do if I am to take Rob to Ledbury tomorrow; so too has Rob. I'll be along early tomorrow. Meanwhile good luck with pulling those cauliflowers!"

Johanna held out her hand to Rob, who took her warm fingers in his. She caught her breath at his touch, and smiled nervously. "I'll see you next week sometime, and will cook you that meal," she whispered.

Rob nodded, and smiled. "I'll look forward to it," he murmured almost to himself as Miles drew Johanna through the door.

Chapter 4

"FATHER, DO YOU THINK I SHOUD MARRY MILES?" ASKED Johanna at the dinner table later that week.

Peter Martin gulped down a spoonful of piping hot soup and immediately regretted the action as it burned its way downward. Hastily he drained his wine glass and poured himself another, which quickly followed its predecessor.

Johanna grinned. "Is it such a shock?" she asked.

Her father smiled back. "Not at all. I am merely surprised that you wish to ask my opinion. You haven't done so on any occasion that I can recall, since you were ten years old."

A sigh escaped her. "Well you should not have raised me to be so independent!" she commented, and then added, "But I suppose there are times when a girl needs advice."

Peter stared at his daughter thoughtfully, not wishing to say or do anything which might prevent her from confiding in him. It was a great pity that Eleanor, his wife, had not lived longer. Johanna was in need of a mother, and he was doubtful whether he could fulfil the role adequately.

"What's the problem? If I can help, then you know I will do my best."

Johanna reached for his hand and squeezed it. "Yes, I know. You have never failed me yet. It's just that I don't know what to do about Miles. Emily was telling me that I should either marry him or stop seeing him. What do you think?"

"I think that Emily is an interfering old woman who takes too many liberties."

"Yes, that's probably true, but she is the nearest thing I have to a mother, so that I cannot precisely ignore what she says. Do you agree with her?"

Peter hesitated. "Well, you do seem to have been living in each other's pockets lately, and I confess that I would not object to him as a son-in-law. However it seems to me that if you are in some doubt as to whether you should marry him, then you cannot be in love with him."

"As usual you have bitten right into the heart of the matter, Father. How can I tell whether I am in love with him? And does it matter much if I am not?"

A frown had gathered upon Johanna's brow, and Peter smoothed it with a grin.

"Your mother and I were very much in love when we wed against her father's wishes. I don't think she ever regretted her choice, even though she had to sacrifice so much in worldly terms."

Johanna noted the faraway look in her father's eyes as he reminisced. It was no secret that Eleanor Highgate had married 'down' and had been disowned by her family as a result.

"What does it feel like to be in love?"

"I can't describe it, Jo. But you will know when it happens to you."

"That's what Rob said," murmured Jo.

Instantly alert, Peter studied her, wondering whether he was about to receive a clue as to the reason for Jo's sudden doubts.

"Rob?" he whispered casually.

Johanna blushed. "I think I mentioned him before. Rob Berrow; he is one of the Lowbands people. Miles and I have been helping him a little."

"Go on," urged her father as she hesitated.

"There is no more to tell. We have met only a few times."

"I was not aware that you were upon such intimate terms with anyone from Lowbands. Tell me more; how did you meet? "

Johanna blushed again and hoped that her father would not notice her burning cheeks. "Miles and I just happened to be riding that way when it was their open day, so that is how we met Rob; Mr Berrow, I should say."

"Yes, you probably should. Your friendship with the gentleman seems to have progressed remarkably quickly considering that you can only have known each other for a few days. What do you know about him?"

"Not a lot. He was a weaver before he came here."

"A weaver? Yes I knew that the inhabitants of Lowbands were mainly tradesmen and factory workers. Does he know anything about the land?"

Jo shook her head. "That's why Miles is helping him."

"I hadn't imagined that Miles would have much sympathy with a group of Chartists," murmured Peter.

"What are the Chartists, Father?" asked Jo. "I have heard of them of course, and I know that they seek some sort of electoral reform, but other than that I know nothing."

"A lot of hotheads if you ask me. They want every man to be able to vote at the election of Members of Parliament, and they want the voting done by secret ballot. I believe they are even demanding that MPs should be paid! It's all a lot of nonsense, I suppose, and they are unlikely to achieve their aims. They would be much better advised to use their energies in doing something more constructive."

"Like the Land Company?"

"I don't know what Feargus O'Connor can expect to gain from such a shatterbrained notion. What is the point in transporting hundreds, perhaps thousands, of people from an environment with which they are familiar to one of which they can have no knowledge or experience? It can only lead to disaster."

"I think he is trying to make a better life for the people."

"A laudable idea, no doubt. However it can do no possible good for anyone. It's difficult enough to scratch a living on the land when you have been brought up to it. Why, the people who work for me have almost as much land for their gardens, and they have their wages to live on! These people don't know one end of a plough from the other. How can they survive?"

Jo sighed thoughtfully. "They don't use ploughs, Father. Feargus O'Connor recommends the use of a fork."

"Feargus O'Connor is a lawyer. He has an idealist's view of the land. What are these people to do if we have a harsh winter and the crops fail? They'll have no means of getting through the winter and will have to resort to parish relief. That would be very expensive for the rest of us, wouldn't it?"

Jo nodded. "I hadn't thought of that. But Miles thinks that with help it might just be possible for them to make a go of it."

"And since when has Miles been such a philanthropist? I've never heard of him taking up lost causes before."

"I think he views it as a challenge."

"That it certainly will be! However we have digressed somewhat. I believe you were telling me about this Rob person."

Jo bit her lip. "I know no more than I have told you. Miles is helping him, by giving him advice and lending him implements when he needs them. He is telling him when to harvest his crops, and when and what to plant. If anyone can make it viable, Miles can."

"That's no doubt true. Miles' own farm is a model to us all."

"Would you like me to marry him?" Johanna returned to the original topic.

"You know that I don't hold with parental arrangements on this subject, Jo. I want you to be as happy in your marriage as I was in mine. You must choose your own husband, for I will not do it for you."

"A lot of help you are, Father!" teased Jo.

"I can't tell you whether you love Miles enough, or whether you would be happy with him. You are the best judge of that. He would certainly be able to provide well for you, and you would live in greater comfort than you do now."

"I don't think that is important to me."

Peter nodded. "It probably isn't, but it should be a consideration."

"Father, first you are telling me to marry for love, and now you are saying that I should marry for comfort. You can't have it both ways."

Peter grinned. "Sometimes it's possible. It depends whether you fall in love wisely or not."

"Can you fall in love where you choose?"

"Perhaps not, but I suppose that the sensible thing to do is to limit the opportunities for falling in love unwisely."

"How?"

Peter thought carefully for a moment.

"By not mixing in the sort of circles where you meet unsuitable suitors," he suggested at last.

"What would you do if I fell in love unsuitably?"

"I should do everything in my power to prevent you from making any match which I felt would not bring you happiness."

"But you said that I must choose my own husband."

"Ah yes, but I am relying upon your good judgement to fall in love with someone who will make you happy."

"Like Mother did?" whispered Jo timorously.

"You have me there, of course! However we have once more moved from the subject of Miles. It seems to me that you are not sure of your feelings, and that's as good a reason as any for delaying any decision about whether or not to marry him. Has he declared himself?"

Jo nodded.

"And he wishes to marry you soon?"

"Yes."

"Well that's to be expected. He is a healthy young man and probably needs a wife. You have not done anything foolish, have you?"

Jo giggled. "Foolish? No, of course not."

"Well then, take your time. Sooner or later you'll know what is the right thing to do. It doesn't pay to rush into these matters. And there's no need to take too much notice of what Emily says. She would like to see you settled, but she probably thinks she knows your feelings better than you do, and she can't do that."

"So you don't think I should either marry him or give him up?"

"No. Not if you are still unsure. 'Though it would be unfair to keep him dangling longer than necessary," he warned.

Jo smiled, her relief evident. "I'm glad you don't agree with Emily. I really am so fond of Miles and I don't feel I want to stop seeing him. I did tell him how I feel , so I don't think I could be accused of leaving him dangling, do you?"

"I might have known that you would have been painfully honest with poor Miles. I'm quite glad I am almost an old man and well past this sort of thing.

"No you're not old, Father!" countered Jo. "Why you are not yet fifty and have plenty of time to find another wife if you want to."

Peter nodded. "But I could never replace your mother and I don't feel I want to try. Young Mollie down at the village inn looks after me admirably. What do I need a wife for?"

Jo blushed a bright crimson. This was the first time that her father had mentioned a liaison of which Jo had been aware for some years.

"Seriously, Jo. You do know what it is all about, don't you? I know that you have no mother to explain things to you, but I don't believe you should live in ignorance of what happens between men and women."

Jo nodded. "There's no need to explain further, Father. I know what you're talking about and shall not go to my marriage bed in total ignorance."

Peter grinned, relieved that a difficult problem had resolved itself without his aid. "Not total ignorance, but total innocence, eh?"

Jo laughed with her father and they continued their conversation on topics of a more general and innocuous nature, whilst Jo dished up the vegetables.

****

Rob woke up the next morning to the knowledge that every muscle in his body ached. Even his fingers and toes felt as if they had been pulled from their sockets.

He stretched wearily, knowing that he should have got up ages ago, but yet unwilling to do so. He had not expected to feel so tired and sore and stiff, and he wondered how long it would be before he became accustomed to his new work; not long, he hoped.

He could not escape the feeling that maybe Liz had been right and it had been nothing but a foolish dream, to give up all that he knew to start afresh on a life which bore no resemblance at all to his previous existence. The work was going to be long and hard, and the living likely to be meagre.

Vaguely he wondered what Liz was doing now; and Jenny. He couldn't think of them without being aware of a pang of guilt. His conscience did plague him at times and he knew that he should not have let them go so easily. His own dreams had, he supposed, been so important to him that he had sacrificed Jenny and Liz to them.

He tried to brush all thought of them from his mind. They were after all far away, and Liz had always been resourceful. Maybe she had found herself a new protector; maybe she had already found one before she suggested that they part. This conjecture brought some comfort. Yes, she would surely have done so, he convinced himself. Even he couldn't believe that their life together had been so dreadful that she would discontinue it without having planned exactly what she would do, and who she would do it with.

Rob nodded sagely to himself. That must be the answer. She had been ready to give up all because she had found a new love. Well, if that were the case, he truly could not blame her. He knew that he had not been much of a husband to her, and Liz was a woman with healthy appetites. He hoped she and Jenny would be happy.

He turned uneasily and groaned as his muscles protested. Crawling out of the dishevelled bed, he grinned to himself as he recalled Johanna doing much the same a few days earlier. There too was a full-blooded woman, eager to be taken by the right man. He knew a momentary regret that he could not be that man. Having lived a fairly celibate existence for some years, he was not totally immune to female charms, and Johanna had them in plenty. He could easily be tempted, but knew that he would not. Johanna was not some wench who could be used and forgotten. She was the daughter of a gentleman, and there were rules about that sort of thing. In any event there could be no place in her life for a poor weaver, or even a poor smallholder, who was already wed.

But that didn't mean that he couldn't look forward to her visits. He had enjoyed her company, and it was a novel experience for him to enjoy the companionship of a woman. There was a refreshing honesty about her, and this, combined with a lively sense of humour, meant that it was impossible not to be cheered and stimulated by her presence. He envied Miles Woodthorpe, who was clearly on close terms with her.

Rob stretched again and rubbed his aching shoulders. Stiffly he made his way to the kitchen and cut a neat chunk of bread, and some cheese, and poured himself a mug of fresh cool water.

Gingerly, his muscles still protesting, he sat down and ate his breakfast.

He had just downed the last of the bread, when he heard the sound of hooves clattering up the road. They stopped outside his gate. As quickly as he could he went to his bedroom and pulled on a shirt and trousers. It would never do for Johanna to find him in a state of undress.

But it was not Johanna who knocked upon the door, and when Rob opened it to find Feargus O'Connor standing there, he realised that Johanna was hardly likely to be visiting him so early in the morning.

Feargus seemed to fill the door frame and his loud voice, with its unmistakable Irish brogue, was as warm as his beaming round ruddy face.

"Good morning, Berrow. I've just called by to see how you are settling in."

"Come in, Mr O'Connor," Rob grinned, still buttoning his shirt. "You're about bright and early. I have only just finished my breakfast."

"I don't believe in wasting the morning, Berrow. Up at dawn is my motto. Especially when I'm working on the land. How goes it, my boy?"

Rob urged Feargus to a seat and carefully sat down himself.

"It goes very well," replied Rob thoughtfully. "I am however feeling rather stiff this morning and I think I may well have overdone it for the first couple of days."

Feargus laughed, a great booming laugh which filled the cottage. "It gets everyone like that. The third and fourth days are the worst, and after that your body starts to get used to it. When you have been here a week you will feel as if you have always worked upon the land."

"Mmm," mumbled Rob doubtfully. "In that case I shall take it easy for the next couple of days. I'm going to Gloucester today anyway, with Miles Woodthorpe."

Feargus nodded. "I'm glad that you have made friends with the neighbours. I confess that when I first came here there were one or two local difficulties. I don't know why some of our neighbours should be so set against us. It was the same at Heronsgate, the first colony I set up."

"What are their objections?"

Feargus shrugged his shoulders. "Who can say? I only know that the owners of the local quarry and sandpit refused to sell me stone or sand. Fortunately we found sand here in Lowbands, and were able to use that for the building. We managed to buy in bricks and these were much cheaper than they had been at Heronsgate, so I'm not complaining. I did get a deputation from local landowners who told me in no uncertain terms that they would not permit their men or horses to work here. That didn't bother me either. I brought in workmen of my own, and lodged them at Redmarley and Staunton; and in six months we have created our own community here. The villagers are no longer opposed to us, even if the landowners are. And now that I have seen you all well settled I shall be moving on to Snigs End, just three miles down the road from here, and there will be a much larger settlement there, with eighty one allotments. It will take a while to have it ready. But I am determined that within five years I shall have all the Land Company members installed in the countryside, as you are."

Rob grinned. "I don't know how you ever thought up the scheme."

Feargus sighed. "It is wonderful in its simplicity, isn't it? The land company buys the estate with the subscription money, and then takes out a mortgage on it, and uses the mortgage capital to buy another estate, and so on until we have bought sufficient estates for all the subscribers."

"But how is the interest on the mortgage to be paid?" asked Rob, thinking that he had found the one flaw in the scheme.

"From the rents, of course," responded Feargus. "One pound, five shillings an acre is a very modest rent, don't you think? And by my reckoning a man can keep himself and a family of six on four acres and still sell surplus produce to fetch in one hundred and twenty four pounds, two shillings a year."

Rob scratched his head and brushed back his hair with his hand. "It all sounds very logical, and as I do not have a family to support I look forward to making a handsome profit," he grinned.

"As a bachelor myself, I do sometimes wonder whether the lack of a wife is necessarily a good thing. Wives are very good at baking bread and making butter and cheese, and the economy here does rather rely on those achievements. You would do well to find yourself a wife before too long," urged Feargus with a fatherly grin.

Rob nodded. "I shall bear that in mind, Mr O'Connor."

Feargus rose as far as his height would permit, and held out his hand to Rob. "Well, I must be on my way. Good luck, Berrow; and don't you be forgetting what I have said about a wife!"

They shook hands and Feargus left with a clatter of hooves, down the lane. Rob felt even more exhausted, as if he had been swept over by a hurricane, such was the forceful vitality of Feargus O'Connor.

His exhaustion didn't last for long, however. Within the hour, Miles arrived to help Rob take his cauliflowers to market at Gloucester.

Rob turned out to be an apt pupil, enjoying the experience of shouting out his wares at market. He learned quickly from watching the other traders, so that within the space of three weeks he had become quite accomplished at setting up his stall and selling his produce.

He kept himself very busy during this period, learning all the time. He was relieved to find that Feargus had been right about the effect of the work on his muscles. His body soon adjusted to the new type of work.

Miles continued to be a regular visitor at Lowbands, but Johanna stayed away. If he were honest with himself, Rob would have to admit that he was disappointed by her continued absence. He knew that she was avoiding him, and this prospect he greeted with mixed feelings. He wanted to see her again, but he also knew that to pursue whatever lay between them would be to tread dangerously. It was as well that she had the strength to keep a distance between them.

Johanna didn't know for how much longer she could maintain that distance. She had heeded her father's words and had removed herself from any possible danger. But it had not helped to quell her inner turmoil. In fact, after three weeks she was no nearer to reaching a decision on the question of her future with Miles, and she knew that before she could make that decision she would have to see Rob again. She had after all, met him only three times, and any danger was probably more imagined than real. She hoped that when she met him again, she would find that all her doubts had vanished, and she would be able to agree to marry Miles without any further delay.

It was therefore with some trepidation that Johanna put together a few items from the larder to take with her to Lowbands. By the time that Miles called for her, the basket was full.

"He won't like it, you know," Miles said when he saw the basket.

"Won't like what?"

"Being treated like an object of charity by the Lady Bountiful."

Johanna halted in her tracks and stared at Miles, struck by this unexpected view of her actions. "Is that what he will think?" she whispered.

Miles nodded. "He is very proud and independent. What would you expect him to think?"

"I don't know. I certainly don't want to appear like Lady Bountiful, but I do want to help him. What do you suggest I do?"

"What have you got in there?"

"Butter, cheese, bread, ham, tomatoes, some pickles, a bottle of elderberry wine, a packet of tea, a teapot, and a plum tart."

Miles grinned. "Well you can take out the tea and teapot, for a start. He bought those at Ledbury a couple of weeks ago. As for the rest, you had best say that we are having a picnic, and invite him to join us."

Disappointed that she had been unable to provide Rob with any comforts, Johanna took out the teapot and the tea, and added a small jug of cream, and one of milk.

Just as she did so, her father entered the kitchen and washed his hands at the sink.

"Where are you two going?" he asked amiably.

"We're going for a picnic."

"It's a nice day for it. Where will you go?"

Johanna was not sure that she wanted her father to know what she was about, but before she could think of a suitable general reply, Miles replied that they were headed for Lowbands.

"I see," said Peter thoughtfully.

Johanna squared her shoulders. "You don't mind, do you, Father?"

Peter Martin hesitated, wondering how best to describe what he felt.

"No," he replied slowly. "I don't object. I think it is highly commendable that you should give the benefit of your advice to one of the settlers. I think the project is ill advised from the start, and from what I hear this Feargus O'Connor has some very strange ideas which can lead only to disaster."

Miles nodded. "I'm afraid that I'm inclined to agree. Feargus told Rob the other week that a family of six can live comfortably off four acres and still make a profit of more than a hundred pounds a year! I should like to know how that can be done!"

"Wouldn't we all? If that were true, you and I would be rich indeed, Miles!" grinned Peter.

"I can't help but feel sorry for them though. They are so full of enthusiasm and determination that they deserve to succeed. They might just be able to do it with the proper advice. Unfortunately, because their neighbours are on the whole unwilling to help them, there is a tendency for them to view my advice with scepticism. I think they suspect me of wanting to sabotage their efforts!"

"That's a pity; because no-one is better placed than you to give advice. Maybe you had best invite them up to Thorpe Hall to show them your methods do really work?" suggested Peter.

"I had thought of that, but it has to be said that farming on several hundred acres is vastly different from farming on four!"

Peter dried his hands and poured himself a mug of ale. "Well, if there is anything I can do, let me know." He downed the ale and wiped his hand across his mouth. Picking up the cask of ale from which he had just poured, he handed it to Miles. "Here, take this. They're not teetotallers, are they?"

Miles grinned. "I don't believe so. Although Feargus would not permit any alcohol at their conference, I think that was more to preserve law and order rather than for any other reason. It is said that Feargus himself is quite partial to the brandy bottle."

Johanna kissed her father's cheek. "I'm glad you don't object, Father. And I'm sure Rob will appreciate the ale. We had best be gone now, or it will be too late for our picnic."

Johanna picked up the basket and Miles followed her out to the stable. Peter watched them go, a worried frown upon his brow. He knew that Johanna had not been to Lowbands since their conversation about love and marriage. He had been sure that she had taken heed of the message he had tried obliquely to convey to her on that occasion. He also knew that in the weeks since then she had grown increasingly restless and tense. Maybe his advice had not been so sound after all, he mused.

When Miles and Johanna arrived at Lowbands, they tracked Rob down to his potato patch. There he appeared to be staring into a large hole, about three feet deep, and three feet square.

"How deep do potatoes grow?" he asked, for once forgetting his usual greeting.

"Not that deep, that's for sure!" responded Miles, frowning. "What's the problem? Haven't you found any yet?"

Rob shook his head miserably.

"Well try further along the row."

"I have," replied Rob, pointing to some more holes in the middle of the patch.

Johanna felt her heart lurch in her chest. If the potato crop had failed, there would be a very meagre living through the winter.

Miles grabbed the spade from Rob's lifeless hands. "There must be something here."

Miles dug up the next plant, and after rummaging around in the soil, he found one small potato, half eaten away.

"Slugs!" he exclaimed."They've eaten their way through the entire crop. It's been such a wet summer! Ideal for slugs! I'm sorry, Rob, but it doesn't look as if you are going to have much in the way of a potato crop this year, We'll have to dig them all up in case they didn't get to all of them, but I have a horrible feeling that you're going to have to manage without any potatoes this winter."

Johanna glanced at Rob's stricken features and fought down the urge to put her arms about him and comfort him, as she would do for a small boy.

"It isn't the end of the world, Rob. You have other crops."

Rob stared at her blankly, and then put his head in his hands. "The turnips," he muttered."I expect they will have had them too!"

"Not necessarily. They probably prefer potatoes, and may have left the turnips alone. Let's go and have a look," called Miles already striding away.

"I don't think I can bear to look," murmured Rob.

Johanna took his hand. "You must. If you want to be a farmer you have to learn to cope with this sort of problem."

His fingers felt cold and lifeless, and Johanna rubbed them with her hand. Rob watched the movement, vaguely aware of a stirring within him.

"Come on, Rob. Pull yourself together!" she whispered, giving him a slight shake.

It seemed to work, for Rob directed his bleak gaze to Johanna, and for a brief moment they stared at each other, Johanna trying to will him to find the strength to deal with the loss of his crop.

A warmth gradually grew between them, spreading from their joined hands, until they each became enveloped in it. A flicker of interest appeared in Rob's eyes. His mouth was firm and strong, Jo noticed, and seemed only inches away from her own. She felt herself drifting closer to him, and his hand in hers was warm and gently caressing.

In the distance she could hear Miles calling to them, but she tried to ignore him, not wishing the spell to be broken. Slowly Rob raised his free hand to her face, stroking her chin and cheek with his long slender fingers.

She wanted to cling to him; to lean against his chest and melt into his embrace. Almost, she did so, but again Miles called to them.

Rob was equally reluctant to end the spell, but he knew that end it must.

"It would do no good," he whispered hoarsely.

"Would it not?" asked Johanna, refusing to remove her gaze from his face.

Rob shook his head. "Absolutely not!" he whispered ambiguously. "Come, Miles will be wondering what keeps us."

Rob's hand moved within hers until he was clasping her, rather than she to him. He squeezed her fingers in a gentle embrace; the most he could offer. And then he turned toward the turnip patch, running and dragging Jo after him.

Miles stared at them, his arms resting upon the handle of the fork.

"What kept you?" he asked mildly, noting Jo's flushed cheeks and her hand resting comfortably in Rob's.

"Nothing that can be of any great moment," murmured Rob, reluctantly releasing Jo's hand with a final squeeze. "Do I have any turnips or not?"

Miles pointed to the pile of big healthy turnips he had pulled, and grinned. "Your turnips at least appear to be safe."

"That's something to be thankful for, then," grinned Rob. "Perhaps I shall not be totally ruined."

"Let's see the extent of the damage, shall we? We'll dig up all the potatoes and see what we get," suggested Miles.

At the end of the day, they had managed to find only one sackful of potatoes, and many of these were of inferior quality and not suitable for keeping through the winter or for taking to market. Whilst Rob and Miles dug them, Jo sorted them; but overall the result was very disappointing.

It was a pity that no-one was in the mood for enjoying the picnic which Jo had put together. The meal passed in a sombre silence, as if some great dark cloud hung over them. Each of the trio was content to rest with his own thoughts and showed no desire to share them.

As they rode home, Miles decided that he must tackle Jo about her feelings for Rob.

"Are you in love with him?" he asked abruptly as they rode side by side.

Johanna felt her cheeks grow hot and her horse, aware of her momentary lapse in concentration, jerked nervously, so that Jo had to pass several minutes in settling her.

"What a strange question, Miles," she sighed when she was in control once more.

"Not so strange, Jo. I saw the way you were looking at each other."

"We hardly know one another," protested Jo.

"Does that make any difference?"

"I don't know. I would have thought that it would."

"You have never looked at me in the way that you looked at him."

"This is nonsense, Miles. You are reading too much into a look."

"Am I, Jo? What should I be reading into it?"

"I don't know, Miles. Please, just don't go on about it. I have met Rob Berrow three or four times; that's all. How could I be in love with him? I know next to nothing about him!"

"You would be making a big mistake if you were to fall in love with him. He is a fine fellow; I like him; but he has nothing to offer you, Jo."

"Do you think I don't know that? He is certainly not the man I would choose to fall in love with, Miles. If I could choose, I would certainly be in love with you, for you are my best friend and I love you very much. I know that you would make an excellent husband, and that I should be very comfortable as your wife. But I don't honestly know if that is enough, Miles. How do I know whether I have fallen in love with this man? And if I have, how could I then marry you? Do you not see what a mess my emotions are in at the moment? Please don't press me, Miles. I just don't know! I wish to God I did!"

Miles reached across and touched her hand in a comforting gesture. "I'm sorry, Jo. I don't mean to push you, and I am grateful for your honesty."

"Oh, Miles; you deserve much more than honesty. I wish I could be what you want me to be, but I don't think I can. At least, not at the moment."

"I'll try to be patient, Jo. Meanwhile, will you promise that you won't do anything unwise?"

Jo giggled. "Do you mean will I prevent him from seducing me? I don't think there is any danger of that. He may be only a poor weaver, Miles, but I'm sure he is a man of honour. I don't think he has any intention of seducing me. Maybe I shall have to seduce him!" she finished with a mischievous grin.

"That's precisely what I mean, Jo! I know you're impetuous, and I wouldn't put it past you to do just that to get your own way."

"Do you really think I would?"

"I don't know. There's no telling what you will do when you get an idea in your head. All I'm saying is please don't rush into anything."

Jo smiled at him. "All right then, Miles. I promise not to rush into anything. But I'm still not sure that there is anything to rush into."

With that, Miles had to rest content, because Jo kicked her horse into a gallop and he had great difficulty in catching up with her.

Chapter 5

By the end of October, Rob had harvested his crops, ploughed his plot with a plough and horse loaned by Miles, and partly replanted with spring vegetables. He had been disappointed with his harvest, for apart from the failure of his potatoes, a problem which had been shared by his neighbours at Lowbands, he had found that his turnips and swedes had not escaped attack from the slugs. In spite of this, however, he had managed a reasonable yield.

He had found the corn harvest difficult and time consuming, and after Miles had shown him how to thresh it, he decided that in future he would buy in corn and flour and concentrate his efforts on vegetables.

Rob felt generally fitter than he had ever done. His long thin body had filled out, and his outdoor existence had encouraged his skin to a golden tan which showed no sign of fading with the approach of winter.

Although Miles continued to visit frequently and advised him on what to plant and when to plant it, it had been some weeks since he had brought Johanna with him. Rob missed her company, much more than he would have thought possible, but he couldn't escape a feeling of relief that she had decided to stay away.

He knew that he wanted her; wanted her more than he had ever wanted any other woman at any time in his life, and yet he knew also that he must not have her. It was safer by far to try to forget her.

His efforts to do so had so far met with a complete lack of success. As he lay in his lonely bed at night, he would conjure visions of her as he had first seen her; dishevelled and uncovered; laughing in spite of her embarrassing predicament.

Sometimes he would dream of her sharing his new life with him; helping him on the land; working by his side; eating and sleeping with him. But he knew that it could be only a dream. Johanna had not been born to work upon the land. She had been brought up to supervise the kitchen and the smooth running of the house. He believed that she had servants to do the heavy work, and he had no right to even think of bringing her to share a life which could mean nothing but hard work from dawn to dusk.

Rob shrugged his shoulders and brushed back the errant lock of sun-bleached hair. He grinned to himself. It was but a dream and where was the harm in dreaming?

The first shafts of sunlight drifted through Rob's window and he turned lazily. He would have liked to linger longer over his dreams, but he knew that he must get up. He had been waiting for a dry day for some time in order to fix some roof tiles which had become dislodged during recent high winds. He had borrowed a ladder from a neighbour, and decided that today would be a fine opportunity.

At last, he jumped out of bed, quickly dressed and swallowed some bread and cheese. He had come to an arrangement with Mrs Lee, the wife of his nearest neighbour, that he would purchase bread from her every other day.

The dislodged tiles were in the middle of the roof, at the front, and near to the centre ridge. By the time Rob had the ladder in position the sun was fully up and promising a warm autumn day. Rob whistled to himself as he climbed the ladder and scrambled over the roof until he reached the damaged part. It did not take him long to fix it, and with a sigh of relief at a job well done, Rob made his way back to the ladder.

Unfortunately he lost his footing just as he was about to step onto the ladder. He knocked the ladder to the ground and he went tumbling after it, ending up in a crumpled heap not far from the front door.

It had all happened too quickly for him to cry out, and when he landed he was immediately conscious of a sharp stabbing pain in his right leg. When he tried to get up the pain was so great that he fainted.

****

Johanna too was awake early that day. She had not slept well for several weeks, and would often wake up heavy lidded, as if she had not been to bed at all. Her father had noticed the change in her but had refrained so far from commenting upon it. What she needed he thought, was some female companionship, and he had written to his brother to enquire whether his niece Jessica, who was a year older than Johanna, would care to make a visit. She was due to arrive in the following week.

Jo, deciding that even if she were to stay in bed until noon she would be unlikely to sleep further, got up and swilled her face with cold water. She dressed in her riding habit and made her way down to the stable where she saddled her mare.

It was not unusual for Jo to ride unescorted about the countryside before breakfast. She could not tell what made her head towards Lowbands on that particular day, unless it was that she had not seen Rob for several weeks.

It had, she supposed, been foolish to consider that she could forget him and the effect he had upon her, merely by staying away. She had spent long hours each sleepless night trying to analyse her feelings, but she had achieved little success. All she knew was that she was miserable and it was not an inherent part of her nature to be dismal.

She stopped at Rob's gate and gazed across his land. She had no intention of actually entering his garden, but she had hoped to have a glimpse of him going about his duties.

There was no sign of him. Jo sighed and would have been on her way when she thought she heard a shout. She turned quickly and stared again, her heart beating rapidly against her breast. Someone was calling, but she could not see from where.

Intrigued, Jo dismounted and wrapped the reins about the gatepost. Light footed, she made her way down the garden path until she found the ladder, and Rob lying awkwardly upon it, his right leg clearly broken.

A startled gasp broke from Jo's lips and she ran to Rob's side, taking his hand in hers.

"Oh, my poor darling! Are you all right? I can see that your leg is broken. Does anything else hurt? What should I do?"

She was completely unaware of the endearment she had used. Rob was not. He grinned through his pain, feeling that the world was suddenly a better place.

"I'm pretty certain it is just my leg. I don't know what to do. I was hoping you would. I can't move; I've tried, and all I did was faint. However I feel much better now."

Jo studied the twisted leg and knew that it should be set in splints without delay.

"Is there a doctor at Lowbands?" she asked.

Rob shook his head.

"Nor a bone setter?"

"Not to my knowledge."

"Then I shall have to fetch Miles. He will know what to do."

She entered the house and came back with a pillow and blanket from Rob's bed. Sitting beside him on the ground she raised his head and shoulders to place the pillow behind him.

"This will at least help to make you ..." Her words were smothered as he brought his lips to hers. She closed her eyes and gave herself up to his kiss. Each clinging tightly to the other, the kiss continued, mouths parting beneath the force of it, tongues searching deliciously, as the long weeks of misery exploded around and within them to be replaced by a surge of emotion more powerful than either could have dreamed possible.

At last it ended. Reluctantly and breathlessly, Rob placed his hands on her cheeks, and gazed into her eyes, shaken by the depth of feelings he had aroused in one moment of unbridled weakness.

"Don't fall in love with me, Jo," he urged in a whisper.

"I'm trying hard not to, but I don't seem to be having much success."

"I'm no good for you."

"Do you not think that I'm the best judge of what is good for me?"

He shook his head. "Not in this case."

"Then why did you kiss me?"

"I couldn't help myself. When your lips were so close to mine I couldn't resist. I've been dreaming of it for weeks, and somehow my dreams became muddled with reality. And I have to be honest and say that the reality was infinitely more satisfying than the dream."

Jo smiled. "For me, too. Can we do it again please?"

Rob laughed and pushed her away. "I would love to, but it is too dangerous a game for you to play. There is truly no place for me in your life, much as I would wish it otherwise. It would be an unforgivable error for me to kiss you again."

A wicked grin split Jo's face. "Ah. yes, but what if I were to kiss you whilst I have you helpless before me?"

"You might get more than you bargained for."

"What, with you with a broken leg? I should like to know how you would manage that!"

Rob grinned. "You have a point there. But don't try it when I'm fit again. I might not then be capable of the magnanimous gesture of refusing you a second time."

"Do you have to be so magnanimous?"

Rob sobered suddenly. "Yes, I'm afraid I do. You can know nothing about me, and I am entirely an unsuitable person for a well brought up young lady. I could never marry you, and I love you too well for any other sort of liaison."

"Do you?"

"Do you doubt it?"

Jo shook her head. Their kiss had been like the joining of two souls. To her it had brought peace and contentment, and the true knowledge that she loved and was loved. No, she did not doubt that he loved her.

"No, I don't doubt it, Rob; and I know that you have no dishonourable intentions. I know that it would be difficult for us to marry, but I don't see why you should write off such a notion so quickly."

Rob sighed. "If it were only that we come from different worlds and there can be no place for me in yours, and I could not bring you down to mine, then maybe we could find a solution, Jo. But it is not, and cannot be that simple."

"What then?"

Rob hesitated, knowing that nothing less than the truth would do. It would be unfair for him to allow her to believe that she would be able to persuade him into something which only he knew was impossible.

"I have heard that bigamy is against the law."

Jo gasped. Whatever she had expected, it had not been that he had a wife already.

"You see the difficulty?" asked Rob gently, cursing himself for inflicting this hurt upon her.

Jo nodded, her cheeks pale, her lips so recently warm from his kiss, now colourless. "Yes," she whispered. "It is a difficulty I had not thought of."

"There is no reason why you should. In your world marriage is forever and divorce is rare. In my world divorce is impossible, but sometimes it is not possible for a couple to continue to live together. So it was with Liz and me."

"What happened?"

Rob shrugged. "I was a poor husband to her and she deserved better. No blame can be attached to her; I don't know what she is doing now, but she refused to come to

Lowbands with me, so I came alone. She urged me to do so. So you see, Jo. I am not a good husband to my wife, and I can be no husband at all to you."

Jo stood up and straightened her skirt.

"Thank you for telling me. I'm not sure whether it helps or not."

"I would not ever wish to deceive you, Jo."

She nodded dully. "I had best fetch Miles, so that he can see to your leg. Are you comfortable now?"

Rob nodded. "The only ache I have is here," he replied, touching his chest dramatically. "And there is no cure for that."

Jo smiled ruefully, and there being no more to be said, she waved and made her way to her horse, who was patiently munching grass at the roadside.

She suffered a further setback when she reached Thorpe Hall because Miles had left early for Gloucester, and was not expected back until evening.

This was an eventuality that Jo had not contemplated, and to the astonishment of Miles' housekeeper, she burst into tears.

She couldn't tell whether she cried for Rob or for herself, but she was completely unable to stem the flood of tears. The housekeeper, Mrs Harper, was quite unused to dealing with hysterical females. After a moment's hesitation she held Jo to her ample bosom and allowed her to cry herself out, a massive handkerchief at the ready. Eventually Jo's sobs subsided and she blew her nose in the proffered handkerchief, apologising profusely for having put Mrs Harper to so much trouble.

"I don't know what's the matter with me," she sobbed. "It's just that Miles being out is the last straw! Is there anyone here who could set a broken leg?"

Mrs Harper stared at Jo, unable to understand why she should make such a strange request. "Set a broken leg?" she repeated blankly.

"Yes. A friend of ours has broken his leg and I thought Miles would know what to do. But I suppose I shall have to find Father. I'm not sure that he has set bones, but maybe he will know who can."

Now that she had decided what to do she suddenly felt much better, and with a further apology she ran back to the stable, leaving the housekeeper staring after her open mouthed.

When she returned home Jo found her father in the kitchen reading a copy of the Times, over his breakfast tea.

"Father, you must come at once. Rob has broken his leg, and I don't know what to do," she cried breathlessly.

Peter Martin put down his newspaper thoughtfully. "Where is it broken?" he enquired, draining his tea cup.

"I don't know. Below the knee, I think."

"Is it a clean break?"

"I don't know, Father. I've not touched it for fear of doing something wrong! Do you know what to do?"

"Possibly. We will need lengths of bandage. Can you find something suitable whilst I search for splints. I'll be in the stable when you're ready."

Vastly relieved that someone had now taken control and could tell her what to do, Jo rushed to the linen cupboard and took out a sheet which was in need of repair. She tore it into strips and stuffed the strips into a pillow case.

Her father had saddled his horse and was waiting in the stable yard by the time Jo was ready. Together they rode to Lowbands.

Peter Martin was pleased that at last he would have the opportunity to meet Rob Berrow. He was almost certain that he was the cause of Jo's recent melancholy, and whilst he was anxious not to pry into his daughter's affairs, he was nevertheless concerned for her welfare, and he didn't like to see her unhappy. Briefly he wondered what she had been doing at Rob's cottage so early in the morning, but decided that this was not the appropriate moment for reminding his daughter of the proprieties.

Peter followed his daughter up the garden path to where Rob lay, his eyes closed and his cheeks white beneath his tan.

Jo took his hand in hers. "Rob. Are you all right? My father is here to mend your leg."

Rob's eyes fluttered open and he tried to sit up straight against the pillow, but this slight movement caused an overwhelming pain in his leg and he lay back again.

"Pleased to meet you, sir," he whispered painfully.

"And I you, Rob Berrow," replied Peter Martin, kneeling beside him and examining the injured leg. "This is going to hurt, I'm afraid."

Rob nodded.

"It feels like a clean break. It should mend with little difficulty. Jo, you sit at his head and hold his hands. He is going to need something to pull against when I put these bones together.

Jo did as she was told and gave Rob's hands a comforting squeeze. He was comforted and managed to grin up at her. Peter Martin caught this exchange, and nodded to himself.

Rob gripped Jo's hands so hard during the next few minutes that she wondered briefly whether her fingers would still be intact. Then as her father made the final manoeuvre to place the broken bones together, he fainted.

Jo mopped beads of sweat from his brow and rested her hand upon his cheek in an intimate loving gesture. She smoothed his damp locks away from his face, and when he regained consciousness, Rob took her hand and kissed the palm.

Although busily engaged with wrapping the bandages about the splints, Peter Martin missed nothing. It was clear to him in every look and every gesture, that his daughter was in love with this man, and he with her.

"I think we'd better get you up to the farm," he said when he had finished.

"Oh no, sir. I couldn't do that," Rob protested.

"You don't have a lot of choice in the matter. You can't possibly look after yourself here, unless you want to be a cripple for the rest of your life. And I won't have my daughter coming here at all hours unchaperoned, to prepare meals for you. No, all in all you will do better at home. At least there I can keep an eye on you and see that you and Jo are properly chaperoned."

"But what about my land?"

"You can't handle that in your present condition. You've got to rest that leg and do nothing at all for three or four weeks. Don't worry about the land. I'll send someone up to keep an eye on things and do whatever needs to be done."

"I don't want to put you to any trouble. There's no reason why you should do this for me."

"Isn't there? Well, maybe I'm the best judge of that. My daughter's reputation is of some importance to me, and I should have thought that keeping her out of trouble is probably sufficient reason, isn't it? Also, now that I have set your leg I don't want you doing anything to spoil my good work. I don't want to be responsible for crippling you, now do I? I shall never be able to hold my head up again if you move that leg and limp for the rest of your life.

"Now then, I'll get off home to fetch a cart to transport you. Jo can tidy up here and keep you company until I get back."

Rob lay back against the pillow and sighed. "Your father certainly knows how to get things done," he murmured.

Jo nodded with a grin. "Yes. He's quite something, isn't he?"

"You're very much like him."

"Me? Oh no! I tend to panic and burst into tears at the wrong time. I wasn't much use to you today, was I? I dread to think what Miles' housekeeper thought of me when I went there this morning. She only said that Miles was not expected back until this evening and I burst into a flood of tears that there was no stopping. I feel positively ashamed of myself!"

"We all have our moments of weakness, Jo. There's nothing to be ashamed of."

"When did you last have one?"

"This morning when I kissed you. I should have been strong, but I gave in to the urge because I wanted you and I did not have the strength to do what I knew would have been the right thing."

"It is a somewhat daunting thought that you can only bring yourself to kiss me when you are in a weakened state. It's hardly flattering."

"You know what I mean, Jo! I have no business kissing you at all, and I don't think your father would be so insistent upon taking me into his home if he knew my true circumstances. I ought to tell him straight away."

"I don't see any need for you to tell anyone, Rob. You have explained it all to me, so no-one could accuse you of deceiving me. I don't think it is anyone else's business."

"Not even your father's?"

Jo hesitated. "I don't know. Certainly not at present. If he starts trying to matchmake, then I can tell him that it will do no good. It may be that he intends to throw us together to see whether our love can stand up to close proximity. Either way, my reputation will be better protected if you are in my father's house."

Jo went into the kitchen, collected up the breakfast dishes and washed them up. She then tidied up Rob's bed, and went back outside to join him.

"It's a good job it isn't raining. You'd catch pneumonia or some other dreadful ague, lying there all day."

Rob grinned weakly.

"How does it feel?"

"It hurts like hell, but doubtless I'll survive."

"Do you need me to pack anything for you?"

"Such as?"

"Well, I don't know. A nightshirt?"

"I don't wear one."

"Oh."

Rob grinned. "You could pack my Sunday best clothing, though. It seems I shan't be working for a while and if I am to live it up in style at your farm, I had better take my best. You'll find everything in a box under the bed.

Jo did as she was directed, and found on the top of the box, a white shirt, bottle green frock coat and black trousers. There was also a change of underlinen. She folded it all neatly and then went to the kitchen where she found Rob's razor and comb. Anything else he lacked would have to be found for him, she decided.

Before long she heard the cart travelling down the lane, and she carried the bundle to the gate. Her father jumped down and looped the reins over the gatepost.

"We'll need a mattress to absorb some of the bumps. Does he have one?"

"Of course he does!" replied Jo indignantly. "Where do you think he sleeps?"

Peter Martin grinned. "Come and show me."

Jo led him into the cottage, and Peter looked about him with interest.

"Not bad little cottages, are they?" he commented.

Jo smiled. "No. Everything is here. Have a look outside; I'm sure Rob won't mind."

Peter stepped out of the back door. The hens and pigs in their enclosures caught his eye; so too did the neatly stacked woodpile, the washhouse and the dairy, as yet unused.

He nodded to himself, impressed by the layout. He went back indoors and picked up the mattress. At the door he asked Rob if there was a neighbour who could see to the livestock.

"I expect John Lee and his wife would. She does some baking for me, and she might feed the livestock instead."

"Where do they live?"

Rob pointed to the cottage just visible behind the hedgerow. Peter headed that way wondering whether he had been hasty in bringing Rob to his home instead of making arrangements for neighbours to look after him. However he shrugged his shoulders realising that it was too late to change his mind, and no doubt Jo found the arrangement more pleasing. She had certainly come to life in the presence of Rob; in her cheeks there was some colour which had been lacking in recent weeks, and the dull look in her eyes had been replaced by a lively sparkle. No, he had to believe that he had chosen the best option.

He spoke to Mrs Lee who gladly agreed to see to the livestock for as long as necessary. Peter gave her a guinea to ensure that she was not out of pocket, and then he put himself to the task of getting Rob to the cart. It was not easily accomplished and proved to be a painful process for Rob. However eventually they set off for Home Farm.

The farmhouse seemed very grand to Rob in comparison with his own small cottage. It was a rambling timbered building, with rooms leading one into another in all directions.

They entered through the yard to the kitchen, presided over by Emily and Hannah, her new young helper. The best guest chamber had already been prepared in expectation of the arrival of Jo's cousin, Jessica. Jo now enlisted Hannah's help in preparing a second chamber for Rob whilst he rested in the kitchen.

It was not long before Rob was once more being helped, this time up the polished oak staircase to the blue bedroom.

"I hope you'll be comfortable here," said Jo shyly.

Rob nodded. "I've never been offered such comfort in all my life." He sat carefully upon the bed. "I'm likely to drown inside this mattress. Will you ever find me again?"

Jo laughed. "It is very soft. I prefer something a little more firm, but I hope it will serve."

"Father I have purloined one of your nightshirts for Rob. I hope you don't mind, but I forgot to pack one for him."

Rob grinned. "The truth is, sir, that I don't possess a nightshirt. I've never felt the need for one, but clearly it wouldn't do for me to be here naked for the next three weeks."

Peter smiled. "No, that wouldn't do at all. You're welcome to anything you need. I'll see if I can find a dressing robe for your use too. Now, Jo, I suggest that you make yourself scarce whilst I help this young man into bed. Perhaps you could see what is happening with lunch? I confess that I'm famished after this somewhat unusual morning."

****

Later that afternoon Rob lay gazing miserably at the ceiling. He was beginning to wish that he had not been brought there. Life at the farm was infinitely appealing, but everything contrasted so much with his own way of life that there could be no comparison. Even the lunch, a simple collation of cold meats and hot vegetables, with a glass of elderberry wine, and followed by apple tart, was the best meal he had ever eaten. This was Jo's world and could never be his.

He didn't need this constant reminder that there could be no future for them. He had never doubted it. The problem was that he needed to convince Peter Martin that he was aware of his own unsuitability, and he had no intention of bringing Jo down to his level.

It made a pleasant dream, though. A future with Jo, here or anywhere was a dream of paradise. She was beautiful and lively and honest, and he loved most of all the way in which she would suddenly burst into laughter.

But it was a dream; could only ever be a dream, and he needed to convince Jo too that it could be nothing else.

There was a knock upon the door, and Jo entered with Emily who was to act as chaperone.

"I've brought the chess set. Do you play?"

Rob shook his head.

"Then I shall have to teach you. Emily, you can sit over there with your knitting, if you please." Jo pointed to the seat by the window. "I shall sit very properly upon this chair here and we can set up the board on your lap, Rob."

The afternoon passed pleasantly. Rob proved an apt pupil, soon mastering the basic moves, and whilst he was no match for Jo, it was clear that he soon would be with a little practice.

Once, their hands touched across the board, and they each raised their eyes to the other to become lost in a world far removed from the blue bedroom, and Emily's clattering knitting needles.

"It's your move, I think," whispered Jo, not taking her eyes or hand from his; not wishing to break the spell which held them, but knowing that broken it must be.

"I don't think I can move. I think you have me in check," Rob replied without looking at the board.

"Do I?"

He nodded. "Is that the end of it, then?"

"Not necessarily."

"What happens next?"

"That rather depends on whether I can get you into checkmate. You would then be helpless to defend your king against the advances of my queen."

"I think I'm there already," Rob whispered hoarsely, still not looking at the board.

His hand tightened around hers, and at last Jo removed her gaze from his, to stare at their clasped hands. Her fingers moved within his in a secret caress, and she knew that the moment must end. Once more she became conscious of Emily at the other side of the room. She sighed heavily.

Jo studied the board reluctantly. "No you're not. You could get out of trouble by moving your knight."

"Maybe I don't want to."

"Have you had enough?"

"I don't think I ever could."

"I know what you mean; but you must either move or surrender."

"I can surrender?"

"At any time. You merely lay down your king," replied Jo, raising her eyes to his once more.

"But wouldn't that be a sign of weakness?"

"An admission of defeat, certainly."

Rob rolled his king onto its side. "I was defeated ages ago. It's time that I admitted it. You have control of the game, Jo."

Jo nodded. "I thought as much. The next move will be a difficult one, I think."

"A lot will depend upon it. But don't do anything without fully considering the consequences, Jo."

Jo picked up Rob's king and studied it intently. "That's the secret of a master chess player, Rob. You seem to have learned fast."

Rob sighed, and picking up Jo's queen, he placed it gently in the box. "We had best play no more for today. I confess that the game has exhausted me."

Jo glanced at him quickly and knew that it was true. "I'm sorry. I didn't mean to tire you," she said, tossing his king into the box beside the queen. She looked at the way the two pieces nestled together, side by side. "It's almost a pity to spoil their fun, isn't it?" she whispered with a grin.

Rob smiled, and added his bishop to the box. "They'll be all right now that they have the benefit of the church," he whispered.

The smile vanished from Jo's face. "Did you have to say that?" she asked, gathering together a handful of pieces, and dropping them into the box. "The game is spoiled, now."

Rob let go of her hand. "A reminder seemed necessary. It wouldn't do to forget what the game is all about, would it?"

Jo shook her head mutely. Just for a moment she had forgotten and for a while nothing had seemed important; nothing that is, except their feelings for one another.

Silently she threw the rest of the pieces into the box and removed the board from Rob's lap.

"You had best get some rest," she whispered as she plumped up the pillows and tried to make him more comfortable.

"If only I could," Rob replied meaningfully.

Jo put her fingers to her lips and then to his forehead. It was the only kiss she could give with Emily not far away. Rob put his own hand to his forehead and transferred the token to his own lips in a gesture which sent little shivers down Jo's spine.

She picked up the board and box of pieces and signalled to Emily that they should leave Rob to get some sleep.

Rob watched regretfully as she left. He knew that the next few weeks were going to be the most difficult of his life.

Chapter 6

JESSICA ARRIVED LATE THE FOLLOWING MONDAY afternoon. Her brother Thomas brought her in his curricle, and stayed the night before returning to Malvern.

Miles was invited to supper and Jo spent a great part of the day organising the food and helping to prepare some of the dishes.

"Good heavens!" Miles exclaimed on setting eyes upon Jessica. "How long is it since we last met, Jessica? I remember you as a gangly schoolgirl with long straight hair and freckles."

Jessica grinned. "It's amazing what one can do with curling tongs and lemon juice, isn't it?" she replied, fingering one of her auburn curls.

"It most certainly is! You look wonderful!"

Jo had to agree with him. She too had been surprised to greet this elegant female, having half expected Jess to have remained unchanged by the passage of time.

Jess had changed for supper into an emerald green velvet gown, cut low over her generous bosom. Jo could not help thinking that the gown was hardly suitable for a small country supper, but she was honest enough to suppose that this acid thought was at least in part due to jealousy. Jess' father, being older than Jo's, had inherited the small family estate near Malvern. The income from it provided Jess and Thomas each with a generous quarterly allowance. Jo, on the other hand, had no regular income, and whilst Peter was quite generous with funds when Jo expressed a need for them, it was not quite the same.

Supper was a lively meal, and Jo was congratulated several times upon keeping such a good table.

Miles passed the evening alternating between ogling Jessica's bosoms and flirting outrageously with her. Thomas proved to be a more serious companion, but he was an interesting conversationalist, and having only recently returned from a tour of Europe, he was only too pleased to regale Jo with an account of his adventures.

When at length Jo and Jessica withdrew, leaving the men to their port, it was Jessica who opened the conversation.

"Miles is a very charming gentleman, isn't he?" she said amiably.

Jo nodded. "The best."

Jessica looked at her from beneath her impossibly long lashes. "Look, I don't want to be treading on any toes whilst I'm here. Miles was a very engaging companion, but if you want me to leave him alone, you have only to say so."

Jo acknowledged a twist of jealousy in her chest, and sighed heavily. She hesitated before replying, choosing her words carefully.

"Miles and I have known each other since we were children. We are good friends and very fond of each other. He has asked me to marry him, but I am not sure that I can."

"Is there someone else?" asked Jess gently.

Jo bit her lip thoughtfully. For weeks now she had been carrying the burden of her emotions alone. If her mother had been alive maybe she could have talked things through with her. As it was, Jess was the nearest female relative she had, and whilst there was nothing in the least matronly about her, Jo considered that it might help if she could unburden herself to someone.

"Yes, there is," she admitted at last. "But he is entirely unsuitable."

"Oh, I see," Jess nodded sagely.

"Do you?"

"Oh, yes. I fell in love unsuitably when I was seventeen. I very nearly eloped with the man, but my father found out and packed me off to Europe to forget him."

"And did you?"

Jess sighed. "I wonder whether anyone really forgets their first love. No, I can't say that I forgot him, but when I came back I didn't want to marry him anymore."

"Why not? Didn't you still love him?"

"Maybe I never had, really. When I was with him everything was wonderful, and when he touched me I seemed to turn to water. But I can't honestly say that I missed him when he wasn't there."

"Nearly all my waking moments I'm thinking of Rob, and I dream about him at night. I can't seem to get him out of my mind at all. Sometimes I think I must be going mad."

Jess stared at her cousin thoughtfully. "You really have got it bad, haven't you?"

Jo nodded miserably. "I think so."

"I don't really see much comparison between your case and mine. I was more bowled over by Edward's good looks than anything, I suppose. He was exceedingly handsome. I think I found his attentions flattering; he appealed to my vanity."

"I don't feel at all flattered by Rob's attentions. It would be difficult to do so as the only time he has kissed me, he immediately wished he hadn't."

"In what way is he unsuitable?"

"In several ways."

"Name them."

Jo hesitated. "I suppose that some people would say that he is of inferior birth," she murmured.

"Mmm; difficult," commented Jess. "Is he 'in trade', as they used to say?"

"Well, not exactly. He was certainly a tradesman; a weaver, to be precise. He is now one of the Chartist land colonists."

"Oh dear. I see what you mean."

Jo blushed. "Yes, but to be honest I don't feel that his origins or the way in which he makes his living in the world weigh very heavily with me. Although I do see, of course, that such material considerations would render him unsuitable so far as most people are concerned."

"There's absolutely no doubt about that, Jo, dear. But if that doesn't weigh heavily with you, what does?"

Jo pulled at a torn finger nail, and appeared to study it intently. "Do you consider that the fact that he already has a wife should count against him?" she whispered, her eyes firmly fixed on her hands.

Jess whistled. "That's a difficult one to overcome."

"Impossible, I'm afraid. Apparently the working class cannot afford to divorce each other. They have no means of ending unhappy marriages other than to part. I understand that it is not unusual for one or other of them to commit bigamy; alternatively many of them live with new partners without benefit of clergy. I don't feel that either course would be acceptable to me."

"No! I'm not surprised. It seems that you have no choice but to forget him. You will have to be strong and not see him again, Jo. The alternative is unthinkable."

"Yes I know. But it is rather difficult when he is at present firmly ensconced in the blue bedroom!"

"What!"

"He has a broken leg, and Father offered him refuge here for a few weeks, thinking that if he did not, I would probably lose my reputation altogether, by spending most of my time at Rob's cottage."

"Does your father know that you love him?"

"I think he suspects it, but he cannot know. I have told no-one but you and Miles."

"What does Miles say?"

"He is very understanding and patient with me. I think he believes it to be a phase that will soon pass."

"And when it does, he intends to be waiting for you?"

"Something like that. Although I couldn't possibly accept him on such terms. Miles deserves much better than that."

"So you don't love Miles, and you cannot marry him. You won't object, therefore, if I try to engage his interest?"

Jo glanced at Jess. "I would not like to see him hurt."

"Oh, I don't intend to hurt him. I should rather like to marry him. He is undoubtedly eligible, and I've had a soft spot for him since I was ten years old. Why do you think I was so eager to come here when I could have been staying with Aunt Mathilda in London."

"I thought perhaps you wanted to see me," Jo replied with a hint of asperity.

"Well of course I did! But I also wanted to see what sort of gentleman Miles had grown into. I like what I have seen so far, better than any of the eligible gentlemen I met in London."

"But you do not intend to let him dangle after you, and then drop him?"

"No. Nothing of that nature, I promise. My intentions are entirely honourable."

"And if you do succeed you do not intend to use him as a means of carrying on a liaison with your ineligible lover?"

"Jo!" Jess sounded genuinely shocked. "How could you think such a thing? My ineligible lover has long since married some heiress or other and is no doubt making her very happy whilst he spends her money. No, I was able to see through him a long time ago. There is truly no-one else."

"Well, if you are prepared to be a good wife to Miles, then good luck to you. I have no right to hold him to me, and I should like to see him happily settled."

"That's me sorted out, then. If only we could solve your problems so easily."

"Well, maybe they will solve themselves in time."

"I don't see how that can be."

"Neither do I at present," sighed Jo, pouring the coffee. "But somehow I feel better for having talked to you. Please though, don't mention it to anyone else. I haven't told Father that he is married, and I don't want him to know just yet."

"My lips are sealed."

They smiled at one another, Jess enjoying the drama in which she suddenly found herself as a bystander, and Jo, feeling grateful to have a friend with whom she could discuss her problems freely.

Conversation turned then to safer topics, covering the dreadful weather and plans for Christmas. The gentlemen entered the room some time later. Miles was in an unusually bright and lively mood; Thomas was slightly the worse for drink. Peter smiled benignly upon the group of young people, and was thankful that he was past his youth.

****

Rob lay painfully in his bed in the blue bedroom, listening to the hubbub of happy voices of people at ease with one another. He felt lonely and miserable. A part of him wanted to join the gathering, to be at Jo's side, to eat at her table, to take a cup of coffee from her hand. But deep down he knew that he would find any social gathering here an uncomfortable experience. He had none of the social graces expected in Jo's world, and he would be afraid of letting her down.

He turned his head against his pillow, and sighed. Maybe he should after all be grateful that he was confined to his bed and could not participate in Jo's supper party. He was safer where he was. On this comforting thought he eventually fell asleep.

He remained completely oblivious to the fact that on her way to bed later that evening, Jo crept into his room to satisfy herself that he was well settled. She held her candle high, shading it with her hand in case it disturbed him. She had never seen him sleeping before, and she was surprised at how young and vulnerable he appeared. She fought down the urge to push that persistent lock of hair from his face, and sighed heavily, before shrugging her shoulders and making her way to her own room.

The next day Jessica could hardly contain her impatience to get to meet Jo's mysterious guest in the blue bedchamber.

"Who takes his breakfast?" she whispered to Jo as they helped themselves to scrambled eggs.

"Hannah, of course. It wouldn't do for me to be visiting a gentleman in his bedchamber before breakfast, would it?"

Jess giggled. "I suppose not. But when shall I get to see him?"

"I usually spend some time with him after lunch. I'm teaching him to play chess."

"Well, that's hardly a romantic occupation."

Jo grinned. "I don't know," she whispered almost to herself. "But it isn't intended to be romantic. I'm trying to put those sort of thoughts out of my mind."

"Are you succeeding?"

Jo sighed. "No; not very well."

"Is he handsome?"

Jo frowned in concentration. "I don't know. He's very tall and tanned and fair haired. Yes. I think he could probably be described as handsome. He has rather nice blue eyes, that crease when he laughs."

"He sounds a regular Adonis."

Jo nodded thoughtfully. "Maybe he is. I rather think that I have taken his good looks for granted."

"So when do I get to meet him?"

Jo laughed. "After lunch! Now hurry up with breakfast and we'll go for a ride. We could head towards Lowbands if you want to."

"I most certainly do!" replied Jess firmly as she tucked into her scrambled eggs.

She was agreeably surprised by the neat appearance of the Lowbands estate, and had difficulty in hiding her disappointment when Jo refused to show her around Rob's cottage, stating that it was not her place to do so.

Jess fully intended to waste no time in securing the necessary invitation from Rob when she and Jo knocked upon his door later that afternoon.

Rob lay back against the pillows and smiled as they entered.

Jo performed the introduction, and as Jess held out her hand to him, he raised it to his lips confidently, almost as if he had daily been accustomed to such courtly manners.

Immediately Jess could understand what Jo had meant about his eyes. As he smiled they seemed to sparkle wickedly, making her feel as if they shared some deep secret.

"I'm pleased to meet you, Mr Berrow," grinned Jess.

"The pleasure is all mine, Miss Martin," Rob assured her, releasing her hand and wishing that he could now take Jo's.

"We've been riding about Lowbands this morning. Jo wouldn't show me your cottage, but I was impressed with what I saw."

Rob nodded. "I'm glad you enjoyed your visit. You must show your cousin around next time you ride that way, Jo. You don't need my permission; you know that."

Jo nodded. "It would have been too much of a liberty for me to show her round without asking you first. However, if you want me to, I'll do so next time."

"I'll hold you to that, Jo! I thought the cottages looked really charming."

Rob nodded. "Mine is certainly adequate for my purposes."

"I suppose things would be a bit tight if you had a wife and half a dozen children there," commented Jess, and then, as she realised what she had said, she put her hand to her mouth and glanced anxiously at Jo. "It's as well that you haven't," she finished feebly.

Rob frowned, aware that Jo was suddenly on edge, and her cousin blushing furiously as if she had committed some dreadful faux pas.

"You've told her, haven't you?" Rob asked quietly.

Jo swallowed quickly and nodded miserably. "I didn't think it would do any harm. The facts can't be changed. We might not want to be reminded of them, but we cannot alter them."

"I'm sorry," murmured Jess. "I don't know how I could have been so thoughtless."

"It doesn't matter," replied Jo. "It's just that I don't want Father to know yet; not while Rob is staying here. It would be too embarrassing."

Jess nodded. "You're probably right. Don't worry; I'll tell no-one. You swore me to secrecy last night, and I've never been known to break my word."

"That's comforting," murmured Jo, not knowing why it should be so.

"Are we going to play chess, or what?" asked Rob at last.

Jo shrugged. "It's a game for two. You two play. I have to organise supper." She stood up and left quickly.

Rob stared after her, aware of a keen disappointment that he was being deprived of her company.

Jess couldn't fail to note the regret in his eyes.

"I'm sorry," she repeated. "You love her very much, don't you?"

Rob stared at her thoughtfully, and nodded.

"I wish there was something I could do to help," continued Jess.

"There's nothing to be done," he said firmly. "Now, how about setting up the game? Or do you think you should go in search of Emily to act as chaperone?"

Jess shrugged. "I don't think we need her, do you? Jo has left the door open, and that will have to do. You don't have any designs upon my virtue, do you?"

Rob grinned. "No disrespect to you, but I should really prefer to improve my chess. I hope you're not too good at it; I would like to win a game at least once in my life!"

Jess smiled. "Let's see what we can do, then," she said as she set out the pieces.

****

During the course of the next few days, Rob received visits from Peter, Jess and Jo at regular intervals. Miles also called frequently, but Rob found that the time hung heavily upon him and he grew increasingly bored and restless . He spent his days reading the Times and playing chess with whoever could be prevailed upon to join him. The nights he found were much worse. It was difficult to relax knowing that Jo was sleeping only two rooms away and he was helpless and alone.

It was at this time that he began to worry about his future at Lowbands. Peter Martin had assured him that one of his men had sown peas and broad beans and onions, and that the sprouts and broccoli were doing well and would soon be ready for marketing. However, during his reading of the Times, he had seen several articles which were severely critical of Feargus O'Connor, accusing him of waste and extravagance. He learned from the Times that the National Co-operative Land Company's provisional registration under the Joint Stock Companies Act had expired. The Company was required to submit a list of all its shareholders, and it had not been possible to obtain this because no national records had been maintained.

Rob didn't know what this meant, and he questioned Miles about it.

"It's a very complex subject," began Miles who had been following the Company's dealings with interest. "The Joint Stock Companies Act of 1844 lays down basic business conduct and account keeping rules. All companies have to be registered. The National Co-operative Land Company was given provisional registration to allow time for a full list of shareholders to be supplied. As the list has not been forthcoming, registration will not be accepted."

"So what difference will it make?"

"It could mean that the Company has no legal basis and is using subscriber's money illegally."

"How could that be? We all know what we are paying for."

"Yes, but people can't just go around using public money for just any scheme. There are legal Regulations they have to abide by. As I understand it there were several options available to the Company, but they have either refused or been refused all of them."

"What were they?"

"I think that in the first place the Company applied for registration as a Friendly Society, but this was refused because no regular benefits are paid to subscribers."

"No, the Company is nothing like a Friendly Society. Don't they pay people when they are unable to work?"

"Quite. Feargus' scheme certainly bears no relation to any Friendly Society that I know of."

"What were the other options, then?"

Miles pursed his lips thoughtfully. "They could have applied for a Royal Charter, but that is enormously expensive and record keeping has to be immaculate, which clearly it isn't. The only other avenue that I know of would be to present a Bill to Parliament. Feargus, as an MP. is in a good position to do that, but it can cost about two thousand five hundred pounds, and there is no guarantee of success. I suspect that many landowner members would be set against it, worried that they might have a Chartist colony on their own doorstep. Feargus probably believes that a Bill would fail."

"Is there nothing else?"

Miles shook his head. "Not that I'm aware of."

"But if the Company is illegal, how will it affect me and the others at Lowbands?"

Miles shrugged his shoulders. "I don't know what would happen if the Company were to be wound up. Presumably the land would have to be sold and you would find yourself a tenant to an individual landlord."

"Would that make any difference?"

"It could do. The new landlord would presumably be able to increase the rent."

Rob brushed his hair from his brow. "Could I be evicted?"

"It would depend upon the terms of your lease. Certainly I should think that as long as you paid the rent you wouldn't be evicted."

Rob sighed. "Well, that's a relief. I really don't know what I should do if I lost my allotment."

"Presumably you could go back to being a weaver."

"Yes, I suppose I could, but it would be a dreadful thing to have to do after enjoying half a year of freedom."

"Do you enjoy it then?"

Rob nodded. "It's hard work, but I'm getting used to that. I enjoy being my own master and being answerable to no-one but myself. I also enjoy working outside."

"You may not do so when winter comes."

"I'm getting used to working in the rain, and I'm sure that working in the cold will be marginally better than that."

Their conversation was interrupted then by a knock at the door. Jess poked her head round.

"Ah, there you are, Miles. Jo said I would find you here. Do you mind if I come in, Mr Berrow?"

Rob grinned. "No. You are welcome."

"How is the leg?"

"It's difficult to tell as Mr Martin will not allow me to put any weight on it yet. I therefore have no idea whether it is mending properly or not. It is reasonably painless at present, so I'm hopeful that all is well."

Jess smiled warmly at him. "I'm pleased to hear it. I understand you fell from a ladder? Was it Jo who found you?" she asked ingenuously.

Rob hesitated, wondering what lay behind the question. Obviously Miles knew that it had been Jo who had found him, and he would already have put some construction upon the circumstances under which she had been visiting him alone so early in the morning. However, if Jo had not wished to compromise herself by telling Jess all the details, then he did not consider that it was his place to do so.

Seeing Rob's hesitation, Miles decided to answer for him. "You know very well that Jo found him. I heard her tell you so yesterday, Jess."

"Oh, I see," murmured Jess knowingly.

"No, you don't see at all," Rob responded quickly.

"Don't I? What is it that I don't see? It seems very odd to me that Jo should just happen to be passing by alone, and so early in the morning."

Miles intervened. "Look, I don't know what you're getting at, Jess, but you must know that I will not permit you to cast aspersions on Jo's integrity, especially when she is not here to defend herself. I am absolutely certain that nothing out of the ordinary is going on, and you will just have to accept my word for it, if it should be so important to you."

Jessica blushed, aware that she had failed miserably in her attempt to drive a wedge between Miles and Jo. Indeed she had succeeded only in harming her own developing relationship with Miles.

She bit her lip. "I'm sorry, Miles. I didn't intend to cast a slur on Jo's character. I'm sure she would not behave with any impropriety. But it does seem to me that she could be placing herself in all kinds of danger if she continues to go careering about the countryside on her own before breakfast."

"Jo is in no danger from me, if that is what you're getting at," said Rob indignantly.

"I know that, silly! But there could be all sorts of unsavoury characters lurking in the hedgerows. I'm surprised that Uncle Peter permits it."

"Of course he does not, and I suspect that he knew nothing of it until this episode. I'm sure that he will be firmer with her from now on," Miles replied.

"I do hope so. I am very fond of Jo and wouldn't like her to find herself in any difficulty. Talking of which, I really came in search of you to see whether you would escort me to Ledbury tomorrow. I am in need of some new embroidery silks and Uncle Peter cannot spare an escort for me. What do you say?"

Miles could do nothing but agree, and in truth he found the prospect of spending more time with Jessica quite appealing. He knew that she was flirting with him, and Jo had mentioned that she had led an adventurous past; but he was convinced that beneath her sometimes brash exterior, the real Jessica Martin lurked.

He grinned. "But you surely cannot intend to go careering about the countryside alone with me?" he questioned.

Jess gurgled with laughter. "No, of course not! I had thought that one of your grooms could act as chaperon."

Miles nodded. "That would seem to be perfectly acceptable, even for the strictest society matrons. What time shall I call for you?"

Rob watched this exchange with interest, wondering why, if Jess were really fond of her cousin, she should be casting out lures to Miles. Still, it was none of his business and Jo was presumably perfectly capable of looking after her own interests.

He lay back against the pillows and closed his eyes. His visitors, believing that they had wearied him, bade hasty goodbyes and left him to rest.

He wished fervently that Peter Martin had not brought him here. Jo had been avoiding him again recently, and he knew that his presence in her home must be placing as great a strain on her, as it was on him. Sometimes he wanted to shout out to the world about the injustice of it all, but he knew that for Jo's sake he must continue to be strong.

Chapter 7

WHEN ROB HAD BEEN AT HOME FARM FOR FOUR WEEKS, Peter Martin announced that the time had come for his patient to try walking with the aid of some crutches he had made.

Rob didn't know whether to be glad or sorry that his stay at the farm was drawing to an end. He was relieved that the torture of being so close to Jo, yet unable to touch her, would soon be over; but he couldn't imagine what his life would be like without the hope or prospect of seeing her again.

For that was what their future must be. Jo had continued to avoid his company, especially since Jessica had returned to her home, and he was left in no doubt that she had decided that their relationship could progress no further.

Jo's absence from the sickroom, except for brief courtesy visits, had not gone unnoticed by Peter. As he helped Rob into a dressing robe, he wondered how to tackle the subject which had been puzzling him for some time.

"Have you and Jo quarrelled?" he asked at last.

"Quarrelled? No, of course not."

"But she is avoiding you?"

Rob nodded.

"Why?"

"It is for the best, Mr Martin."

"Is it? From where I stand it doesn't appear to be doing her much good."

"What do you mean?" asked Rob anxiously. "She isn't ill, is she?"

"No; not as far as I know. But she is listless and sleeping badly; she is clearly unhappy."

"And it's my fault, I suppose," murmured Rob.

"I don't know. Is it?"

Rob nodded. "It would have been best if we had never met."

Peter eyed him curiously as he brushed his hand through his hair.

"Do you really believe that?" he asked.

Rob raised his eyes to Peter Martin.

"I can be no good for your daughter, Mr Martin. I should not regret that I met her and I love her, but for her sake it would have been better if it had never happened."

Peter sighed. "Did she ever mention her mother to you?" he asked at last.

Rob shook his head.

"She died some years ago when Jo was only eight years old. I thought my world would fall apart when she went. I could never love anyone else like that."

Rob watched as Peter gazed ahead of him, unseeing. There was nothing that he could say.

Peter sighed again. "Eleanor's family are very wealthy, you know. They have estates in Kent and Sussex, and an income far beyond anything you or I could imagine."

The fire crackled in the hearth and a clock chimed in the distance. Peter heard none of it, and Rob waited to hear what Peter's revelations could have to do with him.

Peter walked to the window and gazed out. "It didn't seem possible that she could love me as I loved her. I had nothing to offer her; I didn't even have this farm then. I was a younger son, and my father's estate was too small to provide me with any future." His voice dropped away as he remembered.

He turned to Rob. "But she did love me, and she swore that my lack of fortune made no difference; that she couldn't be happy without me. I had a small sum left to me by my grandfather. I bought this farm, and we married and moved here."

"Why are you telling me all this?" Rob asked as Peter seemed to become lost once more in his reverie.

"Why? I don't know. I thought it might help you to know that Johanna is very much like her mother."

"Is she?"

"Oh, yes. But I could never do to her what Eleanor's father did. They disowned her, you know. They never saw her again when they learned that she had married me. I think that was unforgivable, don't you? It caused my wife some unhappiness. I would never do that to my daughter."

"What are you trying to say?" asked Rob.

"I'm not sure. Maybe that love is more important than any worldly considerations. Maybe that I wouldn't stand in my daughter's way if she should want to marry someone who in material terms, might not be her equal."

Rob stared at Peter, realising at last that Peter Martin was giving his permission for Rob to wed his daughter. He turned away, unable to meet Peter's steady gaze.

"Our cases are not the same," he said stiffly. "It may have been right for you; but it wouldn't do for me. The difference is too great. I couldn't expect Jo to accept the life of poverty which is all I can ever hope to offer her. I couldn't do it to her."

"Not even if it were what she would choose?"

Rob shook his head. "She has more sense than to choose it. She knows what it would mean, and it is best that we don't see each other again. It will be easier for her once I have left here. She will be able to forget."

"What about you, Rob Berrow? Will you be able to forget so easily?"

Rob sighed and shook his head. "No; I'll not forget. I don't think I even want to try."

Peter put his hand on the younger man's shoulder, satisfied that Rob would sacrifice everything for Jo's happiness.

He helped Rob to his feet and supported him as he hobbled across the room, testing the crutches.

Peter nodded. "You'll do," he said, more to himself than to Rob.

****

Rob remained at the farm only a few days after that. He soon became adept at getting around on his crutches, and whilst it would be a few more weeks before he would be able to work on his land, Peter and Jo were satisfied that he would be able to look after himself.

Jo watched him leave with her father; her heart felt leaden, and she brushed away a tear.

So many times during the past weeks she had wanted to throw herself in his arms, regardless of the consequences. To look at him; to touch him; these were no longer enough. She had to keep reminding herself that he could not marry her, and they could have no future together.

She had tried to avoid him; but even that brought no ease to her aching heart. She didn't know whether it was better to see him, knowing that was all there could be, or whether it was better not to see him and have nothing at all.

She soon found that his absence from Home Farm brought no release. She went about her duties as if in a dream; nothing seemed to have reality. She slept fitfully and awoke each morning unrefreshed, wondering how long she could go on in this way.

Somehow she managed to live through the days until it was Christmas Eve. The ground lay thick and hard with frost, but a watery sun shone through the afternoon.

For the tenth time that day Jo picked up the parcel which lay upon the dressing table. It was neatly wrapped in a spotted kerchief, and tied with a piece of ribbon. Inside there was a pair of thick woollen stockings which she had been knitting for the past two weeks. They were intended to keep Rob warm during a long winter working on the land. She wanted desperately for him to have them, but she didn't want to take them to him.

This last was not strictly true. Jo knew that she could have given them to Miles at any time, but she had been reluctant to do so. Deep down, she wanted to be the one to give them to him.

She sighed and gazed out of her bedroom window, across her father's fields towards Lowbands.

With sudden resolution she changed into her riding habit and ran down the stairs through the kitchen, ignoring Emily's protests, and out to the stable. Her father was there, examining a grey mare who had recently been lamed.

He stared at his daughter's flushed countenance, and the gift in her hand. He was in no doubt where she was going. She stared back at him defiantly, willing him not to forbid her to go.

"You know I have to go to him," she whispered.

Peter Martin swallowed a great lump in his throat, and was reminded of Eleanor in her youth. She had defied her father in order to marry, and her parents' intransigence had been the only blot on her happiness. He had assured Rob Berrow that he would not do the same for his daughter. She was old enough and sensible enough to know what she was doing. She had tried hard enough to stay away from Rob during the four weeks since he had returned to his cottage, but clearly it had done no good.

Slowly he nodded. "I could come with you," he suggested. It was a last attempt to preserve her from a fate which was increasingly inevitable.

"No," whispered Jo. "This is something we must sort out ourselves, one way or another."

His eyes were unnaturally bright, and Jo reached out to him and put her arms around him. They embraced, a long embrace, full of strength and understanding.

116

Jo kissed her father's cheek. Silently they saddled her mare together, and silently he watched his daughter ride away from him.

The sun was low in the sky by the time Jo reached Rob's cottage. She walked her mare up the path and round the side of the cottage to the stable at the back.

Rob, disturbed by the clatter of hooves, stood at the back door and stared wordlessly as she rubbed the horse down with a piece of straw. Then she stood trembling in front of him and neither knew what to say to the other.

"You should not have come here," whispered Rob, his voice uneven.

"I know. But I couldn't stay away any longer."

Then she was in his arms, where she had longed to be during all the sad lonely long months, and she knew that here was where she belonged.

He held her tightly, kissing the top of her head and the tip of her ear. At that moment to be close was all that they needed; was more than either had expected. It was a moment to be enjoyed and savoured; a profoundly moving moment as if in that embrace they each vowed to love the other for all time. Neither could doubt the extent of their commitment to each other.

"Oh, Jo. What am I to do with you?" whispered Rob at last.

Jo moved against his chest, where she had been lulled by the rhythmic beating of his heart.

"I don't know," she replied into his chest.

He held her from him and gazed into her eyes. "You know that if you cross this threshold now, I shall never be able to let you go?"

Jo nodded. "I don't want you to. My life without you is meaningless. My only chance of happiness is with you."

"Oh, Jo, my Jo! You have no idea what it would mean. I have nothing to offer you; I cannot even marry you!"

"I know; but you do love me, don't you?"

"More than I ever thought it possible for one person to love another. That is why you must think what it would mean. I cannot be the means of your unhappiness. Think

117

what all your friends and family will say if you come here to live with me without being wed. For that is what it must be, Jo; I could never accept anything less. A few snatched moments together is not the answer for either of us. It must be a full and wholehearted commitment between us. A commitment which would be like a marriage, but which could never be a lawful marriage. Think of the hurt your father would suffer. Can you give up everything you have, to come with me to a life of hard work and constant toil?"

Jo nodded. "I have no choice. I need to be with you if I am to keep my sanity. I need you to love me if I am to be a whole person again. Without you I am nothing and can be nothing. With you, I have everything and can need no more."

He held her to him once more and then drew her into the kitchen, kicking the door shut behind him.

The kitchen was warm. Over the fire bubbled a cauldron of rabbit stew. Miles had taken Rob out shooting the previous day, and whilst Rob had not managed to hit anything, Miles had given him the day's bag. The rabbit had been cleaned and skinned, rather inexpertly by Rob, but for a first attempt it had been encouraging.

"It smells good," said Jo lifting the lid.

"I'm getting to be quite an accomplished cook. Would you like to eat now? Miles brought me a bottle of claret to enjoy with my Christmas dinner. I would quite like us to share it. What do you think?"

Jo grinned. "Why not? I'm sure it will be good. Miles has an excellent cellar."

Jo set the table and Rob dished up the stew and poured the wine. Mrs Lee's bread accompanied the meal, and to Jo and Rob it tasted better than the finest banquet.

It was quite dark when they had finished eating, and Rob lit the candles. Jo put the dishes in the sink, and they finished the bottle of wine.

In a warm haze Jo started to wash the dishes. Rob came to her, put his arms about her, and kissed the nape of her neck. His lips moved along her shoulder deliciously, and she turned round within his arms, seeking more.

His mouth found hers in a hungry searching kiss that left them both breathless. As she leaned against the sink and he held her closer still, she could feel his urgent need for her and she moved against him.

"Leave the dishes," he whispered, his lips against hers, his hands seeking the buttons of her bodice. He swore as the tiny buttons eluded his clumsy fingers.

Jo smiled and undid them herself. The candlelight gave her skin a creamy glow, and as she slowly opened her bodice beneath his fiery gaze, he held his breath at the perfection before him. Slowly he reached with trembling fingers, to cup her breasts and with a groan he drew her to him once more.

The touch of his fingers on her bare skin sent fresh quivers of emotion through Jo. She pressed herself more urgently against him and knew that she had passed the point of no return. Her need for him matched his for her.

His lips moved against her neck and down towards her breast. When at last they reached the rosy tip, she wanted him to take more and more of her.

When it seemed that neither could wait any longer, Rob picked her up and carried her to the bedchamber. Leaving the door open so that the glow from the candles reached them, he removed first her clothing and then his own.

He then proceeded to seduce Jo in a manner which was immensely satisfying to each of them. The candles had long since guttered when their loving reached a simultaneous climax, beyond all their dreams or expectations.

Jo was so astounded at the great tide of emotion he had unleashed within her that at the end she was crying.

Rob kissed away her tears and hugged her to him. He too was prey to a profound sense of wonder that their union should have been so perfect; it had been a cataclysmic experience, and he knew that his life would never be the same again.

Not only did he need this woman, but he wanted also to cherish and protect her from all hurt. He would never be able to let her go, now that she had given herself to him so freely and without restraint. From now on, she would always be a part of him.

"I love you, I love you, I love you," he whispered, kissing her brow and her cheeks and her nose.

"And I love you more than words can tell."

"I know. You have just demonstrated your love beautifully."

"Was it good for you too? I had no idea that our union would be like that."

"To be honest, neither did I."

"But you are married. Surely ..." Jo hesitated. She knew it would be in poor taste to seek comparison between herself and his wife.

Rob smiled ruddily in the darkness. "Liz and I were incompatible in many ways. I cannot go into details, but I will assure you that I have never experienced anything like we have shared."

Jo sighed. "I knew that we were right for each other."

"Then why did it take you so long to come to me?" The question was the merest whisper as his lips sought hers once more.

****

Jo awoke to find the first shafts of watery sunlight invading the room. Rob was propped up on his elbow, staring at her.

"I thought I might have been dreaming," he commented with a grin. "Even now I can hardly believe you are really here. This is the best Christmas present I have ever had."

Jo put her hand to her mouth. "Your Christmas present! I've left it in the stable! How could I have forgotten it when it was the reason I came here!"

"You mean you've actually brought me a present as well?" grinned Rob.

Jo smiled. "Well it isn't much; just something I made for you."

"And I have nothing for you. How could I have dreamed that I would even see you again, let alone be given so much."

"You have given me your love, Rob; and that means more to me than anything."

She placed her arms around his neck, and they kissed; a tender, gentle kiss.

Jo moaned softly and withdrew as she began to feel the heat rising between them. "I must get back home before everyone notices that I'm not there," she murmured.

Rob frowned. "I thought you were staying."

"And so I will; but not yet. I have to go to church with my father today, and I need to prepare him for what is to come. You must give me time, Rob. It's no easy matter for a girl to give up everything to be with the man she loves."

He leant down and kissed her, a long warm, loving kiss.

"Can I not persuade you to stay?" he asked, his hands caressing her naked limbs.

"No, Rob. I must go. It will be expected of me."

"Do you not find it incongruous to go from my bed, where you have broken at least two of the ten commandments, to church?"

Jo hesitated, a frown furrowing her brow.

"No, I didn't think of it like that. But I don't see how what we have shared can be sinful. Do you see it as such?"

"Ah, but my sin is the greater, because I already have a wife and cannot take another."

"In that case, I suppose I should tell you to sin no more, but I'm afraid I can't. I still cannot see either how something so beautiful can be anything but a gift from God; something to thank Him for in my prayers."

"Well I'll leave you to say my prayers for me."

"You will not come with us to church?"

"I don't think I could face your father today when I have only just finished seducing you."

Jo shivered.

"You're cold. The fire will have died down. You stay here in the warm while I breathe some life into it."

"I ought to be going."

"A few more minutes will make no difference."

Rob quickly jumped out of bed and dressed. Jo watched him through the open door as he lit the fire and put the kettle on to boil.

She had talked glibly the night before about coming here to live with Rob. She wanted to do so more than anything, but in the cold light of day it did not seem so easy as it had earlier. She would be sacrificing her position and her reputation and would in effect become an outcast. She wondered whether the allottees at Lowbands would readily accept her or whether she would be an outcast from their society too. Would she end up with no place at all, except within the confines of this small cottage with the man she loved? Would it matter?

Rob returned and sat upon the bed, a mug of tea in his hand. He grinned at her, the lines of strain upon his brow seeming to have disappeared overnight. He seemed content and almost boyish in appearance. The lock of blond hair fell upon his face as it always did, and she pushed it back, her hand resting upon his cheek.

He caught her palm in his, and kissed it, his blue eyes fixed to her face.

"You're looking very serious. What are you worried about?"

"I was just thinking how simple life would be if we could just be wed."

He handed her the tea and she took a sip of the warm soothing liquid.

"Don't you think you could be happy here with me without being married?"

Jo hesitated for a brief second.

"You don't, do you? It was all very well last night; it's easy to make promises in the dark, isn't it? But when daylight comes, so does sanity return. Is that what it was for you, Jo, a momentary madness?" His eyes glittered with anger, and his cheeks were flushed.

"If it is madness to love you, then I never want to be sane again," she whispered gently.

He took the mug from her and placed it on the floor before taking her in his arms. "I will do everything in my power to make you happy, Jo. That much I promise."

"I know; I know," she whispered between his kisses as he proceeded to demonstrate just how happy he could make her.

****

Jo arrived home later than she had wished, and still aglow from Rob's love. She managed to evade Emily, who probably thought that she had taken another early morning ride, but her father was waiting for her.

He pulled out his pocket watch and looked at it meaningfully.

Jo blushed.

"When is the wedding to be, then?" Peter Martin enquired mildly of his daughter.

"Wedding?" whispered Jo.

"Yes; wedding! You have been out all night with him. I assume that he does intend to make an honest woman out of you!"

"Please don't spoil it for us, Father."

"Spoil it? How can I spoil it, Jo? How can talk of a wedding spoil it? He does intend to wed you, doesn't he? He didn't strike me as a philanderer."

Jo nodded dumbly, unsure how she could tell her father about the one insurmountable obstacle.

"Well then, we can see the vicar today and make the arrangements."

"There's no hurry, Father."

"How do you know? How do you know that you are not now carrying his child?"

Jo's jaw dropped. "I hadn't thought of that!"

"Then it's time you did, girl! Children are the natural result of what you have been doing, and I'm sure you don't want your children to be bastards."

Jo shut her eyes tightly.

"No, she said faintly. "No, I don't."

"Well then we must see the vicar."

Jo shook her head. "Not yet, Father. We must leave it to Rob. I'm sure he'll come with me to the vicarage as soon as he can."

"He has asked you to marry him, I hope?"

"The subject didn't come up for discussion."

"You mean you have given yourself to him without first obtaining a promise to wed?" Peter asked incredulously.

Jo nodded.

"You are a fool, girl! It's bad enough to fall in love with someone from a different station in life, but then to let him have the benefit of your body without the promise of marriage is the height of folly."

Jo burst into tears.

Her father took her into his arms, and she sobbed against his chest.

"There, there; I don't suppose there's any reason to go getting upset. I shouldn't have permitted you to go there yesterday, but you have been so unhappy these past few weeks, that I thought it would be right for you. It never occurred to me that you would act without there being some assurance as to your future."

"Rob is my future, Father; that must be so, whether or not we can be married."

"Is there then some impediment to marriage of which I know nothing?"

This was Jo's golden opportunity to tell him of Rob's wife, but she could feel her father's anger and disappointment, and she didn't have the heart to disillusion him still further.

Mutely she shook her head.

"Well then, you had best wash your face and change your clothing for church. Happy Christmas, daughter." He wiped her tears with an enormous white handkerchief, and with a weak and watery smile, Jo kissed his cheek and departed for her bedchamber, remembering on the way that she had still forgotten to give Rob his present.

Chapter 8

MILES WAS INVITED TO SUPPER ON CHRISTMAS DAY, AND HE could not fail to notice that Jo was preoccupied throughout the meal. Over the port, he asked Peter what was troubling her.

"You had best ask Jo. I'm blowed if I understand young people anymore. I always thought her a sensible girl, but things have gone from bad to worse since she fell in with this chap from Lowbands."

"You have only yourself to blame. You shouldn't have brought him here when he broke his leg."

"What else could I do? If he had walked on that leg he'd have been a cripple for life!"

"I dare say his neighbour would have looked after him."

"Yes, well you might be right. But I thought I was doing her a good turn. I've always said that she should marry for love. Eleanor and I did, and I want the same for our daughter. I don't hold with arranged marriages. I know that she is in love with this man, so I can't object to their marriage, can I? He seems a sensible fellow; he works hard and has a good head on his shoulders. Apart from his birth, which is not something that I would hold against a man, he will make Jo a good husband. It's plain to see that he loves her."

Miles eyed him thoughtfully from beneath his long lashes.

"So what's the problem?"

"I'm dashed if I know. I believe things have gone a bit far between them, but yet there is no talk of marriage."

Miles bit his lip and was conscious of a twisting pain in his chest.

"How far do you believe things have gone?"

Peter sighed. There could be no harm in telling Miles. He and Jo were like brother and sister.

"She stayed out with him all last night. That can mean only one thing, I think."

Miles nodded slowly. He breathed deeply until the pain subsided. Inside he felt as if he were dying, but he knew that he had to keep going. Jo had never promised him anything, and had always been totally honest with him. He had no right to have expected anything, and yet the realisation that he had lost her completely was not any less painful.

But Jo did not look like a woman who had discovered the joys of love for the first time. Her eyes had the same hollow haunted quality they had borne for the past few months, since she had first learned that Rob was married.

In spite of his own heartache, Miles was intrigued to know what problems Jo was suffering. Clearly her father knew no more than the bare facts; or at least that was all he was willing to say. Miles knew that he would have to talk to Jo to get all the answers.

His opportunity came later in the evening, when Peter announced his intention to take a frosty stroll and smoke a cigar. Miles decided to forego that pleasure, and as soon as Peter left, he turned to Jo.

"What's wrong?" he asked quietly.

"Miles, what do you know about having babies?" Jo asked, her eyes firmly fixed on the floor.

Miles spluttered into his coffee, and put his cup down whilst mopping up his trousers.

"Not a lot, Jo. It's women's business."

"Women can't do it on their own, Miles," responded Jo. "But I don't need you to tell me about having them, so much as not having them."

"What do you mean?" he asked, beginning to see what Jo was getting at.

"Is there some way in which women can stop having babies?"

Miles grinned. "Yes. It's usually called total abstinence."

Jo threw a cushion at him. "I'm serious, Miles! I need to know!"

"I'm sorry, Jo. I don't know much about these things. Do you think you might be in trouble?"

"I don't know. I suppose I could be. It is too soon to tell. Is there something I can take to stop it, if I am?"

"Well, there is a tea, I've heard. A drink of it is said to restore a woman's natural cycle."

"And is it ... safe?"

"That, I truly couldn't say."

Jo shook her head. "I don't think I should wish to take the risk. Anyway, it sounds so heartless. I don't think I could put an end to my child. That's what it is, isn't it?"

"I suppose so."

"Have you ever fathered a child, Miles?"

"Not to my knowledge."

"But you do have women you visit, don't you? I know about Madame Cherbourg's establishment in Gloucester. That's where you go, isn't it?"

Miles blushed. "You're not supposed to know about these things, Jo. Who told you?"

"Jess told me. She seems to know everything."

"Too much, if you ask me."

"It's a pity she's not here anymore. I dare say she could tell me how women prevent getting themselves caught in the family way."

"Do you think Jess needs to know that sort of thing?"

Jo shrugged her shoulders. "I don't know. You ought to ask her, not me."

"But you need to know?"

Jo raised her eyes to his. "I need to know desperately, Miles. I don't want to raise bastards! I don't know what to do. I love him to distraction, but I cannot have his children."

"I believe a sponge soaked in vinegar can help," Miles suggested.

"How can that help?"

Miles explained. Jo stared at him incredulously.

"It isn't totally reliable, mind. It just reduces the risk, so far as I know."

"Anything is better than nothing," replied Jo thoughtfully.

"I suppose so," murmured Miles mournfully.

"Oh, Miles, what would I do without you?" cried Jo suddenly, flinging herself into his arms.

"I dare say you would manage quite well enough."

"Even if I did have a handful of bastards!" she laughed.

Miles gazed at her. "Are you sure you are being sensible about all this?" he asked at last.

Jo shook her head. "No. But when I am with him I am past reasoning. Nothing else seems to matter."

"What will you do?"

"I think I shall live with him as his wife."

"But he already has a wife."

"Most people don't know that."

"But you do."

"It makes no difference to me. I cannot live without his love."

"You can, Jo. It's amazing what one can adapt to if one must."

"Yes, but why must I? He loves me and I love him. I don't care what the world thinks of me. I can be happy with him or unhappy without him. Why should I choose to be unhappy?"

Miles sighed. "I hope you know what you're doing."

"I have thought about it for months. The only problem is that whilst I would choose Rob as the father of my children, I don't want my children to be bastards. I suppose that if we pretend to the world that we are married, then they need never know any different. What do you think?"

"I know next to nothing about bastardy, Jo; but I had always thought the term referred to children who did not know their father. If you are living as man and wife, then your children will know and love their father and it can make no difference to them that you do not have a marriage licence. If you are convinced that you want to go through with this, I should stop worrying about whether your children will be legitimate or illegitimate. No good can come of it."

Jo stared at him. "Do you really think so?"

"I do; most sincerely."

Jo sighed. "It has been worrying me all day and has rather taken the shine off what would otherwise have been the happiest day of my life."

"Last night was the honeymoon, I take it?"

Jo nodded.

"And everything was satisfactory?"

Jo smiled. "Much more than satisfactory."

"There's nothing left for me to say, then."

"You could give me your blessing, Miles."

"That could be asking too much of me, Jo. You know that I had hoped to be the one for you."

"I know. But you deserve someone much better than me, Miles."

"I may be convinced of that in time, but at the moment I shall reserve judgement."

"And you will not give me your blessing?"

He stared down at her upturned face. In the candlelight her complexion was creamy against her dark curling hair; her eyes were velvety dark and her lips tantalizingly red. There was about her an innocence which belied her intentions. He had loved her since they were children playing together, and he guessed that he would still do so when they were both old and grey.

130

He put his hands to her curls and caressed her tenderly. "I cannot withhold my blessing, Jo. I want you to be happy, that's all. Promise me that you will be!"

"I will be happy, I promise."

"Then you have my blessing."

"Thank you. It means so much to me."

He bent and kissed her cheek. "I must be away now. I've been invited to spend a few days with your cousin Jessica's family, and I shall be leaving early in the morning. Would you bid your father goodnight for me?"

Jo nodded, as Miles released her and turned from her quickly. When he reached the door he straightened his shoulders and turned to give her a cheery wave. His heart might be aching, but he was determined that it should recover. He saw no alternative but to put the past behind him and look to his future. It might not be the future he had hoped for, but whatever it held, he would make the best of it. Maybe in time he would be able to be the brother to Jo that she had always wanted him to be.

****

The next day, Jo rode to Lowbands.

"You haven't brought your luggage, then?" Rob queried between kisses.

"Not yet, no."

He held her tightly to him.

"You've changed your mind, haven't you?" he whispered into her hair.

"No, of course I haven't! But it is very difficult to try to explain to my father, you know."

He sighed. "I know, my love. I think it is altogether too much to ask of you. I didn't want to hurt you or worry you. I wanted you to live a full and peaceful life with not a care in the world. And that sort of life is the one thing I cannot give you. I wish to God I had never told you about Liz."

"Who else knows about her?"

"Here, you mean?"

"Yes."

"I've told no-one. Who have you told ?"

Jo blushed. "I have told Miles and Jessica. I'm sure they can be trusted to be discreet."

Rob frowned. "What are you getting at, Jo?"

"Well, if no-one here knows you; or knows that you have a wife already, wouldn't it be simpler for us to pretend that she doesn't exist, and wed anyway?"

Her proposition was met with silence. Rob released her with a sigh, went to the kitchen window and stared out of it.

"Would it be so very dreadful?" Jo asked.

"You are asking me to commit bigamy, Jo. It's against the law, and if it were discovered I'd have to go to prison."

"Oh," murmured Jo, realising the enormity of her suggestion. "It was a foolish idea, I suppose."

She took his hand. "I just thought that if everyone believed we were wed I wouldn't be an outcast from society."

Rob squeezed her hand. "The last thing I wanted was to put you through this, Jo. Maybe it would be better if we didn't see each other again."

She put his hand to her lips. "Don't ever say that, Rob. Anything is better than that."

He took her in his arms, and kissed her; a long hungry kiss. His hands roved her body delightfully.

"There is perhaps another way," persisted Jo.

"What's that?" murmured Rob, his voice heavy with wanting her.

"I thought of it last night. An elopement. We could run away together, stay away for three weeks or so, and come back to tell everyone that we were wed. Although it would be the talk of the village for a few days, at least respectability would be restored."

"Would we have to go to Scotland? We could be married over the anvil at Gretna Green?"

"As I am under age, I suppose it would have to be Scotland. I just hope that if we do that, Father doesn't insist upon a proper wedding when we return."

"Is that likely?"

"I believe it does happen a lot with Gretna weddings."

He kissed her again. "Let's think about it; later. I need you now."

It was late into the afternoon before they surfaced from the bedroom, dressed, but clinging to each other still, each unwilling to let the other go.

Together they prepared vegetables and threw them into the pot. While these were cooking, Jo and Rob sat at the table with mugs of ale.

"We are having a small community celebration here on New Year's Eve. Will you come to it with me?" asked Rob.

"I should love to."

"It will give you the opportunity to meet some of the settlers, and you can decide whether you can be comfortable here. Feargus has promised to come too. He intends to start building his new colony at Snigs End soon. That's just down the road from here, I believe."

"Yes, it is. I wonder how the local people will take to that. Father says that the landowners are worried that they will have to pay a higher poor rate, with all these settlements so close to one another. And I thought there was some doubt about the legality of the company. Has that all been sorted out?"

"No, I don't think so. But presumably Feargus is happy that it will all come about in the end. He is also buying an estate at Mathon, near Malvern. He doesn't believe in letting the grass grow under his feet."

"I hope he knows what he is doing."

"So do I. I couldn't bear to lose this place now."

"And I thought it was me you couldn't bear to lose."

"You and the property are my whole life. Without either I would be only half a person."

"Will there be any dancing at this party of yours?"

"I don't know. Maybe."

"Do you dance?"

Rob shook his head. "I've never needed to."

"Well you will need to now because I love dancing. The country dances are easy and you can learn them as you go along, but you must learn to waltz. I shall insist upon a waltz with you."

"You'll have to teach me, then."

Jo pushed back the table. "There's no time like the present, " she grinned. They then passed a pleasant afternoon waltzing round the kitchen whilst Jo hummed the music.

When the vegetables were cooked, Jo put them into a dish and topped them with cheese which she then melted in the oven. Whilst they were sat at the kitchen table enjoying their supper, opportunities for conversation were limited.

"Rob, what's a bastard?" Jo asked at last between mouthfuls.

Rob hid his astonishment masterfully. He looked across at Jo's embarrassed face.

"You must know the answer to that, Jo. It's a child born out of wedlock."

"Our children will be bastards, won't they?" she whispered, a frown marring her smooth forehead.

Rob finished chewing a mouthful of turnip and potato.

"Does that worry you?" he asked quietly.

"I don't know. I've tried not to let it do so, but somehow I can't forget it, and I can't help wondering whether it is fair to bring children into the world in our circumstances."

Rob put down his fork and stared at her, aware of a creeping numbness in the region of his chest.

"What are you suggesting?" he asked, his voice cool and somehow remote.

"That maybe we shouldn't have children."

Rob's gaze didn't waver from her face.

"It strikes me that it may already be too late for such an issue. Had you thought of that?"

"Yes, of course I have. And I don't think I could do anything to harm a child I was already carrying."

"I'm relieved to hear it," replied Rob equably. "I confess that it hadn't occurred to me that you would wish to murder a child conceived of our love."

Jo raised her eyes to his, and detected shock and hurt beneath the blue surface. Hastily she pushed back her chair so that it tipped to the floor, and she moved to kneel beside him, taking his cool hands in hers.

"You have misunderstood me, darling. It isn't that I don't want your children. I would love to have them, dozens of them if that were to happen. But if we can prevent it from happening, shouldn't we do so?"

"Why? Will they be loved any the less because no priest has said the words of the marriage service over us?"

"No, of course not."

"What then?"

Jo shrugged her shoulders. "I don't know. They won't even be entitled to your name," she said lamely.

"Neither will you, but I shall give it to you all the same. You will be Mrs Berrow to all the world; our children will be my sons and daughters. I don't understand what bothers you, Jo. I can't share your concerns in this matter. I don't see that it makes any difference. It could make none, unless we declared their bastardy to the world, and we wouldn't do that, would we?"

"No," murmured Jo. "Maybe you're right. It is more or less what Miles said."

"You have discussed this with Miles?"

Jo nodded.

"Do you discuss everything with him?" Rob demanded, his voice rising, and his cheeks white with anger.

"Most things, yes. Sometimes when I don't know what to do, it helps to talk to someone. Miles has always been that person."

"I will not have it, Jo!" he shouted, thumping his fist upon the table. "I'll not have you discussing the intimate details of our lives with anyone! Not even Miles! What happens here is between you and me. No-one else has any business knowing. I will not have Miles declaring whether or not I should father children! It is beyond belief that you should even think of talking about it to him. What else have you talked about? Have you compared my performance in bed with his?"

Jo stared at Rob, her mouth agape, trying to recall exactly what she had said that could have sparked off such a storm.

"Well! Have you?"

"Have I what?" she whispered.

"Have you compared my performance in bed with his?"

"How could I? I've never done anything with Miles to compare."

"Have you not? How do you expect me to believe that? You and he were in bed, my bed, when I first met you." He knew that the suggestion was undeserved, but he could not prevent himself from wanting to inflict hurt on her, as she had on him.

"We were not in your bed; we were on it," replied Jo, her own temper rising at the implication behind his words. "And if you recall so much, you will remember that I was not a willing partner!"

"So it appeared at the time. But how many times have there been since? There was no evidence of your maidenhead when I made love to you. Who had that?"

Jo stood up and struck him on the cheek, leaving a red imprint upon his white skin.

"How dare you!" she cried. "How dare you imply that there has been anyone but you! And don't ever tell me what I can and cannot say to Miles. He has been like a brother to me."

"Ha! It didn't appear that way to me when we met!"

"Oh! You're insufferable! I wish I'd never met you!"

"Well if that's how you feel you had best go now. You need never see me again, and you can pretend that I don't exist!"

"Very well! I will!" stormed Jo, and she was halfway home before she realised that her face was wet with tears and she was weeping uncontrollably.

Rob stared through the doorway after her. By the time she had mounted her horse and ridden off down the frosty lane, his temper had dissipated.

He put his head in his hands and cursed himself for having been so foolish. He didn't believe that he had lost her for good. There was too much between them for that; but he had made hurtful comments which it would be difficult for her to forgive or forget. He didn't believe that she and Miles had been lovers, and although it was true that there had been no physical evidence of her virginity, he accepted wholeheartedly that he had been the first. In any event, under the circumstances of their relationship, he conceded that it was hardly important.

He had been surprised by the extent of her concerns about their children. That was something he had not anticipated, and he wanted to alleviate her worries and fears on that score. There was however only one way to do that, and that would be to wed her, honestly, openly and legally. If only he hadn't told her about Liz, he might have been able to do that, but as long as Liz lived, no marriage between him and Jo could be legal.

He wondered what Liz was doing; where she was and who she was with. He hoped Jenny was happy. It was a sad reflection upon his life that he had deserted his only legitimate child and would know more completely his bastards. Poor Jenny; she had been the hapless innocent victim of her parents' antipathy. Maybe Jo was right and they should think carefully about having children rather than just letting them happen.

What had irked him more than anything had been the way in which she had talked over with Miles, matters which had a direct bearing on his life. He liked and respected Miles, but he had to confess to a certain amount of jealousy. Miles belonged to Jo's world; they had grown up together and shared so much. Rob was the outsider, with an alien past and an uncertain future. They both loved Jo, and it seemed incredible to Rob that she should have fallen in love with him, when Miles had all the advantages. He supposed that he would spend the rest of his life hoping that she would not regret the decision she had made.

Rob rubbed his eyes and yawned. Then, still deep in thought, he set about clearing the table.

Chapter 9

Jo PASSED AN UNCOMFORTABLE AND SLEEPLESS NIGHT reflecting upon her quarrel with Rob, and had reached the conclusion that their tempers had been frayed because of the emotional upheavals of the preceding days. It was no reason to terminate a promising relationship. All lovers quarrelled, and in spite of everything he'd said, she loved him and did not want to be without him.

It had hurt that he had been jealous of Miles, for she was confident that had been the root of the problem. It had hurt even more that he had doubted her virginity. It had occurred to her that she had expected some physical signs of the loss of her maidenhead, and their absence was a little mystifying. She would have asked Miles about it, but she was conscious of Rob's wish that she should not discuss intimate details with Miles. How much more intimate could you get, she wondered with a hint of a giggle. The problem was that Miles was a man of the world, and Rob was not. Miles would know more about these matters than Rob would. She suspected that Rob would know nothing about sponges soaked in vinegar!

It was late in the morning when she rode to Lowbands. There was no sign of Rob on his land, so she went to the unlocked kitchen door and let herself into the cottage. The kitchen had a neglected air; the fire had not been lit and it was icy cold. The bed had been neatly made, but the bedroom had a similar uninhabited feel about it.

She felt a rising panic. Surely he would have done nothing stupid after their quarrel? She sat down and forced herself to think logically. It was silly to jump to conclusions. Rob was probably visiting friends, or maybe he had gone to Ledbury or Gloucester for the day.

Hastily she looked under the bed for the box of Sunday best clothes she knew he kept there. The box was empty. She rushed into the kitchen and opened the cupboard where he kept his razor. It was not there. She knew now why the cottage had felt uninhabited. Rob's personal items had gone; Rob had gone.

She would not give in to the despair which she could feel was rising to the surface. Rob could not have gone for good. He was merely out for the day, and had taken his razor in case he should stay overnight. Tomorrow he would be back again, she convinced herself.

But the next day when she rode to Lowbands in the afternoon, Rob had not returned. She began to grow alarmed. If he had gone away for good would he not have left her a note? She sighed. No, maybe he wouldn't have had the confidence to believe that she would come to the cottage again. Maybe he thought that she had gone for good!

Thoughts like those she could do without, she muttered to herself as she made her way to the yard. Fresh corn lay upon the ground in the hen run, and the pigs' trough was full. Someone had fed the animals, presumably acting upon Rob's instructions. That conclusion provided some comfort.

She went back inside the cottage and sat down upon Rob's bed, hugging his pillow to her, as if in so doing she could bring him closer. She sat there for some time, until the chill of the unheated cottage began to sink into her bones, and she decided that nothing could be gained by delaying her journey home.

139

"What's up, Jo?" enquired her father at the supper table that evening. "You have a face as long as Old Meg. It's only a few days since you looked as if you had won the world. Have you quarrelled with your young man?"

Jo nodded miserably. "Yes. You could say that."

Her father smiled sympathetically. "Your first quarrel?"

"Yes."

"I expect it was over something trivial. They usually are."

"No. I don't think it was."

"Do you want to talk about it?"

Jo shook her head. "I cannot."

"Have you thought about riding to him to sort it all out? I don't like to see you so miserable."

"He isn't there."

"Oh? Where is he then?"

Jo shrugged. "I don't know."

"You mean he left without telling you where he was going?"

"Yes."

Peter whistled. "It must have been pretty serious, then."

"Yes."

Peter Martin stared at his daughter's pale drawn cheeks. Her eyes seemed enormous in her thin face, She brushed away a tear with the back of her hand. The gesture reminded him of Jo as she had been when she was a child.

He went to her and put his arms around her shoulders.

"He will be back, you know," he whispered.

"How can you be so certain?"

"Because he loves you."

"Are you sure?"

"Absolutely."

"How can you be sure?"

"He made no secret of the fact when he was staying here in the autumn. It was obvious by the way his eyes lit up whenever you were in the room; then it was hopeless to try to carry on a conversation with him. His concentration would keep drifting towards you. He was totally besotted with you. Did you doubt it?"

Jo shook her head against her father's chest and burst into tears.

"The path of true love never did run smoothly. Have you not heard that said before?"

"Yes, but I didn't realise that it meant that the path would be strewn with hazards at every turn."

"It probably isn't as bad as you think."

"Yes, it is."

"We'll see in a few weeks when all this has blown over. You'll find that this is nothing more than a lovers' quarrel. The best part about those quarrels is the making up."

"Did you and Mother have quarrels?" sniffed Jo.

"Frequently. But we made it a rule never to go to sleep without reconciling our differences. It was a good rule, and you and your young man could do worse than to follow it too. It's more difficult to heal a breach the next morning, and the more mornings that pass, the more difficult does it become."

"What chance have we, then? It has been two days already."

"It does make it more difficult, I agree. But I'm sure your love is strong enough to see you through. If it is not, then it is as well to discover it now."

He handed Jo his kerchief, and she blew her nose loudly.

"Are you feeling better?"

She nodded. "A little."

"Well I suggest you go to bed. You look as if you haven't slept properly for a while, and you could do with a good night's sleep."

She kissed his cheek and made her way to her bedroom. Her heart felt slightly lighter, and she did fall asleep quite quickly, comforted by the knowledge that her father's judgement in most matters was unimpeachable.

****

Miles returned a few days later from his visit to Jessica's family, looking well pleased with himself.

"You had a good time, then?" asked Jo when he eventually called on her.

"Oh, yes. I was very well entertained."

"And Jessica is in good health?"

"In fine fettle. She is an energetic female, isn't she?"

"Yes. She can be quite exhausting if you're not used to her."

"I never found her exhausting; more stimulating, I think."

"Mmm," commented Jo with a sniff.

"Oh, don't be such a sour puss, Jo. You know as well as I that Jess' flirtatious behaviour is largely an act. I have been trying to discover the real Jessica."

"And were you successful?"

Miles grinned. "I think I'm getting there slowly."

"Do you like what you find?"

Miles hesitated, a slight frown upon his brow.

"Yes," he said at last. "Yes, I do." His answer seemed to surprise himself more than it did Jo.

She took his hand. "I'm glad," she whispered with a weak smile.

He squeezed her hand, and nodded wordlessly.

It was as if another door had been closed to Jo. All her life almost, she had been the object of Miles' affection. Now it seemed, he was about to bestow his love upon someone else. She knew that this was as it should be. She was not a worthy recipient, as she had not valued that love as highly as it deserved.

"How do things go with you, Jo?" asked Miles presently.

Jo shook her head. "We had a quarrel."

"All lovers have quarrels."

"Yes, so Father says. However Rob has been away ever since, and I'm beginning to think that maybe he won't be coming back."

"Where has he gone?"

"I don't know. He left without a word."

"Maybe he has gone to visit his family."

"His wife, you mean?"

Miles put his hands in the pockets of his trousers. "No, I didn't mean that. I doubt whether there would be much point in that. He had a sister, didn't he?"

"I don't know. Did he?"

Miles nodded. "Yes. I'm sure he said that he was living with his sister before he came here. Maybe he has gone to visit her."

"I just wish he had told me where he was going."

"Perhaps, as you had quarrelled, he didn't think you would care."

Jo bit her lip. "We did exchange some harsh words. But I didn't mean them!"

"That's always the way with quarrels. What is happening with his livestock?"

"Someone is feeding them."

"Mrs Lee, I expect."

"Who is she?"

"Rob's neighbour. She looked after them for him when he had his broken leg. I'm surprised you haven't met her. I wonder if she will know where Rob is and how long he is likely to be away."

"Do you think she might?" asked Jo, a faint quiver of hope making its presence felt.

"I'll go tomorrow and make enquiries."

Jo felt a keen disappointment, and Miles, always observant to the slightest change in Jo's moods, watched as her face fell.

He put a hand to her chin. "I could go today I suppose, if it were really important to you."

"Oh, Miles; it is important. I have been so worried that he doesn't intend coming back."

"I don't think you have any cause for concern, but I'll go and see Mrs Lee. I suppose you'd like me to go now, this very minute."

"Well, only if there isn't something else you would rather be doing," she replied politely.

Miles grinned. "I dare say I could think of several things I would rather be doing. However as none of them are feasible options, I'll go now. Come and help me saddle Apollo."

She did as he asked, and then she watched him ride in the direction of Lowbands, a nervous fear gripping her stomach. What would she do if Rob were not coming back? How would she be able to accept the knowledge with equanimity? It was all very well not knowing, but at least that left room for hope. How would she be able to go on if that hope were to be destroyed?

She stared after Miles. He had gone too far for her to be able to call him back. She would just have to brace herself for whatever news he brought back to her.

She went inside and paced up and down the parlour. Emily came in to make up the fire, and grumbled about being made dizzy by so much energy.

Eventually she heard Miles trot round the back of the house where the stables were. She didn't know whether she wanted to run to meet him, or stay out of his reach. As it was, she found that her legs would no longer obey her, and she stayed where she was.

It seemed an age before Miles joined her, and she wondered vaguely whether she would have any finger nails left if he delayed much longer.

She watched the door intently as she heard his brisk footsteps in the hall. Time seemed to stand still for her as the door handle slowly moved and the door opened.

Miles' face told her nothing, and suddenly her knees were weak and she sat down heavily in a nearby chair.

Miles walked toward her, each measured step bringing her closer to a reality which she didn't want to know.

She closed her eyes tightly, and put her hands upon her ears.

"No! Don't tell me, Miles. I think I'd rather not know."

Miles grinned, but Jo could not see it.

"Don't be a goose, Jo. Of course you want to know."

Jo took her hands from her ears and opened her eyes, blinking energetically.

"Do I?" she whispered.

"Yes," he nodded, kneeling beside her and taking her hands in his. "It is as I thought; he has gone to Leicester. He didn't know how long he would be away, but he will certainly be back by the end of January, for the early planting."

"Did he say so?"

Miles nodded.

Jo heaved a tremendous sigh of relief. It was as if all her pent-up emotions and fears of the preceding days were expelled in that breath.

She smiled at Miles, a warm sparkling smile, bearing some resemblance to the Jo he had known before she became weighed down by her love.

"Nothing else matters, now. I know that if he comes back we can make up our quarrel. I was so afraid that he had gone for good and there would be no chance for us to repair the damage we have inflicted upon each other."

Miles nodded, aware that as her hopes increased, his diminished. He sighed and stood up.

"I had best be getting home. I have to see some of my tenants this afternoon."

"Will you not stay for luncheon?"

Miles shook his head. It was time for him to make his withdrawal. He could not forever be dangling after Jo, and the less he saw of her, the easier it would be for him to reassert his independence.

He kissed her hand gently and made his departure. Jo watched his retreating back and knew that their relationship had reached a turning point and would never be the same again. She felt as if she had lost a true friend, and she was saddened by the loss. She wiped a tear from her cheek and stamped her foot. Why couldn't life go on as it had before? It was so unfair that in order to gain her love she had to lose a friend.

****

Two days later, Jo knew that she was not with child. She was conscious of mixed feelings of relief and disappointment. She had been preparing herself for the worst eventuality, and now she found that maybe to have Rob's child would not have been such a bad thing after all. It was difficult for her to look upon bearing Rob's child with anything but joy. Now that they were separated, no matter how temporary she hoped that separation would be, it would have helped to know that she carried a part of him with her. She had been foolish to be so concerned about the illegitimacy of their children. What difference could it possibly make to anyone? Their children would be conceived in love and brought up within the warmth of a loving relationship. That was all that mattered. She would tell Rob so when he returned.

He did not return until the last week in January. Jo had continued to visit Lowbands almost daily, confident now that he would return. It was threatening to snow, but still she felt impelled to make the visit.

Smoke was rising from the chimney, and her heart leaped within her breast. She took a deep breath and her hands shook as she opened the gate. She led her mare to the stable, rubbed her down and covered her with a blanket which she had brought on an earlier visit. These mundane routine tasks helped to quell her fluttering nerves.

At last she went to the kitchen door and opened it. Rob was seated with his back to her, his legs stretched out in front of him before the fire. He stared straight ahead of him and appeared not to have noticed her arrival.

Her joy evaporated and was replaced firstly by indignation that he should treat her so shabbily, and then by concern that something was wrong.

The smile of greeting vanished from her face as she stamped her foot and turned to leave. She would not stay where she was not welcomed with open arms. But she found that neither could she leave.

She turned again and walked into the kitchen to stand in front of him. There was no sign of recognition in his eyes and no stirring movement to show that he was even aware of her presence.

Jo frowned. Something was clearly wrong, but at what it could be she could not even hazard a guess.

She knelt before him and took his hands in hers. They were icy cold. She rubbed them between her own. In alarm she wondered if he were dead and pressed her ear to his chest. Rob's heart was beating slowly.

Jo became conscious of rustling in the bedroom and glanced up, realising that she was not alone.

A woman, of middle age, with iron grey unkempt hair stood in the doorway.

"He must have come back last night and fallen asleep in the chair before he could light the fire. That is how I found him not half an hour since."

Jo gulped. "We must get him warm."

"Yes. I've lit the fire. The blankets on the bed are damp, and will serve no useful purpose. I'll go and fetch some from home. Once the kettle has boiled I was going to try to get a warm drink into him."

Jo smiled her admiration, and took off her riding cape to wrap it around his shoulders.

"You must be Mrs Lee."

"That's right. Margaret Lee is my name. I've been feeding his livestock whilst he has been away. He needs a wife to look after him, if you ask me."

Jo smiled. "I couldn't agree more, Mrs Lee."

"I'll be away then to fetch the blankets." Margaret Lee's curiosity was ripe, but she knew that now was not the time to question this beautiful young lady. No doubt she would learn in time who she was and what she did in Rob's cottage.

"Thank you very much."

Mrs Lee turned at the door. "He is a good man. I hope we can pull him through."

"So do I," murmured Jo, as if in prayer. "Oh, God, so do I."

As Mrs Lee left, Jo went to the stable and took the blanket from the mare. It was beginning to warm through and she quickly wrapped it around Rob, taking one of the damp blankets from the bed to her horse. The mare snorted loudly, and Jo patted her rump.

She struggled to drag the mattress from the bed to the floor close by the fire. She was beginning to feel cold herself, and she wondered how long it would take for the fire to warm the room. It had been a bitterly cold night, with a north wind blowing down from the Malvern Hills. It had been that way for a week or so, the frost outdoors lying from dawn to dusk, so that riding through the countryside was like riding through a magical childhood fairyland.

Jo rubbed Rob's hands again. She thought they felt a little warmer, but she could not be sure that this was not wishful thinking.

Margaret Lee returned with two more blankets. She held them against the fire to warm them after their cold journey from her house. Together the women wrapped him up in one of them.

Rob groaned as between them they lifted him on to the mattress on which the second warm blanket had been placed.

"He's beginning to come round, I think," said Margaret, matter of factly. "Of course he would do better if one of us was in there with him. He would then get some of our body heat. I'm quite happy to do it if you will not, but I suspect that he would prefer to come round in your arms rather than mine."

Jo blushed. "Do you really think it would help?" she asked, knowing that there was nothing that she would prefer to do.

Margaret nodded. "You don't need to worry about your reputation. I'll stay to chaperone you; and in any case he is in no fit state to take advantage of you."

Jo needed no second bidding, and quickly she removed her shoes and slipped between the blankets with Rob. She spread herself about him as best she could with Margaret looking on, and put her cheek against his.

"I guess that you and he are good friends," said Margaret with a grin.

"The best," replied Jo, running her hands through his hair.

"Will you marry him?"

"If he'll have me."

"It won't be easy you know. I can see that you're a lady of quality, and you must be used to a different sort of life from us."

Jo laughed. "I don't think 'lady of quality' is a fitting description. I'm a farmer's daughter, and as such I should have thought I am ideally suited to be Rob's wife."

"Well there's farmers and farmers," replied Mrs Lee enigmatically. "I suppose that your father has rather more than four acres."

Jo nodded. "Yes, he does. But he is a working farmer, not one of the landed gentry."

"I don't know much about these things. I'm from the town myself, and in the towns you stay in your own place. We lived in a mill house, worked in the mill twelve hours a day and spent the rest of our time preparing food, eating it, and sleeping."

"Is this life so much better?"

Margaret hesitated. "It is a hard life, there is no doubting that. And when the potatoes failed last year, and the turnips not much better, we did begin to wonder whether it were worth it all. But we did have some crops, the hens kept us in eggs, and I have a sackful of flour. We shall not starve, and we are warm and comfortable. This year it will be better. We shall not grow so much of one crop in case that too should fail. Our cabbages did well, and we shall grow those again, and peas and spinach, parsnips, broad beans, celery, carrots, sprouts, onions, leeks, cauliflowers, potatoes and salad vegetables."

"Quite a variety. But if you grow so many different vegetables, will you have a surplus to sell at market?"

Margaret frowned. "Why should we need to?"

"Well, won't you have rent to pay?"

"I suppose we will, but I can do that by selling my bread. I've become quite a good baker and have been supplying Rob and one or two others. It brings in a few pennies. And there will be surplus vegetables, although not complete crops. Thomas Aclam managed to sell a half acre of cabbage in the ground! That's much better than taking them to market. But what would he have done if there had been a plague of caterpillars? At least our way we do not stand to lose so much."

Jo nodded. She couldn't argue with the logic of Margaret's sentiments.

"And Feargus is going to get us some pear trees. We do lack fruit, and pears grow well here."

"He is a remarkable man, this Feargus O'Connor."

"He is that. We all admire him very much, and believe in him, regardless of what they say about him."

"What do they say?"

"Oh, some newspapers have been spreading vicious rumours about him. We have set up a fund to take them to court to clear Feargus' name."

"That would be very expensive, wouldn't it?"

Margaret sighed. "Yes, I suppose it would. But we have each given a shilling towards the costs, and if all the land company subscribers do the same, there will be a good sum."

Jo hoped that the Lees, and all their neighbours had not wasted their shillings.

Rob stirred, and began to shiver, his teeth chattering.

"That's a good sign, I think," said Margaret. "It must mean that his circulation is getting moving again. You give him a big cuddle and that should do him the world of good."

Jo moved even closer to him and murmured soothing words in his ear. Words which Margaret could not hear, but which she could guess at quite accurately.

"Jo! Jo!" he called out at last.

"Yes, my love. I'm here."

"I'm sorry, Jo. I didn't mean to hurt you."

"It's all right, Rob. You haven't hurt me," she whispered.

Margaret coughed. "I think I'd better be going. My family will be wanting to be fed. I can see that he is in good hands, and I'll come back this afternoon. Is that all right?"

Jo nodded, glad that Margaret could sense that in his halfway state, Rob could reveal unwittingly, more than he would wish.

"Thank you for what you have done."

Margaret smiled. "I think that between us we have saved his life. I'll see you later."

Rob curled himself into a ball, his shivering still intense.

"I want you, Jo. I must have you. I'll do anything to have you for my wife."

"I know, Rob. I'm here; don't worry about anything."

He snuggled up to her.

"Are you really here?" he whispered.

"Yes, I'm really here."

His teeth stopped chattering and he opened his eyes.

"You really are here!" he cried in amazement.

Jo nodded, smiling her relief.

"How do you feel?" she asked.

"Like hell," he replied. "I have dreadful pains in my arms and legs and feel as if I've been run over by a cart. Have I?"

Jo shook her head. "No. You just fell asleep in the cold, and you almost froze to death. Margaret Lee found you this morning."

"Mmm. And how did you get here?"

"I've been here every day, waiting for you to come back, so that I can say I'm sorry for the things I said."

"Not all of them, I hope?"

"What do you mean?"

"You're not sorry that you said you love me, are you?"

Jo kissed his cheek. "No, I shall never be sorry for that."

He took her in his arms, grimacing as the movement of his limbs caused a searing pain.

"Are you all right?" whispered Jo.

"Mmm." He pushed her on her back and leaned over her, his fingers toying with the dark curls, now somewhat dishevelled, on her forehead. He stroked her eyebrows and her cheeks, and his fingers caressed her lips.

"You are beautiful. Has anyone told you that?"

Jo shook her head. "Not in so many words."

"Not even Miles?"

"Not even Miles," she affirmed.

He kissed her gently upon the mouth.

"I'm supposed to be making you some tea."

"Damn the tea," he murmured. "There are much better ways of making me warm than a mere cup of tea!"

Jo stared at him and laughed. "Rob! You were at death's door not an hour since. You surely cannot mean what I think you're meaning!"

"Try me, and see if you cannot warm me up better than this," he whispered with a grin. "Did you not know that you can transmit your body heat much better if you remove your clothes?"

Jo giggled. "I don't believe you, Rob Berrow! This is all a ploy on your part."

"No, it isn't. I speak with absolute truth."

"Yes, but I cannot be found in such a compromising position, Rob. Margaret Lee will be coming back this afternoon."

"How long is it since she went?"

"Less than half an hour."

"Then she'll not be back yet. Come on! Let's see what you can do for me! If I have nearly frozen to death I need to be assured that I am all in working order, don't I?"

There was no doubt about it, and when Margaret Lee returned an hour or so later, she found them sitting at the table drinking tea and laughing together; their cheeks were flushed and Rob was now clearly thoroughly warmed.

"I can see that I'm not needed here; and very pleased I am too that you have recovered so completely, Rob."

"Absolutely completely," replied Rob with a grin at Jo, who blushed a deep crimson.

"I hope you intend to make an honest woman out of her," commented Margaret drily.

"Oh, I do, Margaret. Just as soon as she will have me."

Jo stared at him wordlessly.

152

Margaret nodded. "I'll be on my way, then."

Rob turned to her and took her hand. "Thank you for what you have done for me. I shall be forever grateful to you."

"It was nothing. Say no more about it," whispered Margaret. "I shall be well rewarded when I see you walk down the aisle with your bride."

Rob grinned at her.

Jo collected up the blankets Margaret had brought earlier and handed them to her.

"You'll be needing these. I'm sorry they smell of the stable. I took the first blanket from my mare after she had warmed it up."

Margaret smiled. "It doesn't matter." She took Jo's hand. "You will take care of him, won't you?"

"Of course I will. He's very precious to me, you know."

Margaret nodded and left with a cheery wave. The first snowflakes fell as she reached the gate.

In the kitchen, Rob and Jo failed to notice that the sky had grown darker.

"We have some talking to do, I think," said Rob.

"Yes, I believe we do. Firstly I should like to know how you intend to fulfil your promise to Margaret to make an honest woman out of me. Have you forgotten that there is an obstacle?"

Rob's eyes clouded over.

"No, I had not forgotten. But the obstacle has been removed."

Jo frowned. "What do you mean?"

Rob sighed, and walked to the window, gazing out at the falling snow.

"Liz is dead," he whispered.

"Dead?" queried Jo, suddenly feeling quite cold.

Rob coughed. "Yes."

"But how?"

"Apparently she went to London with a man we both knew. She caught a fever there and died."

"Are you sure?"

Rob nodded.

"So this leaves the path clear for us to wed," he said, turning to face her once more.

"I can't believe it," said Jo, stunned by the knowledge that Rob was free. "When did it happen?"

"I'm not entirely certain. Sometime in October."

"How do you know?"

"I went to see her mother. She told me where to find her. I went to London and spoke with the man who had taken her there. They had apparently been lovers for several years. I had cared so little that I hadn't even noticed. He said that she had been happy with him. I believed him."

"Poor Liz."

Rob nodded and swallowed hard.

"I was not a good husband to her. I shall do better for you, Jo."

"What makes you think that?"

"Because I love you with a love I never felt for Liz. Everything I do from now on will be for your happiness; and because you love me and want to share my life. You do, don't you?"

"Yes, more than anything in the world. I just can't believe that it will all be this easy."

Rob took her in his arms and laid her head upon his chest.

"It will be this easy; it is this easy. When shall we call upon the vicar? Or should I call upon your father first?"

Jo giggled. "Yes, I think you should. He too will be relieved when you have made an honest woman out of me."

She looked out of the window. It was almost dark, and snow swirled about, the flakes large and thick.

"You can't go home in this."

Jo went to the door and opened it. She was almost knocked down by the force of the wind as the door flew from her grasp and banged against the wall.

Quickly Rob grabbed it and pushed it shut.

"You'll have to stay here."

Jo nodded and grinned. "Well, if that's the case I suppose I should make us something to eat."

Rob grinned wickedly, his eyes dancing.

"There's no hurry, is there?" he murmured as his lips descended on hers. "Who needs food anyway?"

Chapter 10

THEY WERE MARRIED ON THE FIRST SATURDAY IN APRIL, IN the village church at Redmarley.

Peter Martin felt a pang of regret as he handed his daughter into the care of Rob Berrow, but he had always known that he could not keep her with him for ever. And when he saw the radiant smile upon Jo's face, he knew that she would be happy. In worldly terms it was not a good match, but Jo was his only daughter and one day she and her husband would inherit his farm. At least Rob would love the land and work hard upon it. Anyone who could make a living on four acres would be able to keep a family in comfort on two hundred.

Margaret Lee wiped away a motherly tear as she watched the two of them walk arm in arm down the aisle into the spring sunshine. Jo looked beautiful in a simple blue gown she had made herself, sitting up late into the evenings with the needle plying to and fro rapidly.

Rob, in his Sunday best, did not look as carefree as Margaret had expected him to on his wedding day. She decided that, conscientious as always, he was probably feeling the burden of being responsible for a family. His days of bachelorhood were now irrevocably at an end.

Miles watched, his features blank. Jessica, standing beside him, put her hand through his arm. He patted it and smiled down at her. He guessed that she knew what he was feeling, and he was glad of her support.

The wedding guests, including most of the Lowbands settlers happy to see one of their number wed to a local, adjourned to the farmhouse where a celebration meal had been prepared on trestle tables in one of the barns. It was a merry occasion, the Lowbands people feeling that the marriage marked their acceptance in the locality at last. This accomplishment had been delayed somewhat due to the imminent opening of a further colony at Snigs End, only three miles from Lowbands. Whilst the local residents had learned to accept the presence of one band of colonists, the prospect of a second colony in the vicinity was, to say the least, worrying.

Rob and Jo left their reception early. There had been little opportunity for them to spend time alone since they had been snowed in together in January. The two intervening months had seemed endless to Jo, and she was as anxious as Rob to leave the celebrations behind.

Jessica kissed her cheek. "Good luck, Jo. I'm so glad that things worked out so well for you. I'm sure you will be happy."

"Thanks, Jess. And I hope you find yourself happily settled soon."

Jessica grinned and cast her eyes towards Miles who was busily talking to Rob. "I'm hopeful," she whispered.

Jo turned to her father and hugged him.

"Be happy, Jo. That's all I ask of you."

"I will, Father. I'm sure I will."

Miles kissed her on the lips; a short sweet kiss. He smiled down at her, his eyes sombre and his cheeks pale, but his heart not so heavy as he had expected it to be.

"Remember, if it hadn't been for me, you would never have met him," he whispered. Jo blushed, recalling the day oh so long ago, when Rob had interrupted them so conveniently.

"I shall always love you and be grateful to you, Miles. You have been my best friend all of my life."

"And I shall be in the future, that much I promise," Miles replied, squeezing her shoulder.

"Thank you."

There were tears in her eyes as Rob took her arm and led her to her father's carriage, bedecked with ribbons and spring flowers.

They drove home in silence. Rob wanted nothing more than to take her in his arms, but knew that he was not yet proficient enough with the horses to do that. He had instead to content himself with the occasional squeeze of her kneecap.

Jo moved closer to him, their thighs touching delightfully as the horses trotted along. His hand upon her knee was surprisingly provocative.

They turned off the Gloucester road and into the lane leading to Lowbands. Suddenly, with a muffled oath, Rob pulled the horses to a stop, and, taking Jo into his arms, he began to kiss her frantically.

Breathlessly Jo accepted his kisses and responded with equal vigour.

"I don't think I can wait until I get you home," whispered Rob hoarsely.

Jo giggled. "Well I think you will have to. I have decided that taking our pleasure in a carriage will not be as comfortable as your bed. And it is after all not much further," she replied, biting his ear playfully.

"Do you think I can make these horses go any faster?"

"Possibly. But I should prefer to get home in one piece. Pray continue, Sir."

"Continue what?"

Jo laughed. "The journey home, of course. I want you to myself."

Reluctantly, Rob turned back to the horses and they finished the journey home quite quickly, Jo running her hands teasingly over him all the way.

Together they settled the horses and Rob carried Jo across the threshold of their home. It was already dusk, and as he carried her into the warm kitchen, she was struck by the delicate fragrance of flowers. She looked about her, but the kitchen looked much the same as usual. However when Rob carried her into the bedroom, she found the room to be full of magnolia blossoms.

"Margaret helped me to do it. It was her idea. She has this beautiful tree close to her house, and this morning we picked nearly all the blossoms from it. It's difficult to find anything really impressive at this time of year," explained Rob.

Jo grinned. "It's lovely. And I'm very impressed. It was so good of Margaret to let me have the benefit of a whole year's blossom!"

He lay her down upon the bed.

"Your father sent your boxes over this morning. I've not unpacked them. I thought that you would prefer to do that yourself. Tomorrow?"

He pointed to some hooks he had placed upon the wall in the corner of the room. "You can hang your clothes there. Margaret told me to make sure I had somewhere for you to hang things. She seemed to think you wouldn't like to keep your clothes in a box, as I do."

Jo pulled him down beside her.

"Stop trying to convince me; I know I shall be very comfortable. I knew it the moment I walked into this cottage with Miles on that first day. Do you remember?"

"How could I forget? It was then that I fell in love with you; with your beautiful long legs flying about, and your breasts enticingly exposed; your hair cascading about you, and your eyes flashing fire. How could I fail to fall in love with you?"

Jo giggled. "But that was just my body. I hope that you love more of me than that!"

He kissed her cheek, his breath warm against her skin.

"Make no mistake, Jo. I love every part of you, and will do always."

She put her lips to his and drew him into a close embrace which was the prelude to a long night of loving.

Dawn was breaking when Jo snuggled lazily against Rob.

"There's something I want to say to you," she whispered.

"Go ahead, love," he replied, dreamily kissing her ear and her neck.

"You are going to be a father."

"I expect so. We can't keep doing this without it happening sooner or later."

"Yes, but I'm trying to tell you that it has happened sooner, rather than later."

He lifted himself from her and gazed into her eyes.

"What do you mean?" he asked stupidly.

Jo giggled. "I mean that I'm with child."

"Already?"

"It's hardly surprising, is it?"

"When?"

"The end of October, I should think."

"Why didn't you tell me before?"

"Before what?"

"Before last night?"

"Why?"

"Why? Well, because I would have been more careful with you if I had known."

Jo hugged him to her. "There's no need to be more careful. I'm not liable to break, you know. I'm perfectly healthy and Margaret tells me that it need make no difference to us; except in the last couple of months when things will be difficult anyway."

"You have told Margaret, but you didn't see fit to tell me," he cried reproachfully.

"There are some things that need to be discussed with other women. Margaret is a very motherly person and we have become good friends in recent weeks."

"I'm pleased to hear it. But I would have liked to have been told about it before."

"I didn't want you to feel that you had no choice but to marry me. Neither did I want our wedding night spoiled. Can you deny that if you had known, you would not have been so energetic with your love making?"

Rob smiled sheepishly. "I would have taken things more gently."

"I didn't want that. I needed you, as much as you needed me. It has been a long time since we have been together like this. You can't imagine how much I have looked forward to this night, and it was exactly how I had dreamed it should be."

"Mmm. For me too, Jo."

His kisses became more urgent and demanding.

"Wait a minute, Rob," cried Jo, pushing him away from her. "You haven't said how you feel about becoming a father."

Rob shrugged. "I'm sure that our child will be quite delightful, especially if it takes after its mother. However, it's you I love, Jo, and a child cannot make me love you more or love you less. It will be a part of us that we will love and care for. It's not necessary for my well-being to either have or not have children. You are necessary for my well-being and I don't want anything to come between us."

"You don't mind?"

"No, of course not. The child will be as much mine as yours. You didn't make it on your own, did you? Why should I mind?"

"I don't know. I had hoped that you would be pleased. I've known for a month or more now, and have been bursting to tell you."

He looked into her face, her dark eyes pleading with him to be pleased. He felt a momentary remorse. It was her first child; she was bound to be excited. She didn't know that he had a child already, a child whom he had loved in a detached sort of way; a child whose presence he still missed almost a year since he had seen her. A child whom he had failed as certainly as he had failed her mother.

"Was there any reason why you and Liz had no children?" Jo's voice penetrated his mind.

"We did."

Jo sat up. "You never told me that!"

"It didn't seem important to us."

"What happened?"

"What do you mean, what happened?"

"Where is he?"

"Where is she, you mean. It's a little girl, called Jenny."

"Where is she then?"

Rob hesitated. "With Liz's mother."

"Shouldn't she be here with you?"

"No. She needed to be with her mother."

"But when Liz died?"

Rob got out of bed, and pulled on his trousers.

"I don't know. It seemed better that she should stay with her grandmother. I couldn't have cared for a seven year old girl, could I? Who would have looked after her while I am working? Who would have put her to bed when I'm out till ten o'clock at night in the summer?"

"Well, I suppose that's all very true. But you have me now, and your daughter should be here with you."

Rob shook his head. "Her grandmother loves her very much and would miss her dreadfully if I were to take her away now. Besides, I want you to myself for a while. I don't know how we could be expected to have any privacy with not one but two children arriving almost at once."

His lips were at her breasts and she could feel herself yielding to him.

"Doesn't she miss you?"

"I don't think so. I was always working and she saw little enough of me. I don't suppose she would have noticed much difference when I left."

"Don't you miss her?"

"Yes. But it has been a long time now, and to tell the truth I never really learned how to deal with her. We were almost strangers."

"Can she come here to visit you?"

Rob shrugged his shoulders. "I suppose we might be able to arrange something when the time is right. For the moment she stays where she is."

With that, Jo had to be content, but later in the day, when she was making a batch of bread, and Rob was out on the land, she reflected upon his strange attitude both to his daughter and to her forthcoming child. His reaction had in a way taken the edge off her own excitement. She could not help wondering why he had never mentioned Jenny before. It couldn't have been that it was unimportant, but she supposed that while Liz was alive and Jenny had been settled with her mother, there would have been no reason to mention her. She was however very disappointed that he had not seen fit to discuss her future with Jo when he had discovered that Liz was dead.

She realised that not all men were totally enamoured with the prospect of fatherhood, seeing the care of children as women's work with which they needed to have only a minimal involvement. Jo didn't see fatherhood in that light at all, her own father having played an active role in her upbringing, taking on the role of mother as well as father when Jo was just eight years old. She had hoped that Rob would have wanted to be an equally interested parent, and she was disappointed that this was not the case.

Rob meanwhile was aware that he had been less than enthusiastic about Jo's condition. As he steadily worked through staking his quarter acre crop of peas, he thought how he could make amends. He had to admit that her bold statement that morning had come as a shock to him. He had not the least suspicion that she was already in the family way, having thought that she would have told him if there had been any results from their loving earlier in the year.

Now that he'd had the chance to get used to the idea, he did not dislike the prospect of sharing a child with Jo. He knew that he had not played much of a role in Jenny's childhood, but he was honest enough to admit that he rather than Jenny had been the loser for that. The more he thought about it, the more inviting became the prospect of bouncing their child upon his knee, cuddling it, and helping to feed it. There were of course some aspects of babies that were less enthralling, but he didn't feel that he needed to go so far as to get involved with changing linen, and mopping up when the child had been sick.

On the whole, he reflected, it would be a pleasing experience, and anything shared with Jo could not be bad.

He whistled to himself as he hammered the stakes in. Of course, a part of the problem had been their quarrel at Christmas. He was almost convinced then that Jo didn't want children; and if she had not wanted the child he had given her, what could or should he have done about it? It was an overwhelming relief to him that she at least seemed pleased. And if she were pleased, how could he be otherwise?

He vowed to make his feelings clear to Jo that night, before there could be any serious misunderstandings.

Rob finished work at dusk and made his way back to the house.

Supper, which consisted of a potato, swede and carrot pie, followed by stewed apples which Jo had raided from the cold store at the farm, was a pleasant meal, and much better than the plain vegetables that Rob had become used to.

Jo took the dishes to the sink when they had finished, and they washed them up together.

"I'm sorry about this morning," Rob whispered into her hair.

"Sorry about what this morning?"

"About my reaction to the baby. You took me by surprise. I must have sounded cold and unfeeling, and believe me, I am neither."

Jo nodded and turned her face to his chest.

"I know that."

"I am pleased, you know. I have always wanted you to have my children."

"Always?"

Rob grinned. "Well, since we first met and I saw Miles trying to do the same thing."

"Poor Miles."

"Is he very disappointed? I've missed him. He's not been here since before Christmas."

"He'll get over it. I'm still hoping that he will discover that he loves me like a sister and not like a wife."

"It didn't look that way to me."

"That was not a true portrayal of our relationship. I think on that day we were more like two people trying to find out what their relationship was."

"I don't think Miles is yet convinced."

"He will be," Jo replied confidently. "Jess will see to that."

"Ah yes, Jessica! A flirt if ever I saw one."

Jo giggled. "She can appear that way, but Miles is convinced that it is only a veneer, and that underneath she is warm hearted and generous and reliable."

Rob whistled. "Well anyone who can believe that of your cousin must be all about in the head."

"Or falling in love," reminded Jo.

"Miles and Jessica?" Rob sounded incredulous.

Jo laughed. "Yes! Seriously, Jessica wants to marry Miles and she has assured me that she will be a good wife to him. She has only to convince Miles that he cannot live without her."

"Maybe she will, at that!"

Rob kissed his wife thoroughly. "But I don't know what we are doing discussing the love lives of our friends. What about us? It's at least fifteen hours since we last made love, and I need you now."

His fingers slid to the buttons of her bodice.

"Am I forgiven?" he asked, pressing his lips to her throat and her breasts.

"Of course," murmured Jo. "There's nothing to forgive. Let's go to bed."

****

During the course of the next few weeks, their lives together settled into a pleasant routine. Rob would get up at first light and make a cup of tea for Jo who was suffering a certain amount of sickness in the mornings. He would return to the house after a couple of hours' work, by which time Jo had a breakfast waiting for him. Jo would then do some washing or baking or whatever other domestic chores were needed in the morning, and if the weather was fine she would take some bread and cheese and cider to Rob and they would sit and eat together outdoors. Sometimes the meal break would be extended as they were tempted into taking more than mere food for luncheon, but then Jo, feeling the need to help make up for lost time, would work beside her husband for a few hours.

She would then return to the house to prepare the evening meal. Rob returned at dusk. It was a long, but varied day and neither had any complaints.

Twice a week Jo rode to see her father. Rob had at first forbidden her to ride, on account of her condition, but when she burst into helpless tears which nothing seemed to alleviate, he had withdrawn his opposition.

Peter Martin was pleased at the prospect of being a grandparent, the more so since Rob's wedding band was firmly upon Jo's finger. He missed his daughter as much as he had thought he would, and in order to get through the long lonely evenings he would often ride to Ledbury and pass a pleasant few hours in the Feathers Hotel.

It was he who drew Jo's attention to an article in the Times stating that the House of Commons had appointed a Select Committee to enquire into the affairs of the National Co-operative Land Company.

In March 1848, Feargus O'Connor, realising that his company could never comply with the requirements of the Joint Stock Companies Act, had asked Parliament to amend the Benefit Societies Act so that the Land Company could register as a Friendly Society. He suggested that all members could receive an interest of 1% on their paid up shares until they had been allocated a place in the ballot for allotments. The interest would be left to accumulate in the member's name and would be put towards paying off the member's purchase price of the land. Feargus had purchased several other estates by this time, and it had been agreed that members could purchase allotments at cost price. In order to qualify for Friendly Society status, Feargus was also suggesting that a separate subscription should be raised for a fund for medical and sick benefits and funeral expenses.

Further, Feargus, in his petition to Parliament, stated that if they were not prepared to amend the Benefit Societies Act he wanted them to consider passing a separate Act to cover the Company.

The article went on to criticise Feargus personally. He had for some weeks been living and working at Snigs End, and there was amongst the workers there, some concern and speculation about the state of his health. He was showing signs of exhaustion, and there was little evidence at all of his former vitality. The personal criticisms in various newspapers had depressed him, so too had his seeming inability to have his company legalised. He was drinking quite heavily, and sometimes seemed hardly conscious. The workmen at Snigs End, busily engaged in getting the estate ready for occupation by the allottees in June, could not tell whether these lapses were due to drink, or exhaustion, or some other deeper cause. One newspaper article had drawn attention to the fact that Feargus' father had died in an asylum for the insane.

Whatever the newspapers might say about Feargus O'Connor, his people, the settlers, were fully in support of him. The Commons Select Committee would be told quite firmly what they thought of the Land Company.

It was therefore in this uncertain atmosphere that the Lowbands settlers held a visiting day on June 12th, to coincide with location day at Snigs End.

It was raining heavily, and Rob was reminded of location day at Lowbands, which had not been much better. In the morning, Feargus O'Connor himself arrived, accompanied by the company's stockbroker, and Sharman Crawford, the pro Chartist MP for Rochdale. Rob's was one of the allotments chosen for inspection, and he and Jo were able to see for themselves the extent of Feargus' decline in health. He was perfectly lucid and coherent, and there was no evidence that he had been drinking, but his hair, which until recently had been bright red, was now streaked with grey, and his face was haggard and drawn, the flesh hanging in folds below his eyes and about his jowls. It was true that there was little

167

comparison between this man and the Feargus Jo had seen almost twelve months earlier.

As he walked about the allotment with Rob, commenting upon the lay out and complimenting him upon the state of his crops, Jo rushed into the bedroom and burst into tears. It was not an unusual situation these days; she blamed it upon her condition. Margaret had told her that she suffered the same when she had been carrying her firstborn. There was no helping it or accounting for it; Jo would have to learn to live with it until after the child was born.

She was learning to live with it, but she didn't like it. She had always been a strong-willed person, fully in command of her emotions. She had rarely been given to emotional outbursts in the past, and she didn't like the loss of control which her condition had brought.

Still, she wiped away her tears and made herself a cup of tea. She was drinking far more tea than Rob could afford. At one shilling a quarter, her purchase of it was eating into Rob's savings. Unfortunately she found that there was little else she could drink at present. The well water had a peculiar taste and she was not at all keen to drink it, and she had never been very partial to ale.

Vaguely she wondered whether she should ask her father for his teapot leavings. That would protect Rob's savings, but she quickly discarded the idea, knowing that it would do nothing for his dignity.

Feargus O'Connor and his friends pronounced themselves impressed with Rob's husbandry, and they congratulated him on his recent marriage.

"Well, not all that recent, perhaps," said Feargus kindly, noticing Jo's disappearing waistline. She had long since given up wearing all the petticoats worn by aspiring ladies of fashion, in favour of plain skirts, more suited to the work in which she was engaged.

Rob smiled and took his wife's hand in his.

"Recent enough for us still to be in love," he said. Jo blushed and smiled her gratitude for this public pronouncement of love and support.

Feargus smiled too, and then sighed heavily, perhaps for his own perennial bachelorhood. It was said that he had been thwarted in love at an early age and had never since succumbed to it. Jo could believe it, and felt an overwhelming sorrow for this generous, well intentioned man. She went up to him and kissed his cheek.

"I should like to thank you for what you have done. You have brought hope and pride to people who were formerly short of both. May God bless you."

Feargus seemed touched by this and patted her head in a paternal manner. His eyes were unusually bright as he rode to Snigs End with his companions.

Following the location, the settlers at Snigs End had been invited to the schoolroom at Lowbands for tea, and it was intended that afterwards they would tour Lowbands and discuss mutual problems, the new settlers thus gaining help and advice from their more experienced neighbours. Each household at Lowbands had been asked to produce a contribution for the tea, and Jo had spent the previous day making bread and buns.

The Lowbands settlers were all assembled in the schoolroom, the trestle tables were set out with a wonderful array of food, when a messenger arrived to explain that the Snigs End party would probably be unable to come after all. Feargus had arrived just as they were leaving, and he wanted to tour each house on the estate and give the allottees their documents of possession.

The young lad who had brought the message stared hopefully at the mass of food.

The Lowbands settlers stared at each other, wondering what to do with it all.

"Well I don't know what we are dithering about," cried Rob. "We've made all the arrangements. Let's have a party. I'm sure we can enjoy ourselves even if there are fewer than we have catered for!"

His pronouncement was met with a loud cheer. The sole representative from Snigs End was invited to join them, and when he had eaten, to travel back to Snigs End to spread the word that if anyone were free to call before dusk they would be welcome to join the party.

Everyone began to tuck into the food with great gusto. They toiled from dawn to dusk each day, and when the chance for a diversion from work presented itself, they knew how to make the most of it.

When they had eaten their fill, someone produced a fiddle, and without any bidding, the dancing began. There followed a series of country dances. Not everyone knew the steps but amid much hilarity, they enjoyed it immensely.

When everyone was exhausted and about to fall in a heap on the floor. the fiddler slowed his pace to something resembling a waltz.

Rob took his wife in his arms.

"Do you remember when you taught me to waltz for the New Year party?" he whispered in her ear, taking the opportunity also to kiss it.

"Yes, I do," Jo replied. "And after all my trouble, you went away and we missed it."

"Well, let's make sure the effort was not wasted. Let me see if I can remember how to do it."

He led her to the middle of the room, and they waltzed around, watched by a hundred pairs of eyes. It was not the most elegant example of a waltz, but as Margaret Lee said to her neighbour, the way those two looked at each other was enough to send shivers up and down your spine.

Jo and Rob were oblivious to the watchful eyes of their neighbours and friends. The movement of the dance, the way they were holding each other, the effect of the music, all combined to form a magical moment. They gazed into each others eyes wordlessly, breathlessly, as they moved about. Occasionally, Rob's eyes would lower to Jo's lips, red and warm, and inviting. He had to fight the urge to kiss her.

The music came to an end at last, and Rob did steal a chaste kiss, thinking that no-one would notice. As he did so, a loud cheer echoed round the room and the assembled company applauded them good humouredly.

Rob and Jo looked up. They stood alone in the middle of the schoolroom. Everyone was looking at them.

Jo blushed furiously, and Rob too was embarrassed. He grinned ruefully and led Jo from the floor.

"We must have made a dreadful exhibition of ourselves," murmured Jo as the fiddler began another lively country dance.

Rob nodded. "I'm afraid so, my love. I'm sorry; I should have realised."

Jo grinned. "It was no more your fault than mine. We were both carried away. At least we have afforded some amusement."

Rob smiled and hugged her to him.

"Let's go home," he suggested.

"No, we can't go yet," argued Jo. "Everyone would think we were too embarrassed to face them. And they would know what we had gone home for!"

"I don't care," murmured Rob against her ear."I want you now. Please come with me. We can come back later if you want to."

Jo gave in gracefully and allowed him to take her hand and lead her from the schoolroom along the lanes until they reached their cottage. They stopped often on the way to exchange hungry kisses, so that by the time they reached home they were well and truly ready for each other.

Chapter 11

Jo awoke to the sound of an eerie cry. It was pitch dark and for several seconds she couldn't think what had disturbed her. Rob's arms were enclosed tightly around her, and his breathing was fast and laboured. Clearly he was in the midst of a dream, and one which was causing him some torment.

Gently Jo extricated herself from his vice like grip and put her arms around him.

"No! No!" Rob cried indistinctly.

Jo held him to her.

"It's all right, Rob. Don't worry. Everything will be all right," she whispered soothingly.

Her words seemed to have a calming effect on his sleep filled brain. She continued to hold him, stroking him gently, and whispering words of comfort, as she would to a child experiencing a nightmare.

Suddenly, Rob's breathing stilled and then he cried out again. The words were muffled by Jo's shoulder and she could not catch all that he said. She thought he cried that he was sorry, and finally on a sob he murmured, "Liz, Liz; what have I done?"

The world seemed to stand still for Jo. She felt an ice cold hand creep around her heart. Why should Rob be tortured by dreams of his dead wife, now? It had been almost a year since he had left her, and several months since her death. He had said that there had been no love between them, so why should he think of her in his dreams? And what could have caused the pain which he evidently suffered?

Jo patted his arm absently, but she no longer wanted to offer maternal comfort. She was engulfed by jealousy that Rob must have truly loved his first wife and she could never occupy more than a small corner of his heart. His words when he had told her that he and Liz had nothing in common, and that their relationship had borne no resemblance to the love he and Jo had for one another, must have been empty words. How could she believe them when Liz continued to occupy his thoughts and his dreams?

Rob seemed quiet now, his breathing shallow and regular.

Jo felt the need to remove herself from him so that she could think more clearly, unimpeded by his touch and the very distraction of his proximity.

Gently she eased herself out of bed and pulled the cover up over him. In the darkness she felt for and found a woollen wrap which she shrugged over her naked limbs.

She felt as if she wanted to die. The happiness which she had found so complete since she and Rob had come together was now indelibly marred. It was as if Liz had been sharing their bed, living and sleeping between them. She wondered whether even in their most intimate moments, Rob had imagined himself with Liz.

She had been so sure that he had loved her as much as she loved him. How could she have been mistaken? Had it all been lies?

Restlessly she paced the bedroom floor, and finally her misery became so acute that she could do nothing to control the flow of tears which would fall.

She sobbed silently at first, but then the trickle of tears became a flood and loud sobs racked her body.

She was leaning against the window sill, beyond caring whether she woke Rob. She could not have stopped the tears even had she the will to do so.

Rob awoke to the heartrending sound of Jo's misery. Her silhouette clearly visible against the window.

"What's the matter, Jo?" he whispered, his concern and alarm evident.

Jo shook her head on a sob, and Rob scrambled out of bed to her side. His arms were about her, offering her comfort, but she was beyond being comforted.

"What's the matter?" he repeated at a loss to know what could cause such upset in the middle of the night, especially when they had made love in such a mutually satisfying manner not more than an hour earlier.

Jo couldn't speak. She just shook her head again.

"I didn't hurt you, did I?" Rob asked, a sudden fear that in the heat of their loving he had been too rough.

Mutely she shook her head again.

Rob sighed. "Good. I couldn't bear it if I should hurt you. I could never forgive myself."

He pulled her to him in a more comfortable embrace and held her head against his shoulder.

"Don't cry, Jo," he murmured. "There's nothing to worry about. We shall make out all right. Is that what you are bothered about? Do you regret marrying me?"

Jo's sobs stilled suddenly. Did she regret it? She could feel his heart beating beneath her, and his arms were warm and comforting about her. His lips were upon her hair, his hands upon her back sent delicious shivers up her spine.

"No, I don't think so," she whispered at last.

Rob's hands ceased their caressing movement.

"You don't think so? What sort of answer is that? I had hoped for a more emphatic denial than that. Is that the best you can do?"

Jo nodded.

Rob frowned into the darkness. "Do you need more convincing?" he whispered.

Jo looked up at him, his features dimly apparent in the pre-dawn light. She put her hand to his cheek and her heart lurched. Her hands slid around his neck and she pressed her face into his chest.

"I love you so much that it hurts," she whispered.

Rob's arms tightened about her. "It's the same for me."

"Is it?" she asked, lifting her face to his, in desperate need of reassurance.

Rob read the doubt in her eyes and was overcome by the urge to protect her and envelop her in his love. Gently he kissed her eyelids.

"Don't you know that I would do anything to keep you with me, because I couldn't live without you, Jo. My life would be nothing without you, my love," he murmured as his lips moved over her cheek.

Jo was reassured by his words and by his actions. The turmoil resulting from his dream receded until she was able to cast it from her mind, putting it down to no more than night-time fears, as Rob led her back to the bed. There he completed the act of reassurance.

****

During the summer months of 1848, Rob worked hard upon the allotment, often from dawn till ten o'clock at night, weeding, hoeing, planting and harvesting his acres. They were rewarded with a good crop of beans, onions and early potatoes.

The long hours of labour took their toll on Rob, and often he would fall asleep at the supper table, and it was only with great difficulty that Jo managed to get him to bed.

Sometimes his sleep was disturbed by nightmares, and he would awake sweating and shivering at the same time. On these occasions Jo would comfort him and her very presence seemed to be all that was needed to enable him to fall back into a peaceful slumber.

Jo however found it more difficult to return to sleep after these dreams. She was unable to forget the night when he had sobbed Liz's name, and the fact that he continued to torment himself worried her. She no longer feared that he loved Liz and regretted his marriage to Jo. If their marriage was based upon an illusion, then Jo herself was totally fooled by it. Deep within her she knew that Rob loved her and needed her as much as she loved and needed him.

If Rob had no doubts about his love for Jo, she could not help but wonder why the nightmares about Liz should be so persistent. There appeared to be something that he regretted, for had he not muttered, "Liz; what have I done?" In the still darkness of the night Jo began to dwell upon these words, and worried over their cause.

She couldn't tell when her worst fears began to take root in her brain, but before long she had convinced herself that Liz's death had been very convenient for her and Rob, and she could not avoid the suspicion that maybe Rob's journeying at the beginning of the year had been carried out in order to smooth the path for them. He had stated at the outset that divorce was out of the question, so that the only way he and Jo could marry would be when Liz was dead. Could it be mere coincidence that on his return he brought the news that her death had indeed taken place?

Jo tried to still her racing heart as the awful conclusions to her ramblings settled upon her brain. Surely Rob wouldn't have done anything to hasten Liz's end. In the dawn light she turned to study Rob's profile as he lay sleeping, now peacefully. A lock of hair fell boyishly upon his brow, and in repose he appeared younger than his thirty years. There was however a determined set to his jaw, and had he not once said that he would do anything to keep Jo with him?

Jo realised that she hadn't enquired deeply into Liz's death. At the time she had been overcome with a sense of relief that the obstacle to their marriage had been removed. Maybe even then she had not wished to know the details. Rob had been somewhat vague about the circumstances, and Jo had accepted what he had said.

But what about his daughter? Jo had been surprised that he had been content to leave his daughter with Liz's mother, and now that they were wed, surely it would be more appropriate for Jenny to live with her father. The Lowbands school had opened in July, with the arrival of Mr and Mrs O'Brien from Exeter. Patrick O'Brien taught the boys and Mrs O'Brien the girls. Jo was sure that Rob would be able to afford to pay the few pence needed to send Jenny to school.

She vowed to tackle the subject with Rob at the earliest opportunity, putting from her mind the dreadful possibility that her husband had murdered his wife. She couldn't really believe that Rob could have done anything like that.

The next day dawned bright and sunny, and when Rob came into the house for his breakfast, Jo decided that she must find out more, if only to quell the fears building within her.

"Rob, now that the school is open here, don't you think it would be a good idea to arrange for Jenny to come to live here with us?"

Rob put down his fork and stared at Jo as if she had taken leave of her senses.

"Why?" he frowned.

Jo shrugged. "Surely she would be better with her father than with an aged grandparent. And Jenny will be a sister to our child."

Rob smiled. "Liz's mother is not in the least aged, and she loves Jenny as if she were her own daughter. How could I deprive her of the child when she has looked after her all this time?"

Jo pouted. "I don't know, but I can't help feeling that you should take responsibility for your child."

"I told you, Jo, I had little to do with Jenny when Liz and I were together, and she and I would be strangers now. The child is much happier where she is, although that must be a matter of some regret to me. I should have made more effort to get to know her when Liz and I were together."

"Why did you part?" asked Jo at last. "I know we have never discussed Liz, and in most respects I have no right to ask. But I can't help wanting to know what she was like and what happened between you. It is a part of your life that I can't share, and yet I should like to understand it."

Rob nodded, and took Jo's hand.

"I understand, love, but I still find it difficult to talk about. I was not a good husband to Liz or a good father to Jenny. In fact, I failed both of them abysmally. I know that, and I have tried to put my past behind me to ensure that I don't also fail you, and this child within you." He pulled Jo closer as he spoke and rested his head against her increasing stomach. "You are everything to me, Jo, and what happened in the past is something with which I must live, and I have no intention or desire to burden you with it. It was all a mistake and I don't want to be reminded of it every day by having Jenny here. Do you understand?"

Jo nodded, unsure whether she did or not.

"I think so," she murmured, knowing that the opportunity for further questioning was lost. She had to trust that he was right and that he knew what was best for all of them.

Rob kissed her stomach, and pulled her down upon his lap.

"Now then, what have you made for the anniversary tea tomorrow?"

Jo smiled. "Nothing yet; I'm doing the baking today. I thought a fruit loaf would be good. What do you think?"

Rob grinned. "That sounds wonderful. Can you make one of your pork pies as well? We don't often have meat, and it would be nice to share it with the others. You do realise don't you, that whilst the occasion is the first anniversary of the Lowbands settlement, it is also of some significance to us."

Jo smiled, gratified that he had remembered the anniversary of their first meeting. She looked across to the bedroom door, recalling the circumstances with some embarrassment.

"Whatever did you think when you saw me with Miles?" she asked, her cheeks delightfully pink.

Rob hugged her to him. "I had great difficulty keeping my eyes off you, and I was mightily envious of

Miles. Little did I know then that within months you would choose to come to me. Sometimes I think I must be the luckiest fellow alive. Maybe one day I'll wake up and find this is all a dream."

Jo took his hand and placed it on her stomach.

"No dream, Rob, but very much alive; here, can you feel your child kicking?"

Rob gazed up at her in wonder as he felt the insistent pressure against his hand.

"Does he hurt you?" he whispered.

Jo grinned. "No, of course not, silly. It is the most wonderful feeling to know that there is a life inside me and we put it there."

"It is rather wonderful, isn't it?" whispered Rob, still somewhat in awe, as he buried his face against her breast.

****

The celebration tea the next day was held in the schoolroom. The men spent the morning setting up trestles which their wives then loaded with food. One hundred and twenty people sat down to tea, and while they ate they listened to Patrick O'Brien's brass band playing some lively tunes.

"Not bad, are they?" shouted Rob to Jo. "Especially when you consider that they have hardly played together before."

"No; they're quite entertaining. I've told Mr O'Brien that you would be interested in learning to play the ophicleide."

"The what?" exclaimed Rob in some horror.

"The ophicleide."

"It sounds like some dread disease. What is it?"

Jo laughed and pointed to a serpent like instrument in the brass band. "Mr O'Brien was telling me that he was short of ophicleide players for his band and asked me if I would tell him if I knew anyone willing to learn."

"You didn't seriously tell him I would, did you?"

Jo winked at him. "No, not really. You won't have time for brass bands. I want all of your spare time to myself. Does that sound greedy?"

Rob kissed her ear. "No. It sounds highly diverting. When can we leave?"

"Not yet," whispered Jo. "There are speeches."

"Oh dear, and now I don't think I shall be able to concentrate on them at all."

Jo removed her gaze to the platform at the end of the room and stared innocently ahead whilst her hand stroked Rob's thigh beneath the tablecloth. However it was not too long before Rob banished her composure by repeating the gesture to her; and when their eyes met they both fell about laughing, to the general bewilderment of their neighbours.

When the vast mounds of food had been demolished, Edmund Kershaw, one of the allottees with a four acre allotment, strode to the platform and proposed a toast to the prosperity of the Land Plan.

Mr O'Brien, the schoolmaster and newest resident of Lowbands, stood up and drew attention to the difficulties the Land Plan was currently undergoing. The House of Commons Select Committee which had been investigating the company had published its findings at the end of July, and these were a general condemnation of the company in its present constitution. However O'Brien was confident that the Land Plan would either be legalised or altered.

"Those of you who persevere here at Lowbands will succeed in making a living and paying your rent," O'Brien continued. "Such a man as Feargus O'Connor has never existed in any age or clime."

At a signal from O'Brien, his two children stood up and sang "We'll rally around him," a Chartist song about Feargus O'Connor. The chorus was taken up by the whole of the assembled company until it echoed around the rafters.

Jo glanced around the room. All of the allottees seemed to be inspired by the occasion, and there were many eyes suspiciously bright at the end of the chorus.

Edmund Kershaw stood up again and added that they would need to stick at their allotments for three years before they could expect to get full reward for their hard work.

Following these speeches, the tables were cleared away and a quadrille band settled itself on the stage. Rob and Jo did not stay long for the dancing as Jo was now well advanced towards her confinement and subject to extreme tiredness.

Arms entwined, they made their way back to the cottage, the sound of the band echoing on the evening breeze.

"Do you think it will work out all right in the end?" Jo asked. "Will it be legalised?"

Rob shrugged. "I'm not a politician and have no idea how they work. However the plan must be legalised, because I don't dare to think what it would mean to us if it isn't."

"Would we lose our allotment?" Jo asked wide eyed.

Rob squeezed her shoulder. "I shouldn't think it will come to that. But I am worried that no-one seems to be bothered about paying their rent. It will be difficult, I know, but if they don't pay rent I don't see how their tenancies can be protected if there should be any trouble."

"When is the rent due?"

"It must be about now. We have been here twelve months. I don't see how the scheme can continue without the rent income. The land has been mortgaged to buy further settlements. The mortgage must be paid or the land will be repossessed. Miles explained it all to me some months back."

"Have we got the rent money?"

Rob nodded. "We shall manage, never fear, love. I'm determined not to lose my land."

****

If Rob worried about the future of the Land Company he kept his fears to himself after that. Jo worried that her husband worked too hard, leaving little room for play. However, his efforts seemed to be paying off because Rob's allotment produced a series of good crops of beetroot, cauliflower, onions and beans, and they were able to send a steady flow of vegetables to the Birmingham market using the fly boats on the canals from Gloucester.

Jo settled into the last few lazy weeks before her confinement; too large and cumbersome to be of much help to Rob either on the land or in his bed. She began to feel awkward and unlovable, and she couldn't think how Rob could possibly want her in the way that he had before she had become so gross. Rob tried to assuage her fears as best he could, but working from dawn to dark each day left him tired and sometimes too worn to give her the reassurance she needed.

Jo had too much time to think and it was during this period that her earlier suspicions concerning the fate of Liz once more surfaced in her mind. She didn't know what she should do about them; or indeed what she wanted to do about them. When she was with Rob she couldn't believe him capable of any act of violence, but when she was not with him she remembered his determined approach to life, and she recalled the timeous news of Liz's demise. It was really too convenient.

She debated whether to discuss the matter with Miles, but she had seen little of him since her marriage, and they had inevitably grown apart. She thought of talking to her father but decided that she didn't want to burden him with her doubts and suspicions.

She knew only that she loved Rob, and whatever he had done, he had done for her, and therefore he must have her support. If only they could talk about it together, it would surely help, but Rob continually refused to enter into any conversation concerning either Liz or Jenny.

In September Feargus visited Lowbands and issued demands for rent payments. This caused a stir amongst the allottees, most of whom did not have the means to pay, having made no provision throughout their twelve months residence.

Rob tipped out the contents of the crockpot in which he had been saving for the rent and found the six pounds he needed for the half year's rent. There was precious little left, but Rob felt that it would just about suffice for the purchase of seed for the following year. Additionally he hadn't yet sold any of the pigs and they should yield a profit.

Jo ambled from the bedroom.

"Well, will we manage?"

Rob smiled up at her. "Of course we will, and maybe next year there will be something left over for me to buy you a new dress."

Jo kissed the top of his head and then sat down beside him. "I need no new dresses Rob. I have all I need."

"Do you, Jo? Still no regrets?"

Jo smiled. "No regrets, I promise. How could I have, when I have you?"

Rob touched her hand, and leaned toward her. As his mouth moved close to hers they were disturbed by a loud knocking at the door.

Rob lifted her hand to his lips instead, and pushed his chair back. He grinned at her ruefully as he opened the door.

"Margaret, good morning," greeted Rob cheerfully, and then he frowned as he saw Margaret's anxious expression. "What's wrong?" he asked.

Margaret looked beyond him to Jo, sitting heavily at the kitchen table.

"I don't know," she whispered. "Perhaps you should come to my cottage. I have a visitor asking for you."

"For me?" queried Rob. "Then why didn't you bring him here?"

"It isn't a him; it's a her; and she's not in any fit state to walk further."

The colour drained from Rob's cheeks. He pulled the door behind him in an effort to shield Jo from the conversation.

"Where is she?" he whispered hoarsely.

"In my parlour. I didn't know what else to do with her. She has a child with her as well."

Rob turned quickly to see how much if any of this whispered conversation Jo had heard. She had her eyes closed and her hand upon her stomach as if she were in some discomfort.

"I'll be with you in a minute, Margaret," he whispered. "You go on."

Margaret nodded and left quickly, her curiosity unrewarded.

Rob returned to Jo's side, his face pale and grim.

"Are you all right, love?" he asked, putting his hand upon Jo's shoulder.

Jo smiled up at him. "Yes, I'm fine, but you look a little pale. What's the problem?"

"Nothing for you to worry about, love. But I must go with Margaret to sort it all out. I'll be back as quickly as I can."

Jo reached up and kissed his cheek. Rob drew her to her feet and enclosed her in a firm embrace, kissing her neck warmly.

"Remember that I love you, Jo. I want you to know now that whatever I have done, I have done it because I love you."

Jo frowned. "Is there some trouble, Rob?" she demanded, alarmed at his pallor and the tension evident in his expression.

Rob nodded. "I think there may be, love."

Jo put her arms around his neck. "Let me come with you, then."

Rob shook his head regretfully. "No. You have the baby to think of. I may be able to sort it out with no bother. We'll talk later."

She kissed his cheek. "I love you, Rob. Whatever you have done; I love you."

He sought her lips and crushed her to him. "I may remind you of that, later. I'll try not to be too long."

He left quickly and Jo watched through the window as he caught up with Margaret Lee at the front gate. She sighed heavily and sat down at the kitchen table once more, her legs suddenly unable to support her weight.

Her heart felt like lead. Trouble could only mean that someone had found out about Liz. Maybe even now Rob was being arrested by the Peelers. But surely they would have come to his door rather than Margaret Lee's.

She was inexplicably weary. Rob had asked her to stay at home because of the baby, but she knew that she couldn't sit there whilst he might be dragged away to some filthy gaol. She must at least know where he was to be held and what was to happen to him.

She felt the baby stir inside her, and was once more overwhelmed by her love for the child's father. She could not let him go without a fight. Miles would help her to hire the services of a good lawyer. Miles would know what to do; but Jo must be with Rob now to know what was happening to him.

Heavily she stood up and plodded wearily down the garden path toward Margaret Lee's cottage.

She knocked upon the door, and it was some minutes before Margaret opened it.

"I must see Rob," whispered Jo, pushing past Margaret who was totally bemused by the day's happenings. Voices came from the parlour, and Jo hastened toward it, pushing open the door.

Three astonished faces stared at her. A woman, small and dark, her thin body swollen and distorted, lay upon the sofa. A child of about seven cried silently, and Rob stood somewhere between the two, unsure as yet what to do.

Chapter 12

"LIZ?" JO WHISPERED.

Rob nodded silently, his lips as white as his cheeks, his stricken eyes showing signs of the guilt and fear which laboured within him.

Jo stood still, leaning against the door frame, her heart thumping rapidly in her chest, its rhythm echoing in her head as she tried to take in what was happening. Once the numb, shocked sensation had passed, she was conscious of an overwhelming relief that Liz was alive, and Rob was not about to be arrested for her murder. But fast upon the heels of her relief came the knowledge that she could not really call Rob her husband anymore. Jo sighed, knowing that one problem had merely been replaced by another.

She turned to Margaret Lee whose features were agog with curiosity.

"Has Rob introduced you to his sister, Liz, Margaret?" she asked at last.

"His sister?" queried Margaret, unable to rid the doubt from her voice.

"Yes, of course his sister. Shame on you, Margaret if you thought she could be any other."

"Well yes, of course. I'll go and make some tea. I think we could all do with some."

"That would be wonderful, Margaret. While you are doing that I'll make the acquaintance of my new sister-in-law."

Jo closed the door firmly behind Margaret, and stepped toward Liz.

Close to, Jo could see that she was in worse case than had first been evident. There were dark shadows beneath her sunken eyes and her arms were stick thin.

"I hope you hadn't told Margaret anything before I got here," Jo whispered.

Liz shook her head painfully. "No. I don't want to cause any difficulty for Rob. It's just that I had nowhere else to go. I didn't know what to do."

Tears rolled down Liz's emaciated cheeks.

"Then you won't mind being Rob's sister?"

"No, not at all," Liz murmured.

Jo turned to the child. "And you must be Jenny," she said with false confidence.

The child stared at her, refusing to respond.

"Are you hungry, Jenny? You look as if you haven't eaten for a while. Would you like to come to my house and I'll make something for you to eat?"

Jenny looked at her mother who nodded weakly. The child was clearly torn between leaving her mother and the prospect of something to eat. Her clothes were torn and her thin limbs sticking out so that Jo guessed that she and her mother had been travelling for a long time with little food.

Jo took the child's cold skeletal hand in her own and led her out of Margaret's house. Halfway down the path Rob joined them.

"I just wanted to say I'm sorry," he whispered huskily.

Jo smiled weakly and put her hand to his cheek.

"Don't worry. You can have no idea what I thought had happened, and nothing can be as bad as my worst imaginings. We'll survive this, I'm sure."

A gleam of hope registered on Rob's face.

"Do you think so?" he whispered.

She put her arms around his neck and hugged him to her, as far as she was able in her advanced state.

"I can face anything except the prospect of losing you," he murmured against her hair.

"Then you have nothing to fear because I couldn't give you up, Rob. We will find some other way; we have to."

Jo was conscious of the child staring at them curiously, and of Margaret Lee standing at her front door.

"We'll talk later, Rob," she whispered, reluctantly letting go of him and taking the child's hand. "You had best bring Liz to the house as soon as she has the strength to get there. I'll have a meal ready, she obviously hasn't eaten for days, and who can say what that will do for the baby she's carrying. Come, Jenny, let's get something to eat, and then I'll show you how to feed the chickens. Would you like that?"

Jenny nodded. "I'm very hungry. I've had nothing but mouldy bread for ages."

"I'm sure we can do better than that, then. How about some cauliflower with cheese and potatoes. Do you think that will fill a hole?"

"Well I'm not sure whether I like cauliflower, but I do like cheese, and potatoes are all right."

"I love cauliflower. Have you never tried it?"

Jenny shook her head.

"Well in that case you are in for a rare treat," said Jo when they had returned to the cottage and she had started to break up the cauliflower head.

"Would you like to have a wash before you eat?" Jo asked.

Jenny looked at her hands which appeared to have several days grime encrusted on them.

"I suppose I am rather dirty," she said.

Jo smiled. "Just a little. I think you could do with a bath."

"I don't like baths."

"I don't know many little girls who do, but you need one just the same."

"I haven't had a bath for ages."

"No, I expect you've been travelling?"

Jenny nodded silently. "It seems as if we've been travelling for ever," she commented sadly. "Mam hasn't been very well."

"Now that you're here, maybe she'll get better soon."

Jenny shook her head.

"If she dies, what will happen to me?"

Jo halted her chopping in order to look at the child whose face was so serious and so sad.

"I don't suppose that anything will happen to your Mam, but if it did you could always live here with your father."

"Da doesn't love me anymore. He left me and Mam," Jenny said wistfully.

Jo put down her knife and knelt beside the child, so that her face was on a level with Jenny's.

"Your father didn't leave you because he didn't love you, Jenny. I think that he and your mother had some differences, but I know that he has always loved you and missed you."

"If he had loved me, he wouldn't have left."

"It isn't always that simple, Jenny. When he and your mother decided that they couldn't live together anymore, your father had no choice. He didn't want to leave you behind and yet he couldn't take you with him; your mother would have been lonely without you."

"No she wouldn't. She had Uncle George."

"Uncle George?"

"We went to live with him after Da left."

"Oh, I see," said Jo beginning to understand. "And where is Uncle George now?"

Jenny shrugged. "Heaven, I think."

"Oh."

"He didn't like me very much."

"Whatever makes you think that?" asked Jo, her sympathy for Jenny growing by the minute.

"He said I was a cumbrance."

"A cumbrance?" asked Jo, thinking it must be a dialect word.

"Yes. I don't know what it is, but it must be something like a nuisance. I expect you will think I'm a cumbrance too."

Jo smiled and hugged the child to her.

"I don't think I should ever think you are a nuisance, Jenny. It would be very nice to have another girl about the house, to help me and to talk to me. Would you like that?"

Jenny nodded.

"I get lonely sometimes," Jo added. "Your father works very hard on the land, and sometimes I don't see him all day. It will be nice to have a companion, and I shall be glad of some help when the baby comes."

"Mam is having a baby soon. She's big, like you."

Jo nodded. "Do you know when your mother will be having the baby?"

Jenny shrugged. "Any time now, I think. That was why she wanted to get here. She wanted to make sure I had somewhere to go in case she ..." Jenny gulped and swallowed hard. "In case she dies," she finished on a whisper.

"There's no reason to think that your Mam will die, Jenny. Women have babies all the time."

"And sometimes they die."

Jo nodded. "Yes, sometimes they do, but usually because they haven't been properly looked after. We can look after your Mam now, and there is a good midwife at Lowbands."

Jenny nodded. "She isn't very well now, and the baby isn't here yet."

"Well we'll just have to give your Mam the best care we can, won't we Jenny?"

"Yes," sighed Jenny.

Jo levered herself upright after giving Jenny a cuddle, and continued preparing the cauliflower and potatoes. Jenny watched, her eyes following the food wistfully.

"Are you Da's mistress?" she asked at last, breaking the companionable silence which had grown between them.

Jo's hands came to a standstill. "What do you know about mistresses?"

"Mam was Uncle George's mistress. I heard Gran say so."

"What is a mistress?"

"I'm not quite sure. Do you think it is something to do with them not being wed?"

Jo nodded. "It might be, but if that's the case I can't be your Da's mistress, because we are married."

Jo frowned. "Does that mean that he and Mam weren't married?"

Jo sighed, finding it difficult to explain to a seven year old the complications of her parents' relationships.

"No. Your parents were married. But since then they have stopped living together, and so your Da married me, and now I am his wife."

Jenny smiled. "Oh, I see! So now Da has two wives!"

Jo sighed. "Well in a way, I suppose he does. Grown-ups do sometimes get into some very complicated situations, don't they? But while it is all right for you to talk about this to me and to your Mam and Da, it would really be best if you didn't mention these matters to anyone else."

"What matters?"

Jo shrugged. "Well about your Da having two wives and such."

"Why not?"

"Well, it would cause him some problems with the people here. They don't know that he was once married to your Mam."

"Oh, you mean it's got to be a secret?"

Jo nodded. "Yes. Our secret, between you, your Mam and Da and me. No-one else must know."

"I'm very good at keeping secrets."

"Are you? Have you had many?"

Jenny screwed up her eyes and thought hard. "Well, not very many, but I can keep them."

"Good. This is an important secret."

"I won't tell, I promise."

Jo bent and kissed the top of Jenny's head. "It's a long time since I had a friend to share secrets with. Do you have a special friend at home?"

Jenny shook her head. "I did have, in Leicester, but we left there ages ago and I didn't have much time for making friends in London."

"Why was that?"

"I had to help Uncle George with the bobbins."

"Was Uncle George a weaver, then, like you father?"

"Yes. But he made me work more than Da did. It was probably because I was a cumbrance."

"I should think that if you were winding bobbins all day you would have been a great help to Uncle George, and certainly not an encumbrance."

"Will I have to wind bobbins here too?"

Jo smiled. "No. Your Da doesn't do any weaving here. It might be nice if you were to help him with the hoeing sometimes, but I don't think we need you to work too much."

"What shall I do then?"

"I told you; you can help me with the baby when it arrives, and be my friend."

"I don't know anything about babies."

"Well, neither do I," grinned Jo. "I never had any brothers or sisters and this will be my first baby. Do you think that between us we will be able to manage?"

Jenny nodded. "Mam will know what to do. That is if she ..." Again Jenny's voice fell away as she failed to put into words her thoughts and fears.

Jo didn't feel that she should offer too much reassurance. It was as well for the child to be prepared for the worst, although she didn't wish to nurture a lapse into morbidity. Clearly the long journeying without food had taken its toll on Liz and she had certainly appeared frail when Jo had seen her so briefly.

"Where will we sleep?" asked Jenny at last.

Jo frowned. "I'd not thought about it. Maybe when Rob comes back with your mother we can discuss it. We should be able to borrow a mattress and put it in the parlour for you and your mother."

Jenny nodded. "Do you sleep with Da?"

"Yes. Married people usually do sleep together."

"Maybe Mam should sleep with you."

Jo coughed awkwardly. "Well, I don't think the bed is big enough, Jenny. I'm sure your Mam will be quite happy in the parlour with you."

"I expect so. We have been sleeping together since Uncle George died."

At that moment Rob came in, carrying Liz who appeared if anything to be even more frail than Jo had first thought.

"She fainted almost as soon as she left Margaret's house. I shall have to put her on our bed, Jo. Do you mind?"

"No, of course not," Jo replied, opening the bedroom door for him.

Gently Rob laid his burden upon the bed. Liz stirred slightly but immediately fell into the deep sleep of total exhaustion.

Jo dished up the cauliflower and potatoes with cheese sauce and watched as Jenny started to tuck into it. Rob stood behind Jo and put his arms around her.

"We must talk," he whispered.

Jo nodded.

"Jenny, you'll be all right for a few minutes, won't you? Your father and I have something we must do in the garden."

Jenny raised her large grey eyes from her plate.

"Yes, of course."

Rob and Jo walked from the kitchen to the dairy, arms still entwined. He pulled her close to him.

"God knows, Jo, I would have spared you this if I could. I never intended you to be hurt." His voice cracked with emotion.

"I know, Rob," she whispered.

"What are we to do?" Rob cried, his despair evident in his voice and in his face.

Suddenly Jo knew that in this she would have to be his strength and support. She sensed that Rob was weighed down too heavily by guilt and despair to think clearly.

"No-one knows that you had a wife, do they?" Jo asked.

"You told Miles and Jessica, remember?"

Jo bit her lip. "That's true. I can be sure that Miles will not speak of it. I'm less certain of Jessica, but she lives a distance away so can do us no damage."

"You told Miles everything, didn't you? Maybe you would have done better to marry him. He wouldn't have led you into this sort of coil. You could be sure that no-one would turn up claiming to be his wife."

Jo put her fingers over his mouth.

"No. That's true. But neither would he have given me all the months of happiness that we have shared, Rob. No matter what happens now, I cannot regret it."

Rob gazed into her eyes, unable to believe that she could have no regrets.

"I want you to know that I could think of no other way, Jo. When I left at Christmas to go to Leicester, I discovered that Liz was living with her lover in London. Her mother said that she was quite happy without me. Apparently their relationship was one of longstanding. There is even some doubt as to whether Jenny is my child or his. I must have been blind not to have noticed what was going on right in front of my nose!"

"Did it bother you to learn that she was living with another man?" Jo had to know the answer, although she didn't think she could bear it if she discovered that he had come to her still feeling the wounds as a result of losing his wife.

Rob shook his head. "No. I was glad to learn that she was happy and had no need of me. It relieved me of some of the guilt I had been feeling concerning her. I was reasonably certain that she would never come seeking me out, and so I decided to tell you that she was dead."

His voice fell away to a whisper as though he didn't wish to speak the words.

"I'm sorry, Jo. I shouldn't have lied to you. I thought it would mean that we could be together and you would not suffer from the knowledge that our marriage was not a true marriage."

"Oh, Rob, my love. Our marriage is a true one to me. It doesn't matter anymore that it is not lawful. You are, and will always be my husband. To think that you have borne the burden of this knowledge alone for all this time."

"It seemed a small price to pay to keep you with me," he whispered against her ear. "I didn't do it because I wanted to deceive you, Jo. I did it because I wanted you to feel free from any guilt or worry. Can you understand? Can you forgive me?"

"Yes, I understand, Rob. I would not have been able to live without you, and you made it easier for me to live with you. None of it seems important anymore. I don't know why I was so worried about becoming your mistress in the first place. It can make no difference. I love you and must be with you."

Rob buried his face in her hair and squeezed her close to him. "I don't think I could live without your love, Jo."

They held each other in silence for a few minutes.

"What should we do now that Liz has turned up?" Rob whispered.

"We must make sure first of all that no-one suspects her of being your wife. I told Margaret that she was your sister, and I think that everyone will believe that." Jo giggled. "I think she thought Liz was a discarded mistress, don't you? No wonder she was at a loss what to do."

"I don't know how you can laugh, Jo. This is a serious situation. I have committed a crime in marrying you."

Jo looked up to his tortured face and smiled. "Well I don't think bigamy is such a serious crime. I think it will be much easier to live with a bigamist than with a murderer."

"A murderer?"

"There were moments when I wondered whether Liz's death had been a mite too convenient."

Rob stared at her, incredulous. "You mean you thought that I had done away with her?" he gasped.

"I'm sorry, Rob. I knew really that you couldn't have done. However I confess that when I saw her I felt an overwhelming relief that the suspicions that would keep nudging their way into my brain were totally unfounded."

"But I don't understand! Why didn't you ever tell me what you suspected? How could you live with me even thinking that I had killed my wife?"

Jo shrugged, as if it were all of no importance. "I love you," she said simply. "I was concerned only for the burden of guilt under which I thought you suffered."

Rob pulled her roughly to him, his eyes bright with unshed tears.

"My God, Jo; I should be angry with you for even thinking that I could do such a thing. But somehow I can't think beyond the fact that you loved me that much."

"Not loved, Rob; love. I still love you that much; nothing can ever change that."

"We must think of a way out of this, Jo. You are my very life ..."

"Da!" The shrill cry disturbed them. "Da! Mam says the baby's coming!"

Jenny stood at the doorway of the house, wringing her hands in agitation.

"Oh my God," murmured Rob. "This is all we need!"

Jo smiled. "Don't worry! Go and fetch Margaret and Mrs Skinner, the midwife. They will know what to do. And when that is done, see if you can borrow the cart and go to my father. We shall need to borrow a mattress and bedding from him. You can use the ones from my old bed. Tell Father it is an emergency as your sister has arrived unexpectedly."

Rob kissed Jo firmly on the lips. "God knows what I would do without you, love. Thank you for being so understanding and loving."

With that he ran down the garden path towards Margaret's house. Jo plodded heavily to Jenny and took the child's hand. The small fingers trembled and Jenny's thin shoulders shook.

"There's no need to worry, Jenny. Things will turn out all right; you'll see. Let's see how your Mam is, shall we?"

Chapter 13

Liz was in a poor state; her thin body racked with pain which she seemed too frail to withstand. She clutched at the bedpost and stifled a scream.

Jo found a cloth and asked Jenny to go to the pump and fetch a bowl of water. Whilst she was away at this task, Jo set Liz more comfortably on the bed.

"It shouldn't be happening this fast, should it?" Jo enquired.

"I've been having these pains for two days or so now. I don't think it can be much longer."

Jo stared at her. "But how have you coped?"

"Jenny has helped," smiled Liz weakly. "She is a good child, Jo. Will you promise to take care of her for me?"

Jo shook her head. "You'll be able to take care of her yourself in no time."

Liz grasped Jo's hand. "Promise!" she cried.

Jo glanced down at Liz's bony fingers clutching at her own. "Very well, I promise that should the need arise I will look after Jenny."

Liz sighed and let go of Jo's hand.

"She is Rob's child, you know," she whispered.

"Is she? Are you sure? Not that it makes any difference to me, but Rob seems to have some doubts on that score."

"It's not surprising really. I've not been a good wife to him and he was such an innocent. I'm glad he has found you. You will be good for each other."

"What happened to George?" asked Jo, suddenly needing to know what had brought Liz to this.

A look of sadness crossed Liz's features.

"Typhus," she whispered.

"I'm sorry," murmured Jo, not knowing what else to say.

"He was a good man, Jo. We did truly love each other. I should never have married Rob, but you know how it is when you are young," she shrugged.

Jo nodded. Yes, she knew exactly how easy it was to fall in love.

Another contraction swept through Liz and she doubled up in pain. She grasped Jo's wrist in a grip the strength of which surprised Jo.

Jenny arrived with a bowl of water and Jo wiped Liz's brow. Margaret arrived shortly and ushered Jo from the room.

"This is no place for you, with your own time so near," she said firmly.

"But I can help."

"No. It's best that you do not. Mrs Skinner and I will do all that needs to be done. You can look after the child."

Meekly Jo took Jenny's hand and led her from the room. The thin walls of the cottage did nothing to muffle Liz's cries of pain and when Mrs Skinner arrived, Jo took Jenny outside into the sunshine. They threw corn for the chickens; Jenny not altogether certain that they wouldn't bite her. Then they walked through the allotment to Fortey Green, where a couple of horses grazed peacefully.

Jenny, a town girl through and through, was at first reluctant to wander too close to the horses which seemed much larger than they did when pulling coaches in the street.

"Would you like to learn to ride, Jenny?" asked Jo once the child had ventured to pat the mare's body.

"No, I don't think so."

"I could probably arrange it. My father has a farm not far from here and my old pony is still there. She's a lovely old thing, and I'm sure she would be able to take your weight."

Jenny shook her head. "I don't think I need to learn. I expect I'll be going back to Leicester when Mam gets well enough."

Jo was pleased that Jenny was now more optimistic than she had been about her mother's recovery. She only hoped that the optimism was not misplaced. Certainly Liz seemed to think that she would not pull through, but didn't all women have such fears during childbirth? Perhaps nearly all, Jo thought, but she herself had no intention of falling prey to such qualms. She was going to sail through her confinement without any trouble at all; she was determined that it would be so.

The afternoon passed slowly. In the distance Jo saw Rob returning home with the cart, and she and Jenny returned to the cottage.

The baby had been stillborn. Liz was in such a weak state that neither Margaret nor Mrs Skinner held out much hope of her survival.

"Maybe it's for the best," murmured Margaret. "I gather she has no husband to support her."

"He died of the typhus," Jo informed them, anxious that they should not think Liz unwed.

"Well she has no claim on this parish. She'll have to go back to where she came from if she is to get any Relief," said Mrs Skinner.

Jo hadn't considered what Liz would do if she survived her present ordeal. She realised that she had been concentrating her thoughts upon the dilemma in which Liz's arrival had placed Rob and herself. Maybe deep inside her she had not thought that Liz would recover. Quickly she wiped the thought from her brain before it could take root. She couldn't possibly wish for anything other than Liz's quick recovery.

Rob entered the kitchen and was immediately informed of the situation. He and Jo together went to the bedroom to see if there was anything they could do for Liz.

Her eyelids fluttered open as they entered.

"I'm sorry about the baby," murmured Jo.

Liz nodded. "Poor little bastard. Perhaps it's for the best."

"What will you do now, Liz?" Rob enquired.

"Rob! You must give her time to recover before asking what she will do."

Liz smiled. "Don't worry, Rob. I'll not be staying here to embarrass you. You can keep your little love nest. I can see that you are well settled."

"What will you do?" Rob ignored the teasing note in Liz's voice.

"I think I'll return to London. I'm bound to find something I can do there. There are plenty of opportunities for a girl."

Rob's eyes narrowed. "What about Jenny?"

"Ah! There's the rub! It would be very difficult for me to take a child with me. I love her dearly but I cannot keep her. Now that you are about to become a family, can't you take her? She will after all be a sister to your new child."

"Will she?" Rob demanded. "I need to know, Liz."

Liz nodded weakly as if the conversation had worn down her energy.

"Yes, Rob. She is your child, of that I am certain. It was necessary for me to tell George that she was his, otherwise he wouldn't have taken her with me. And indeed she could have been, had she been born a month earlier. I had to change Jenny's birth date to fit in."

"But why, Liz? If you and George were lovers before me, why did you marry me?"

Liz sighed. "It was all a big mistake, Rob. I thought George had left me, and you do have a certain amount of charm, don't you? When I knew that I was expecting, what else could I do but wed you? I couldn't pass off your

201

bastard as George's child, that wouldn't have been playing fair, would it?

"George returned to Leicester two months after our marriage. He concluded that I had found myself in trouble after he had left and had found it necessary to find myself a husband. I didn't disabuse him of the notion. How could I confess that I had been deliberately unfaithful within a month of his departure?"

"So all along you and George were lovers and he believed Jenny was his daughter."

"I didn't intend to be unfaithful to you, Rob. But when you joined the Chartists you seemed to have no time for me or Jenny, and George was very persuasive."

"What happened to him?"

"He's dead," muttered Liz bleakly.

"Typhus," added Jo.

"So now you want me to take Jenny while you go whoring in London?"

Liz winced. "Well, what else is there for me to do? Can you afford to support me, Rob? Can you support two wives as well as your two children? Do you want me to stay? That should cause a few eyebrows to raise."

Jo glanced quickly at the thin wall between the bedroom and the kitchen, thankful that Liz's voice was too weak to carry.

"No, I don't want you to stay, Liz. I wish you had never come here, but I do understand your concern for Jenny and we will take her in. However we will only do so on condition that you don't come here again, and that you have no further claim on me. I don't feel responsible for you anymore, Liz, knowing that you lied and cheated throughout our marriage."

His voice was a harsh whisper, clearly heard by Liz, and understood to the letter.

She sighed. "I promise, Rob. It's fair enough. We have I think each wronged the other and are probably even. As soon as I'm on my feet I'll be on my way."

"That's settled then," said Rob with some satisfaction.

Jo looked from one to the other. "I'll get us something to eat. When did you last eat, Liz?"

"Yesterday we had some stale bread."

"I'll make you a vegetable broth. I don't think it would be wise to overdo it too soon."

"That would be fine, Jo. And thank you for not turning me away. I would have understood if you had done so. I would never have come here if I had known that Rob had taken a new wife. To be honest, I didn't think he was that interested. He seemed quite happy to live a celibate existence. We must have been all wrong for each other."

"I must have come as something of a shock for you, then," responded Jo, wondering whether if she hadn't been there, Liz might have tried to make a fresh start with Rob. She frowned, not wanting to pursue the thought further, as it would inevitably involve consideration of what Rob's response would have been.

She turned quickly and re-entered the kitchen to find that Mrs Skinner had left and Margaret was well advanced with the preparations for supper. Jenny was helping.

"Thank you, Margaret for starting the supper. I don't know what I would have done without you today."

"That's what friends are for, Jo, love. But I should be getting along now. My own menfolk will be wanting their supper."

Jo saw Margaret to the door, and there the older woman seemed suddenly at a loss for words.

"Look, Jo, I don't know what's going on here, and I don't think I want to know. I never have been one to delve into other people's business. If you say that Liz is Rob's sister, then I believe you. God knows I don't want to believe any different. But you will have to do something about the child. She calls that woman Mam, and your Rob, Da, and if that isn't going to cause some gossip, then I don't know what will!"

Jo felt her cheeks flush, wishing that she had thought to tell Jenny not to call her father Da. But how could she have explained it all to a seven year old?

She smiled. "It's easily explained, Margaret. Jenny never knew her real father, he died before she was born. Liz kept house for Rob in Leicester before he came here, and Jenny grew up thinking of him as her father."

Margaret looked doubtful. "Well that's as may be, Jo, but if you take my advice you'll tell the child to call him Uncle Rob."

Jo smiled weakly. "It doesn't sound very credible, does it? Maybe I'll take your advice after all. I'll discuss it with Rob. I wouldn't want anyone to misunderstand the situation."

Margaret nodded, and then as an afterthought, she hugged Jo to her.

"I'm sure things will work out for you. Anyone can see that you were made for each other. He loves you to distraction, and don't you ever believe otherwise."

Jo nodded. "I know, Margaret. And thank you for being our friend. I know we can rely on you."

"That you can. Now I'll be away before my lads start sending out a search party!"

Jo watched her walk down the path, turning at the garden gate to wave. It was one more person in on the secret, and she could but hope that Margaret was as discreet as she said she was.

Jo sighed and returned to the kitchen to find Jenny asleep at the table, a large piece of bread clutched in her hand, but evidently too tired to stay awake long enough to eat it.

Rob took Jo in his arms.

"It's been a long eventful day. Supper is ready. I think then you should turn in. You look exhausted."

Jo smiled. "It has been a strange day. I'm wondering whether tomorrow I shall wake up and find that it was all a dream. It doesn't seem real somehow."

"I wish it were just a dream, but I'm afraid it isn't, love. Unfortunately tomorrow we shall be faced with the same problems. I think though that we are all too tired to talk about them tonight. Shall I put Jenny on the mattress I've put in the parlour? You can sleep there with her."

Jo shook her head. "I want you near me. I need you near me, Rob. Put Jenny in our bed with her mother. We shall sleep in the parlour."

Jo set the table whilst Rob lifted the sleeping child and carried her to the bedroom.

They sat down to a silent supper together. Words now seemed unnecessary, so long as they were together and were each able to take comfort from the physical presence of the other.

****

"What's wrong, Rob? can't you sleep?" Jo asked later after Rob had been tossing and turning for what seemed to be half the night.

"No. But it's hardly surprising, is it?" There was a harsh quality to his voice, almost a touch of disgust.

Jo frowned into the darkness and propped herself up on her elbow to try to see him.

"What's wrong?"

"Come on, Jo; you know what's wrong. You surely don't need me to spell it out."

"Apparently I do. I thought that we had decided that we would see this thing through together. Why then should you be so upset? After all, so far as you are concerned, the situation hasn't changed, has it?"

"What do you mean?"

"Well you knew when you married me that you were not free to do so."

"Yes, but you didn't!"

"That's true, but the fact remains that you were not free, you knew you were not free, and the situation hasn't altered."

"You don't understand at all, Jo, do you?" Rob cried in exasperation.

"No. I can't see how my knowledge of the truth can have any effect on your situation. I've told you that I want to remain with you, surely that should set your mind at rest?"

"How can it, when we are not truly married?"

Jo sighed, thoroughly confused. "I'm sorry, Rob, but I don't understand what the problem is. We've never been truly married and you have always known that. If I'm not going to enact some Greek tragedy, I certainly don't see why you should!"

Rob sighed. "It was different then."

"What was different?" Jo asked, feeling a growing alarm.

"I could live with the knowledge that I had dishonoured you when you thought yourself my legal wife and could live secure in that belief. I'm not sure that I can live with myself now that you know that we are living in sin. I really don't know how you can remain so calm."

"Do you think our living together is sinful?"

Rob shook his head vigorously and drew her to him. "How could it be?"

"Then why should I think so? I don't feel any different about you now than I did before, unless I love you more. And in any case, you never dishonoured me! You made love to me when I had thrown myself at you, and it was the most wonderful thing that has ever happened to me."

"Was it?"

Jo moved to kiss his cheek, and then her lips sought his. "Did you ever have any doubts?"

"Sometimes," he sighed. "Sometimes I think I must have been so selfish to deceive you into marrying me, merely because I couldn't bear to lose you."

"Oh, Rob! You poor silly man! Think back a while. When I came to you and threw myself at you, I knew you couldn't marry me, and yet it made no difference. I still wanted you to love me, and I couldn't have given you up even if you hadn't told me that Liz was dead. I would still have been here, even without your small deception."

"No you wouldn't," he said firmly.

"What makes you say so?"

"I wouldn't have permitted it. I could never have kept you here as my mistress, dishonoured not only in fact, but in name and reputation. Your father wouldn't have been able to face his neighbours and friends, and you would have had no friends. No, Jo; you would not have been here without 'my small deception.' I would sooner have killed myself than bring you to such a state. Why, that would have made you no better than Liz, and doubtless you would have ended up a whore, just like Liz."

"That would have been a much more likely consequence in the scenario you have just painted. For if I couldn't be your mistress, what else would there have been for me? I could not in all honesty marry some upright gentleman, for I had already lost my virginity, remember? And what gentleman seeks a soiled bride? And yet, having known love with you, I couldn't see myself living a totally celibate existence, could you? If I couldn't have you, then what was my life worth anyway? Do you not think that I would have sought some sort of happiness with someone else, maybe anyone else to help me to forget the love I had lost?"

"You paint a bleak picture, Jo. But I don't believe any of it. You would have returned to your father and eventually made a respectable marriage. The small problem of a lack of a maidenhead can be overlooked, you know," he finished bitterly.

Jo bit her lip, recalling that Rob had not been the first with Liz.

"Sometimes I think it would have been better for everyone if I hadn't come here."

"Oh no, Rob; I won't accept that. If you hadn't been here I would have lost my good name to Miles that day, because you wouldn't have been here to stop us from going further than we ought. And then what would my future have been?"

"You would have been happy enough if you hadn't met me."

"Perhaps I should have been contented with Miles, but who wants contentment when there is passion and love such as we have known together?"

Jo found Rob's ear and began to nibble it. Rob groaned and pulled her to him.

"I don't deserve you, Jo."

"Possibly not," she grinned. "But you are stuck with me, so I want to hear no more morbid meanderings. Is that clear?"

"Mm," he murmured deliciously against her breast. "I wish this child of ours would hurry up and be born so that I can get to you again. I'm missing your body so much."

Jo turned toward him, grinning in the darkness. "Well we'll just have to be imaginative, and see what we can do, won't we?"

****

The next morning Liz developed a fever. Jo and Jenny bathed her in order to try to keep down her temperature. Mrs Skinner called and pronounced childbed fever, giving an altogether gloomy prognosis. Margaret arrived and helped Jo with the nursing.

"She's very frail, Jo. I don't much fancy her chances of getting through this. I've seen childbed fever carry off many that are stronger to start with."

"We'll just have to do the best we can, won't we?"

"I suppose it would suit your purpose better if she didn't pull through, wouldn't it?"

Jo looked sharply at Margaret. "I don't know what you could possibly mean by that, Margaret. I want nothing but a full and complete recovery for my sister, and if you think anything else, then you are entirely mistaken."

Margaret grunted.

"Did you talk to Rob about the girl?" she asked.

"The girl?"

"Jenny! Did you talk to Rob about Jenny?"

"What about Jenny?" asked Jo blankly.

Margaret sighed. "About her calling him 'Da'!"

"Oh, that!" Jo shook her head. "No, I haven't spoken to him. So far as I am concerned Jenny can call Rob what she will. If people insist upon putting some peculiar interpretation upon it, then I cannot be held responsible for their imaginings."

"Bravo, Jo!" clapped Rob from the doorway. "I don't know what you are trying to get at, Margaret, but if you value our friendship you will cease these innuendos. If Jenny looks upon me as her father, then I am proud of it. I've no wish to discourage her. She has had little enough love in her life, and I'm prepared to love her as much as any father could."

Margaret shrugged her shoulders. "I was only trying to protect you from gossip, Rob."

"Gossip cannot hurt us, Margaret. Nothing can hurt us so long as we have each other."

Margaret nodded. "I believe you're right at that. Oh well, not a word shall pass my lips; of that you may be sure."

Rob nodded, indicating that the subject was closed. He looked at Liz who was still hot and feverish. She cried out several times in her delirium, and although her words made no sense to those nursing her, Jo couldn't help wondering whether she had been altogether wise in accepting Margaret's help with the nursing. Suppose in her fevered state, Liz started to talk about matters which were best kept quiet?

As the day drew on, Jo became more nervous and agitated, until at last she suggested that she had taken up too much of Margaret's time, and she should be allowed to return to her family to prepare their tea.

Margaret nodded. Her sons, Henry and Thomas, were renowned for their huge appetites, and she had to admit that it was a full-time job trying to keep up with them, not forgetting her husband John, who toiled from dawn to dusk working up a good appetite too.

And so, Jo was left alone with Liz, while Rob took Jenny out with him on to the allotment.

Jo busied herself sponging Liz down, and holding her hand when she felt that this helped. Liz continued to thrash about, but occasionally she became more lucid. Once she opened her eyes and stared at Jo.

"I would have got him back, you know; if you hadn't been here."

Jo nodded and smiled. "I'm sure you would; if I hadn't been here."

Liz sighed. "Oh well, it was worth a try."

"Certainly," agreed Jo equably.

"Does nothing rouse you?"

"Oh, yes. I can be quite passionate when the occasion demands."

"Did he wed you? Properly?"

Jo blushed. "Why do you ask?"

"I just wondered how he had managed to get you. Did you think you were wed?"

"I knew he had a wife, if that's what you are getting at."

"You surprise me. You don't look the type to settle for anything less than marriage."

"How do you know what type I am?"

"Cool and unruffled. A bit of class; I'd say. What is Rob to you? A bit of rough?"

Jo stood up, her cheeks burning with anger. "How dare you speak so about him. There is nothing, absolutely nothing rough about Rob! If you think so then you don't know him at all."

"We lived together for five years. How long have you been together?"

"Not so long in time, but our relationship is altogether on a different level."

"Well yes; I can't deny that," murmured Liz with a sigh. "I'm sorry, Jo. Do get off your high horse and sit down. I didn't mean to be rude. Maybe I'm a bit jealous of your obvious domestic bliss. Maybe I'm just not cut out for that sort of life. Do you think I'm attractive?"

Jo studied her too thin face, sunken eyes and greasy unkempt hair.

"It's difficult to say. It cannot be denied that you are not at your best at present. How do you expect me to judge? And why should I anyway? My opinion of you can't be any more important than yours of me, can it?"

Liz shrugged. "No, I suppose not. I'm just wondering how long it will be before I'm over this and in looks again. I'm not one of those women who bloom when they have a belly full. In fact, most of the time, from the beginning to the end I look a mess. You don't, do you? You are blooming. How I envy you."

"There's no reason why you should. You would soon be dissatisfied with a life like mine."

"Would I? Yes, I suppose I would. I never did like the country, and that's why I refused to come with Rob. Talk about boring! I'd be out of my mind within a week."

They sat in silence for a while.

"Would you like me to get you something to eat? What is it they say; starve a fever, feed a cold! I'm not really trying to starve you to death but I'm never sure when it is good for you to eat. I could make some more vegetable broth for you. Or do you feel up to something more substantial now?"

"Vegetable broth will do nicely, thank you. Where's Jenny? I miss her."

"She's about the allotment with Rob. How will you manage if you go to London without her?"

Liz bit her lip. "I don't know. That will be the hard part. I do love her, you know."

"Then why part with her? Why not take her with you to some more respectable existence?"

A cloud seemed to form in front of Liz's normally clear grey eyes.

"What could I do that is respectable? We'd both end up either in the workhouse or on the streets. I can at least save her from that fate. You see, that's how much I love her. I love her enough to give her up. Rob will be a good father to her. Will you be a good mother?"

Jo shook her head. "She has a mother and I shall not seek to replace her. I will however promise to be her friend, and treat her as I would my own child. Is that good enough?"

Liz smiled. "Couldn't be better."

"I'll get some tea, then."

Jo left the bedroom and busied herself in the kitchen, feeling that she and Liz had reached a good understanding of each other.

Chapter 14

Two weeks elapsed before Liz was fit enough to leave.

"Are you sure you wouldn't like me to stay until your baby is born?" she enquired.

Jo shook her head vigorously. The last person she would need around her would be Rob's wife.

Liz took a tearful farewell of her daughter, and Rob prepared the cart for market. It had been agreed that he should take Liz to Gloucester Railway station before going on to market. The money put aside in the jar for rent had been used to purchase Liz's rail ticket, with sufficient left over for her to establish herself in London. Jo had donated a travelling gown and an evening gown from her premarital wardrobe. Between them they had managed to turn them into a creditable fit for Liz, who was shorter and thinner than Jo.

Jenny had made friends with a little boy who lived on a neighbouring allotment, and once she had recovered from her tears following her mother's departure, she went to play with James.

Jo, watching her skip down the road, marvelled at the resilience of children and decided not to delay making arrangements for Jenny to attend school.

When Rob returned from Gloucester, his face was grim.

"What's the matter, Rob? Didn't you get a good price for the cauliflower?"

He nodded. "We did all right. I've just been worrying where we go from here. You know I had to use the rent money for Liz. Heaven only knows when we shall be able to save enough again."

"Patrick O'Brien is advocating non-payment of the rent," Jo pointed out.

"I know; and I don't like it. It was a mistake engaging him. He's nothing but an agitator. Just look at how he was singing Feargus' praises a few weeks ago, and now he hasn't a good word to say for him. I don't like this rent strike. It isn't fair that we should work the land for nothing. I'm used to paying rent. Everyone here has been paying rent. How can they expect to get away with not paying?"

"Maybe like us, they have used the money for something else."

"Maybe they didn't save enough in the first place. The problem is, do we or don't we join the rent strike?"

"What choice do we have if we don't have the money?" asked Jo.

"Not a lot. We could borrow, although it goes against the grain to do so. Or we could sell up," suggested Rob tentatively.

"Sell up?"

"Yes; sell up. Some of the allotments are already for sale. They can fetch as much as one hundred and twenty pounds."

"That's quite a consideration."

"Yes. That's what I thought. We could cut our losses and we could move back to Leicester or somewhere up north where my weaving skills could earn us a living."

"Is that what you want to do?" whispered Jo, appalled at the prospect of moving from her beloved countryside to some dirty smelly industrial city.

"No, damn it! It's not what I want, but I can't seem to see the way anymore. This is what I want. But how can

I keep it? I'm in danger of losing everything that I hold dear, and I don't know how to stop it happening!"

Jo put her hand to Rob's tormented face. "Oh, Rob, Rob, my love; it cannot be that bad," she soothed. "Let's join Mr O'Brien's rent strike for the moment and if we can recover the rent money we will pay it to Feargus. Does that help? Don't let's sell up. That would be the end of your dreams, wouldn't it? This was your very own dream, Rob, and you've worked hard to achieve it. I won't see you give it up at the first setback. We can come through this together. We can come through anything together!"

Rob hugged her, his anxieties temporarily allayed. She always managed to make light of his problems, and for the thousandth time he thanked God for her. He still couldn't quite believe his good fortune in finding her, but he could never be entirely convinced that something wouldn't happen to disturb their present joy.

Jenny came trundling in, singing a rude ditty which James had apparently taught her.

Rob grinned, and Jo blushed.

"Goodness, Jenny; if you must sing rude songs, you should always make sure there are no ladies present. They are easily shocked you know," smiled Rob.

"What does it mean then?" asked Jenny.

"Well," hesitated Rob," I'm not sure that it means very much, but some of the words are not really very nice."

"Like swearing?"

"Yes. And we don't swear in polite company, do we?"

"You do!"

"I do?"

"Yes. I heard you say damn. That's a swear word isn't it?"

"Well yes. But sometimes I do things I'm not supposed to do."

"Do you?"

"Don't look so surprised! Nobody's perfect!"

"I thought grownups were supposed to be."

"Supposed to be, perhaps, but Jo is the only perfect person I know."

Jenny looked at Jo with awe, as if seeing her in a new light. "I didn't know you were perfect, Jo."

"Neither did I. I think your father has a rosy image of me."

Jenny smiled. "Yes you are all rosy. You have rosy cheeks and you smell like roses."

"Well it's better than smelling of goats. Have you and James been playing with the goats again?"

Jenny sniffed her hands. "Yes. Does it smell so bad?"

"Pretty bad. I think we'd best get the bath tub out, don't you?"

"Oh no! Not another bath! I seem to have done nothing but have baths since I got here."

Rob laughed. "Didn't you know that cleanliness is next to godliness? And I'll let you into a secret, she makes me take baths too!"

Jenny laughed. "Do you really?" she asked Jo.

"Of course!" laughed Jo. "It is one of my imperfections, I'm afraid. I do insist that the people I live with are reasonably clean."

Jenny resigned herself to her fate with good grace.

It was whilst Jo was drawing the water from the copper that she felt the first pain of her labour. She stood up, clutching herself, and at the same time she felt a warm dampness about her legs.

"Oh dear," she murmured, catching her breath.

"What is it?" asked Rob, immediately at her side, his arm supporting her.

"I think the baby is about to arrive."

"I'll go and fetch Margaret and Mrs Skinner," said Rob, his voice a few tones higher than usual as he headed for the door.

"You'll do no such thing, Rob. I have had but one pain and it could be hours yet. Perhaps you could finish getting Jenny's bath ready, and I'll sit in the kitchen and watch."

Rob looked at her doubtfully. "I'd prefer to get Margaret."

"What's the matter, Rob? Are you afraid that you'll end up delivering the child yourself?"

"Of course not!" Rob replied anxiously. "It's just that I don't know what to do."

"Don't worry. You won't have to do anything. And first babies are notoriously slow in coming. It could even be tomorrow before we need Margaret and Mrs Skinner. I'll tell you when I need them."

Rob seemed pacified, but as he prepared Jenny's bath, it was clear that his mind wasn't on his work.

It wasn't long before Jo's pains were following quickly one upon another, and she sent Rob to fetch Margaret and Mrs Skinner, while she and Jenny put together the nightdresses Jo had embroidered for the baby.

It was an easy labour, but Jo, wanting Rob to feel as close as possible to his new child, especially in view of the doubts he had suffered concerning Jenny's parentage, insisted that he stay and hold her hand throughout the confinement.

Margaret and Mrs Skinner were horrified as they had never heard of such a thing. Rob too was alarmed at the prospect, but when Jo told him that she needed him, he knew that he couldn't refuse.

He held her hand and offered words of encouragement, and when his second daughter was born he found the experience so moving that Margaret swore afterwards that he had cried.

When Mrs Skinner had cut the cord and pronounced the baby plump and well, she wrapped the child in a clean towel and handed her to Rob. He stared at his daughter in amazement and held her tiny hand in wonder that he and Jo should have performed this miracle.

When Jo had been tidied up she immediately asked Margaret to fetch Jenny to see her new sister. Jenny had felt rather left out of the proceedings and was prepared to dislike her sister on sight. However when Rob placed the miniature bundle in her arms she too was overcome with wonder and she knew that she would love and protect the little girl for ever.

"What is her name?" asked Jenny.

"Name?" queried Jo and Rob together.

"Well she must have a name," said Jenny sensibly.

Jo laughed. "Of course. It's just that we hadn't thought of any names; we've been so busy."

"What would you like to call her, Jenny?" asked Rob.

"Me? You mean I can choose her name?"

"Well she's your sister. You can choose so long as it isn't anything too outlandish," confirmed Jo.

Jenny studied the baby's face.

"I think she looks like a Lucy."

Jo smiled. "What a delightful name. Lucy she shall be. Now, Rob has held her, and you have held her, can I hold her? I did all the work, after all!"

Jo gently took her daughter from Jenny and held her to her breast. She knew now that no matter what happened in the future she would always have a part of Rob with her. She frowned wondering why such a thought should have occurred to her when they were all so happy together. A shiver ran down her spine, and it was Rob who drew a wrapper round her shoulder, and she smiled at her own stupidity.

****

In March of 1849, Rob and Jo received an unexpected visit from Miles. They had seen little of him since their marriage almost twelve months earlier, and they greeted him warmly.

Jo rushed forward, her hands outstretched, smiling a surprised greeting. Rob followed behind, not quite so eagerly, but nevertheless pleased to see the one person who had helped him more than any other.

Rob watched as Miles took Jo in his arms and kissed both her cheeks. He knew it to be no more than a brotherly gesture, and one which was welcomed and accepted as such by Jo. However he couldn't help but feel a surge of jealousy within him. He knew it to be ridiculous, certain that there was no cause for it, but still he couldn't rid himself of the fear that gripped his heart.

He stepped forward at last, and shook Miles' hand.

"This is an unexpected pleasure, Miles. We quite thought you had forgotten all about us."

"No, Rob; never that. But you know how it is," mumbled Miles, unable to explain that he hadn't had the strength to visit Jo in the early days of her marriage, and as time went on it had become more difficult to bridge the gap that had developed between them.

"You know that you will always be welcome here, Miles," said Jo. "I missed you."

Miles smiled down at her, and Rob couldn't fail to note his wistful expression.

"I missed you too," Miles whispered.

Rob coughed to break the spell which was in danger of holding them.

"You must come in, Miles. Jo will make you some tea, or we have some elderflower wine."

"Thank you, but I can stay for only a short while. I'm on my way to Gloucester to meet the train from Worcester."

Miles appeared unable to take his eyes from Jo's face.

"Well you must at least come and admire our daughter, Lucy."

"Has it really been so long since I last saw you?"

Jo smiled. "Well perhaps not that long. But Lucy is now almost six months old."

Miles grinned mischievously. "So old? Had you forgotten that I can count as well as the next man?" he whispered confidentially to Jo.

Jo blushed. "It is not gentlemanly to pass any comment, Miles. You will embarrass me."

Rob watched this whispered conversation with growing suspicion. Jo appeared so much more lively in Miles' company. He was aware that her social life had taken a downward turn when she had married him, and whereas in the early days he had hoped that their love could provide adequate compensation for this, he was now not so sure.

To see Jo blossoming under the attention of Miles, as she had once blossomed under his own love, caused his heart to lurch wildly within him.

Miles duly admired Lucy; she was indeed a bright happy little girl who had brought much joy to them all.

"Well maybe this time next year I shall be able to show off my own offspring. Jessica and I are to be wed next month. I have called today to invite you to our wedding."

Rob watched Jo closely and noticed how the happy smile was fleetingly replaced by a lost, stricken look. She quickly recovered herself and smiled, although Rob could see that the smile failed to mirror itself in her eyes.

"That's good news, Miles. I hope you'll be very happy," he heard her say.

"I hope so too, Jo. I shall try to be a good husband to Jessica. I don't deserve her."

Neither of them seemed to notice that Miles had taken Jo's hand, but Rob had not missed any detail. He felt like an outsider, superfluous in his own house.

"You will come, won't you?"

Jo shook her head. "I don't think so, Miles. Although I am glad that you have asked us."

Rob stepped forward, no longer content to be an onlooker.

"Why can't we go?" he asked, not knowing what drove him. He had no desire to go.

"What?" asked Jo absently.

"Why can't we go?" he repeated.

"Well, er ... there are several reasons."

"What?" he demanded.

Jo gazed about her, seeking inspiration. "Um ... I don't think I have anything suitable to wear."

"I'll buy you some cloth for a new gown. I wouldn't want anyone to think that I can't afford to clothe my wife."

"Well.. there are the children."

"Children?" asked Miles.

"Rob's sister's little girl, Jenny, lives with us. She's at school at present."

"Oh, I didn't know."

"There's no reason why you should have done."

"Is there any reason why you can't bring her? And Lucy as well, of course," asked Miles.

Jo shook her head mutely, unable to think of any more excuses.

"You should be there. You are Jessica's cousin, after all."

"Yes, I suppose so."

"Look Jo, I don't want to cause you any difficulty. Suppose you talk it over with Rob, and let me know some other time. I'll ride over for your answer next week."

Jo nodded. "Of course," she replied mournfully. "And thank you for thinking of us."

"I have done so often, you know," he murmured, caring not that Rob was still present.

Quickly Miles remounted and Jo and Rob watched him ride away. When he was out of sight, Jo turned mutinously to Rob.

"Why did you do that?" she demanded.

"What?"

"You know what! Make it so that I couldn't refuse!"

"Did you want to?" asked Rob innocently. "I thought that you and Miles were like brother and sister and that you would want to go to his wedding."

Jo hesitated. "Well, yes I would."

"Then why did you make excuses?"

"I wasn't making excuses!"

"Sounded like it to me."

"I only said that I have nothing to wear. That's true! I'm not quite as slim as I was before Lucy was born and none of my gowns fit me properly."

"I know, love. But surely you could trust me to provide you with a gown?"

"How can you? All we have saved is for the rent. You can't afford to buy me some cloth."

"If you need a gown, you shall have a gown. I'll not see my wife in rags!"

"It doesn't matter, Rob! It doesn't matter if I don't go to Miles' wedding. It doesn't matter if I don't have a new gown. Can't you see that? Why are we quarrelling?"

"We are not quarrelling! And I will not have my wife thinking that she cannot go to her cousin's wedding for lack of a gown."

Jo sighed, seeing that it was useless to argue further. "Well, it's for you to decide, Rob. I shall of course do whatever you say in the matter, but I want you to know that I truly don't mind if I do not go to the wedding, and I would rather you didn't spend the rent money on clothing for me."

"Why don't you face the truth, Jo?" sneered Rob. "You don't want to go to the wedding because you don't want to see your former lover married to someone else."

Again Rob didn't know what devil within him drove him to make those hurtful remarks. He was not in any doubt that Miles and Jo had never been lovers, and when he saw the shock written on Jo's white features, he immediately regretted the accusation.

As soon as the words had been uttered, he moved toward her to apologise, but Jo, too astounded and angry to take heed of his conciliatory gesture, struck him.

"How can you say such a thing, when you know that it isn't true?" she cried, her cheeks now red with anger and hurt.

"Oh, I know that it isn't true in fact, but in your heart you have wished to be his lover. I saw the way you looked at each other just now. Admit it, Jo! I'm no good for you. You were born to a better life than I can offer. Here we are scratching a living from a measly four acres; not knowing whether or when we shall be evicted for non-payment of rent; unable to afford decent clothes, and working from dawn to dusk! For what?"

Jo stared at him in growing alarm and dismay, her anger dispersed by the hurt evident in his words.

"You surely cannot think that any of that matters to me? You are what matters, Rob. I chose you and the life you had to offer because I loved you. You didn't force me into it."

"No, but then I had my dreams, didn't I? I didn't realise that I could never be in a position to give you anything. Before long we may not even have a roof over our heads. I never thought that would happen. I believed that all I had to do was work hard and we would always have sufficient for our needs. But we haven't, have we? This is no life for you. You should be with your own kind; people like your father and Jessica and Miles. You shouldn't be here with me, and neither should your daughter. She deserves better than I can give her. Lawfully I can't even give either of you my name!"

"Rob, what are you saying?" Jo whispered.

"I don't know, Jo. But I don't think I can carry on much longer. I have no chance of getting the rent money, and I don't wish to see you and the children homeless. I guess that what I'm saying is, let's call it a day."

"What do you mean?" Jo asked dimly.

"I can't go on with it. The dream is over and it's time to face reality. I want you to go back to your father. I want you to take your rightful place in society."

"What is my rightful place?"

"You are your father's daughter. No blame can attach to you if you have made an unfortunate marriage."

"But I haven't, have I? We discussed this before and decided that I have no place, except with you."

"And I'm saying that there is no place for you with me from now on. I shall have to give up the allotment and return to Leicester. What sort of life can I offer you there?"

"Is it that bad?"

Rob nodded. "It's far worse than anything you can imagine. It is truly no life for you, Jo. You would be stifled by the close quarters, the smells, the lack of fresh air. So too would the children. Ask Jenny if you don't believe me. I couldn't bear to watch you slowly wither and die like a flower that is cut from its roots."

"I didn't know you could be so poetic, Rob."

"There are lots of things you cannot know about me, Jo."

"I still don't know what you are saying to me."

"What I'm saying is that this is the end of the dream. You were a part of that dream for me, and the dream is no more."

"Are you saying that you don't love me anymore?" she demanded quietly.

Rob hesitated. He knew that what he had to do would bring her unhappiness, but he hoped that one day she would get over it. Better that, than to watch her slowly shrivel and die in the poverty which he knew was all he could offer her. At one time he had hoped that matters would have turned out differently, but seeing her with Miles today had brought home to him just exactly what she had given up for his sake.

"Are you?" she repeated.

Slowly he nodded.

"Then say it!" she cried.

He looked at her blankly.

"Tell me you don't love me and maybe then I will believe it!" she demanded.

Rob swallowed and closed his eyes. Trust her to make it difficult for him. Could he bring himself to say the words needed to deny his love?

"I don't love you, Jo," he heard his voice but didn't know how he had framed the words. "I don't love you, Goddamn it!"

He opened his eyes briefly, saw the stricken look upon her face, and closed them again. There was nothing more he could say, so he turned and walked toward his allotment.

"Remember you did this, Rob Berrow!" she called after him. "You did this all by yourself!"

Jo gasped for air and caught her breath on a sob. She became aware that Lucy was crying and Jenny would be home from school soon. She couldn't believe that it was all over. And for what? The cost of a dress to attend Miles' wedding? It was nonsense! It couldn't be true. Why, she and Rob never quarrelled. How could their relationship end after their first quarrel? It must have been a bad dream. She tried to convince herself that she would wake up soon and Rob would be there to comfort her.

Dully she went into the cottage and picked up Lucy, putting her to her breast. She always found feeding the baby relaxing, but on this occasion she felt as if her life was ebbing away with the milk the baby took from her.

Her tired brain could make no sense of it. Rob wanted her to go; he didn't love her anymore. The words echoed around her head until she thought she would go mad.

Jenny arrived home from school.

"What's wrong, Jo?" she asked, immediately aware that all was not well. "Are you ill?"

Jo shook her head. "No. Not ill; just tired."

"Shall I help you with the tea?"

Jo shook her head again. "No. We have to go."

"Go? Go where?"

Jo shrugged. "My father's farm. You know you like it there, Jenny."

"Are we all going, then?"

"Yes."

"How long for?"

"I don't know. Maybe for good."

"But what about our farm?"

"Our farm?"

"Yes. This place, silly!"

"Oh, I see. No, this isn't a farm, Jenny. This is an allotment. It was allotted to Rob, and now we have to leave."

"Why?"

"Because we can't afford to pay the rent and it is better for Rob to sell his interest now rather than be evicted with nothing later."

"But what will we do?"

"You and I and Lucy will go to live with my father."

"But what about Da?"

"He plans to return to Leicester and take up his weaving again."

"I knew this would happen. Every time I get to like where I am, something awful happens and it all comes to an end."

Jo hugged the child to her. "I'm sorry, Jenny. I don't want it to end either, but we don't seem to have any choice. Rob is convinced that we cannot go with him."

"Can't we change his mind?"

"I don't think so."

"Well then, when do we go?"

"Go?"

"To your father's farm," said Jenny as if she were a grownup talking to a child.

"Now, I suppose."

Jo sorted through a change of clothes for each of them and folded them into a basket. She picked up Lucy and wrapped a shawl around her.

"You'll have to help me carry the basket, Jenny," she stated, feeling all the time a great coldness deep within her.

Jenny nodded, taking a handle of the basket. At the front door Jo looked back at the cottage in which so many of her dreams had found fulfilment, still not understanding why it should have ended so suddenly. She sighed and pushed her shoulders back, as if by so doing she could withstand the sorrow.

Slowly she marched out of Lowbands towards Redmarley.

Chapter 15

"IS IT VERY FAR?" ASKED JENNY WEARILY.

"Not to a little girl who once walked all the way from London," said Jo resolutely.

"Well we didn't walk quite all the way," replied Jenny. "Sometimes we rode in carts. But it isn't as far as that, is it? Will we be there soon?"

"Yes, of course," Jo smiled, regretting that she had found so little time to visit her father during the long winter months. He had called at their cottage once or twice, but even those visits had fallen away since the beginning of the year.

Jo heard a horse trotting behind them, and the rumble of cart wheels. She drew Jenny into the side of the road so that they could wait in safety for the vehicle to pass.

Jo kept her eyes to the ground, and was therefore surprised when the cart drew to a halt in front of her.

"Get up, Jo," Rob said.

She looked up at him, his features cold and hard. Her first hope that he had come to take them home withered away as she saw Jenny's mattress and more clothing piled into the cart.

"We can manage on our own," she said mutinously, not wishing to accept his help now that he no longer wanted her.

"You can, but Jenny can't. Come on, be sensible. I'll take you," he said curtly.

Jo looked down at Jenny, who was indeed already tired, her pale strained face showing her confusion.

Jo nodded and handed the baby to Rob. She lifted Jenny up beside her and jumped on to the board herself, holding her arms out silently for the baby.

Rob gazed down at his daughter's sleeping face, almost hidden inside the shawl, and bent to kiss her cheek. The baby stirred but didn't wake. He handed his daughter to Jo.

Silently they drove through the late afternoon to the farm where Jo had been born and lived most of her life. The driveway seemed neglected and Jo noticed that several more fields were lying fallow than was usual. She frowned, but Rob, less familiar with Peter Martin's farming methods, appeared to notice nothing.

At the front door he set them down, unloaded the goods from the cart, leaving them at the door. If he was surprised that no-one, save a dog barking at the back of the house, had noted their arrival, he said nothing.

His heart felt too heavy to notice anything, and he couldn't understand how he had brought this situation upon them. Following the argument with Jo, if that were indeed what it had been, he had walked determinedly about his allotment, trying to shake the cobwebs from his brain. Somewhere he had taken a path not of his choosing. It was almost as if he were being driven by something beyond him.

He had been ready to apologise, half hoping that when he returned to the house she would be there, waiting for him, almost as if nothing had happened. But she had been gone, and the cottage was empty to him already. The fire burned in the kitchen, but a damp chill seemed to have descended upon him.

He had been right then. She did need to return to her own world. It had indeed been too much to expect her to be able to accept the life of poverty he had outlined to her. He must now try to rebuild his own life as best he could without her.

But he felt so weary, and vaguely he wondered whether it would be worth the trouble. Was his life worth rebuilding? What had he got to show for his thirty one years? A daughter whom he had now deserted twice, and a baby who would grow up not knowing her father at all.

Poor Jenny. He hoped she knew that he loved her and would not willingly leave her again. But she would have a better life with Jo than she would with him. He imagined her struggling on her still thin weary legs up the long hill to Redmarley. It was no good. He would have to make sure that she was all right.

And so he had borrowed the cart, thrown in a few items which Jo and Jenny would need, and now here he was, leaving them yet again.

He took Jenny in his arms, his eyes unusually bright.

"I'm sorry to do this to you again, Jenny. Sometimes grownups make a complete mess of their lives, and unfortunately it is the children who suffer. Jo and I will not be living together anymore, and whilst I would dearly love to have you live with me, I don't know where I shall be or how I could work with a little girl to look after. You do understand, don't you? You will be happier here with Jo, but I want you to know that I do love you, and I shall be thinking about you all the time."

Jenny nodded, unwilling to allow her hurt to show. It seemed to her that for as long as she could remember she had been passed from one person to another, each swearing to love her, but in the end leaving her just the same. Well, she wouldn't love anyone else, and then it wouldn't matter. So long as she didn't have to leave Lucy, nothing else would matter.

Jo looked at Rob, her face a careful mask of indifference. She wouldn't show that she cared either; she was beyond that.

"I suppose that you will be in touch sometime, to see how the children are growing up. They will need to know where their father is, and what he is doing."

"Maybe. But maybe a clean break is best. It would only prolong the agony if I remained on the edge of the picture."

Jo felt like asking whose agony would be prolonged, but she didn't do so. Instead she held out a cold hand to him.

"Well, good-bye then, Rob," she whispered, her voice breaking.

Rob gazed blankly at the outstretched hand. He couldn't take it. If he touched her he would have to draw her into his arms, and if he did that he would end up pleading with her. He closed his eyes, imagining the warmth of one last kiss, but it was too much for him. With a stifled groan he turned quickly and reboarded the cart, whipping the horse up to a dangerous gallop, and disappearing down the drive in a cloud of dust.

Jo watched him go with a heavy heart. There seemed nothing more she could do. She turned to the door, wondering anew why no-one had come to investigate their arrival.

Taking Jenny's hand she led her to the back of the house where she knew the kitchen door would be open.

When she entered the kitchen she was surprised to find that the stove was unlit and there was an assortment of dirty dishes about the place. The dog seemed thin as she jumped up to greet her.

Jo bent to stroke her.

"What's the matter, Bess? Where's Father?" she murmured. "And Emily and Hannah?"

Jo sat Jenny down at the table, and placed Lucy in her arms.

"You wait here, love, whilst I see what is going on here."

She went into the parlour, calling to her father and Emily. Her voice seemed to echo around the chilled house.

Satisfied that there was no-one on the ground floor she made her way upstairs, conscious of a muffled sound from the direction of her father's bedroom. She knocked upon his door, and entered. Her father coughed feebly from the bed, and Jo ran to him. The room smelt of sickness and stale odours she preferred not to think about.

"What's wrong, Father? How long have you been like this? Who's looking after you? Why didn't you send for me?" she demanded breathlessly.

Her father smiled weakly. "So many questions, Jo. Always you were the same." He sighed and leaned against the pillows. "But I am glad you're here," he added, reaching for her hand.

"Where's Emily?"

"Her sister fell sick and she went to look after her."

"While you are ill?"

"No, I wasn't ill then. That was in January."

"How long have you been like this?"

"A few days; I can't remember." He coughed again, his whole body caught in the spasm.

"How long have you had the cough?"

"Ah, the cough has been with me for a while, now. Since I caught a chill a couple of months ago."

"Have you seen a physician?"

"Mmm. He gave me some dreadful liquid to cure me, but it has done no good."

"What about Hannah? Where is she?"

"Hannah? She was a flighty piece. I think she has got herself into trouble. I don't know, she hasn't been here for a couple of weeks, and everyone says she has run off with a stable lad from Miles' place."

"So you've been alone like this for a few days?"

Peter Martin nodded.

"Then it's as well that I came."

"Why did you come?"

"It's a long story, Father, and one which I don't feel able to cope with today. I'll tell you all when you are feeling better."

"I feel better already; just knowing that you're here."

Jo smiled. "Good. Now, let's get you cleaned up and some fresh air in here. You may have a cough, but I don't think it can do you any good at all to be breathing in this atmosphere."

She set about opening the windows, changing the bed linen and her father's night shirt, and clearing out the slops.

When she had seen her father well settled, she installed Jenny and Lucy in her old room. Then she fed Bess, who had apparently had nothing for a couple of days, and set about lighting the fire and tidying the kitchen.

At last she went to bed, too exhausted to worry about her own plight. She fell immediately into a deep dreamless sleep.

****

During the next two weeks, Jo worked tirelessly to see to the comfort of her father and her two children. Peter made a quick recovery from the fever which had kept him to his bed, but the cough remained, and Jo couldn't help wondering whether that would be with him always.

It was a bright sunny spring morning with the first hint of summer warmth to come. Peter was settled, well wrapped, before a small fire in the parlour. Jenny was playing outside with Bess, who seemed to have attached herself firmly to the child. Jo had just removed a batch of bread from the oven and now she settled down opposite her father to feed Lucy.

Peter eyed his daughter curiously. He was worried about her. She had been working hard, but that alone couldn't account for her thin drawn appearance, nor the blue circles surrounding her hollow eyes.

He sighed. "You've been here two weeks now, Jo. I've seen nothing of your husband during that time, and I'm wondering when you are going to see fit to talk about what has happened between you."

Jo shrugged her shoulders. "I can't talk about it, Father. I don't understand it; all I know is that it is over between Rob and me."

"Over?"

Jo nodded. "He doesn't love me anymore."

Peter frowned. "Just like that?"

"Yes. Just like that."

"Is there someone else?"

Jo shook her head. "No. I'm sure there isn't. I would have known if there were."

"So when did he stop loving you?"

"I don't know. I didn't know that he had. I thought we were fine; happy. And then suddenly he told me to go away; he didn't want me anymore."

"When was this?"

"The day I came here."

"What happened?"

"Nothing happened! He just told me to go and so I came here. I was shocked. Only the night before we had ..." Her voice drifted away as she recalled the love she thought they had shared on their last night together.

"Come on, Jo! This doesn't make any sense! One day he loves you, and the next he doesn't! I don't believe it. Rob never struck me as being shallow. I could have sworn his was a deep and lasting love, otherwise I would never have agreed to your marriage. Something must have happened for him to send you away."

"No it didn't! We had an argument, that's all. Miles came and invited us to his wedding. I didn't want to go. Rob said I was making excuses."

"Ah," murmured Peter, a glimmer of light appearing before him. "Miles then was the catalyst."

"The what?"

"The catalyst. The cause of it all."

"No, he couldn't have been. He only came to invite us to his wedding."

"And you didn't want to go."

"No, I didn't."

"Why not?"

"Well, I have nothing to wear!"

"I see why Rob thought you were making excuses."

"It isn't an excuse! It's the truth!"

"Ah, but I wonder if Rob would have seen it that way."

"Clearly he did not."

"So Miles turns up, a reminder of your past. A past which, from Rob's point of view, presents a lifestyle which is in contrast to that which he shares with you. If you had married Miles, you wouldn't have had to worry about having nothing to wear. Even if you had stayed with me you would have had no such concerns."

"But I didn't want to marry Miles! I wanted to be with Rob!"

"You know that, and I know that. But how can Rob ever be sure that what little he has to offer means so much more to you than all the rest?"

"I told him! He must know that!"

"You can tell him over and over, every day of your life, but he will still worry that he has brought you down. Believe me, Jo, I know; for did I not suffer the same qualms with your mother?"

"But you never sent her away, telling her that you didn't love her anymore."

"How do you know?"

"Did you?"

"Yes. Once. I was filled with guilt and jealousy and I thought to return her to her old station in life."

"What happened?"

"She refused absolutely to go."

"Even though you told her you didn't love her?"

Peter Martin smiled. "She didn't believe me. She knew I thought the world of her. She knew that I was offering her a way out in case she wanted it. She knew that I would be a broken man if she ever were to leave me. Little did we know then that soon she would be taken from me." He sighed.

"I shouldn't have left him, should I? I should have stood my ground."

"Your mother certainly did."

"But I couldn't stay, believing that he didn't want me."

"Do you believe that? Do you believe that the love he bore you could vanish so quickly?"

"No," she murmured. "No, I can't believe it. We have shared too much together for it all to have been for nothing."

"Has it been very difficult?"

Jo nodded. "We were doing well until Rob's sister came. We had to use the money we had saved for the rent to see her settled. It has been difficult trying to save it again, and Rob thinks we will be evicted."

"This land scheme cannot last, you know. Parliament has declared it illegal and it will be wound up sooner or later."

Jo nodded. "Rob knows that. He believes the only choice is for the allottees to pay their rent, but O'Brien has them all stirred up and no-one is paying. Without the rent income, Feargus O'Connor stands no chance of ever getting the scheme onto a proper footing."

"He was criticised for his accounting methods, you know. Is it wise to put more money in his hands?"

"Rob says that although his methods were criticised there was no question of the money being misused by him. Indeed he has put much of his own money into the scheme and lost it."

Peter nodded. "Yes, I had heard that."

They sat in silence for a while.

"What will you do then?" Peter asked at last.

"I don't know."

"What plans did Rob have, if he thought the allotment was doomed to failure?"

"He talked about selling his interest and returning to Leicester to take up his weaving again."

"Ah, I see."

"What do you mean?"

"He would doubtless have worried about how a well brought up farmer's daughter would take to the teeming slums of Leicester."

Jo frowned. "He said I would wither and die."

Peter nodded. "There you are then. There can be no question of you going to Leicester with him. He is probably right; you could never settle in that environment."

"What choice do I have if I want to be with Rob?"

"Stay here."

"How? We can't afford to stay, and as you have said, the Land Scheme is doomed to failure."

"Yes. But I'm getting to be an old man, Jo. I can no longer cope with my acres. I need someone to help me, and who better than my daughter's husband? The farm will one day belong to you, Jo; and to your sons."

"Are you suggesting that we should stay here with you?"

"No, not exactly," said Peter slowly. "I don't think Rob would accept that. He would consider it to be living off his wife's family, and that would smack of charity to someone like Rob."

"What then?"

"Every girl is entitled to a dowry, isn't she?" .

Jo frowned. "I don't understand."

"When you married Rob, you should have taken a dowry with you. It was something I didn't do at the time because I thought that my motive might have been misunderstood. Rob would certainly not have wanted me to think that he was marrying you for your money!"

"He wasn't!"

"Of course he wasn't. And he has proved it to himself and to me every day since. But nevertheless you should have your dowry in the form of your mother's jewels."

"I don't have any need of jewels! What would I do with them?"

"Well you could sell some to pay the rent."

"Rob would never let me."

"Then you must talk him into it. You managed to talk him into marrying you, didn't you? Surely you can use your powers of persuasion here."

"I could try, I suppose," Jo muttered doubtfully.

"It's not as if you would have to sell them all. One of the brooches should be sufficient to pay the rent for a while, and enable you to buy a dress for Miles' wedding; and a coat for Rob too!"

"Do you think I could do it?"

"Yes, of course you can, child. And at the same time you must tell him that I will make him a full partner in the farm, or pay him day labourer's wages if he would prefer. Either way you must make it clear that I need his help, and that someone must protect your inheritance, and that of my grandchildren."

Jo smiled. "You have an answer for everything, don't you, Father?"

Peter patted her hand. "Not quite everything Jo. Sometimes I wonder why Rob's sister's child should address him as 'Da', but at other times I feel I would rather not know the answer to everything."

Jo kissed his cheek. "It can't make any difference, can it, Father?" she asked anxiously.

"No difference whatsoever. Now, what are you going to do?"

"Saddle my old mare and ride to Lowbands of course. Will you be able to take care of Jenny and Lucy 'til I get back?"

"Of course I will, Jo. I may be old but I'm not yet in my dotage. Give me Lucy and tell Jenny to come in and bring her playmate with her!"

"Thank you, Father."

He winked. "Don't forget the jewels."

"Where are they?"

"I put them in your room this morning."

"You knew all along, didn't you?"

"Not much escapes me, Jo."

****

The cottage at Lowbands had a deserted appearance when Jo arrived there later in the afternoon. She tied her mare at the gate, hoping that Rob had not already carried out his intention to leave. She would never be able to find him in Leicester.

The front door was unlocked and so she walked in. The bedroom door was open. The bedcovers lay in a crumpled heap as if Rob had passed more than one restless night in them. She plucked at the covers, hoping that touching something of his would bring him closer. She sat down upon the bed and pulled the coarse blanket to her cheek. So many happy memories did she have of this room.

She didn't know how long she sat there, alone with her memories, before she became aware that she was alone no longer. He was leaning nonchalantly against the door frame, his lean face unshaven, and his long hair unkempt.

She felt a gnawing ache spread from her breast to her stomach, and she thought she would suffocate, so difficult was it to breathe.

They stared at each other silently, drinking in the memory of that moment. Through bleary bloodshot eyes, Rob thought at first that she was a mirage, a vision conjured up by his overwhelming longing for her. He couldn't move, lest she should vanish in the clouds of his mind.

Jo started to get up.

"Don't move!" he commanded roughly. "Just let me look at you."

His speech was slightly slurred, and Jo realised that he must have been drinking. She smelt the brandy fumes and stared in surprise.

"You've been drinking!" she accused.

Rob blinked and then frowned.

"That's true. I've been drinking now for two whole weeks; seeking oblivion, but it doesn't seem to work."

"Doesn't it?"

He shook his head and then wished he hadn't.

"Wherever I look, there you are still. I don't think I can ever be free of you."

"Me neither," whispered Jo.

Rob frowned again, as if her words were echoing in his brain incomprehensibly.

"What did you say?"

"I said that I could never be free of you either."

Rob blinked again and put his hands to his head.

"That was what I thought you said, but it doesn't make any sense."

"Nothing has made any sense to me for the last two weeks," Jo smiled nervously.

He stared at her, a small measure of hope igniting within him.

"Me neither," he whispered.

"What?"

"I said that nothing makes any sense anymore."

They gazed at each other, the width of the room lying between them, the distance melting away in the warmth that spread through each of them.

Rob stumbled forward, feeling the need to touch her to assure himself that she was real and not some figment of his disordered imagination.

He put out a hand and touched her cheek, kindling his burning need for her and hers for him.

"You are real then," he whispered.

Jo nodded, putting her hand on his and cradling his large calloused palm against her cheek.

When she placed her lips against his palm he drew his hand away quickly with a groan.

"Don't do that, Jo. I'm drunk and not answerable for my actions."

"You don't have to answer to anyone but me," she whispered.

"You and my conscience. Which one will give me the most trouble, do you think?"

"Let me be your conscience and then you will have no problems."

"Why are you here?" he groaned.

"Did you think I came to plague you?"

"You do plague me whether you are here or not. You have no idea what you do to me, Jo."

"I think I do."

"How can you?"

"Because it is the same for me."

"Is it? Do you lie awake each night reliving every moment we were together and wondering where it all went wrong and what you could have done to prevent it? Do you dream of my body beside you and the things that we did together in the secret darkness? Do you, Jo? Do you remember how I could touch you and we would forget everything but our need for each other? Do you relive every kiss we ever shared, the exquisite fulfilment each time we made love? Is that what it is like for you, Jo?"

Jo knew that she could not match his eloquence, and the time had come for action. She stood up and stood close in front of him, so that their bodies almost touched.

"Like this, you mean?" she whispered, standing on tip toe and drawing his mouth down to hers.

With a deep groan his arms crushed her to him and he feasted hungrily upon her kiss. Jo felt as if she would drown as the passion which had of necessity been contained for what seemed like an eternity, burst from her uncontrollably.

Clumsy fingers tore at the buttons of her gown as she pressed herself against him. She could not tell how she became separated from her clothes, and neither did she care so long as she could feel him ever closer to her.

With equally nervous fingers, as if she had never done it before, she unfastened his breeches and without further preamble they were taking their fill of each other, assuaging their need, together in a crescendo of passion which left them both exhausted and breathless.

"Yes, just like that," Rob whispered contentedly against her ear; their bodies still entwined, each reluctant to draw away from the other.

"What shall we do about it?" asked Jo.

"I thought we had just done it," murmured Rob. "There's no turning back, now, love. You know that, don't you? I won't have the strength to let you go again."

"Good. For I don't want to go; ever. This is where I belong."

Her words stilled him and brought him back to reality. He turned from her and swung to the side of the bed, searching for his breeches.

"I have found a buyer for my interest here," he said bitterly. "We cannot stay here."

"Then tell him you have changed your mind."

"I can't. There is no money left for the rent."

"Well, let's just join the rent strike and see what happens."

Rob shook his head. "That would be to lose everything. We would be evicted sooner or later. At least this way I get something for my share. One hundred pounds to be exact."

"We could use my dowry to pay the rent."

"Your dowry? What dowry? I signed no marriage settlement; and neither did I wish to."

"I know. That's why Father didn't draw up a deed when we married. He figured that you would take it the wrong way."

"Well and so I would."

"But not now, Rob, surely? I have the jewels my mother left me, and you don't need to prove to me or anyone else that it is only me you want, and not my money! Can we not sell just one of the jewels to keep our home?"

Rob hesitated. "I know that in your world a dowry is expected. It isn't, where I come from. A man is expected to keep and support his wife."

"Oh, where I come from, too; believe me. But sometimes the husband uses the dowry to invest and increase its worth, and sometimes the wife is allowed to keep her dowry to grant her a little independence from her husband; you know, to purchase a new gown or two; that sort of thing. Little things to keep her happy and comfortable; sometimes the husband borrows from the wife's dowry and settles the debt when times improve. You know; for richer, for poorer and all that."

Rob sighed and put his arm about her shoulder.

"Are you offering me a loan?" he grinned.

"Well, only if you won't take it any other way."

"I won't."

"All right then, it's a loan!" she sighed. "I do charge interest you know," she added wickedly.

"Will I be able to manage it? I hope it's not an extortionate rate."

"It depends upon your point of view. The interest demanded is that you inspire me to passion at least once every night until the capital is repaid. And if you miss a payment you are expected to make up the deficiency."

"Then I shall have to make sure that I never repay the capital, and I look forward to paying interest on the interest. Can I start now?" he asked as he threw his breeches down again and moved toward her.

****

Meanwhile back at the farm, Peter Martin gazed out contentedly into the dusk. He wondered how he was going to feed his granddaughter and decided it was high time she learned to drink cow's milk from a cup.

Epilogue

April 1858

"QUICK! HURRY OR WE'LL BE LATE," CALLED ROB impatiently from his position at the horses' heads.

Jo kissed each of her three daughters and her baby son, and hugged Jenny. Lastly she hugged her father.

"I've no idea where we are going for this mystery tour to celebrate our anniversary, but Rob assures me that we shall be back tomorrow."

"Yes, yes; don't worry, Jo. You know that Jenny and I will manage perfectly well without you both. I expect that Rob has in mind something of a second honeymoon," her father replied, winking in Rob's direction.

Rob grinned. "You could indeed say that. Now, come on Jo."

She jumped up into the phaeton and Rob tugged at the reins expertly, with a crisp order to the horses.

"Just where are we going?" asked Jo, enormously proud of her farmer husband, in his new frock-coat and trousers.

"Somewhere I have wanted to take you this ten years past."

"Where's that?" asked Jo with a frown.

"Church."

"Church?"

"Church."

"But we go to church nearly every Sunday. And today isn't Sunday."

"No."

"Then why?"

They had reached the main road to Gloucester, and Rob drew the horses to a halt.

"So that I can marry you, of course," he whispered, taking her in his arms and giving her a resounding kiss.

"Marry me!" exclaimed Jo. "But there's no need for that, Rob. I am as married as I need to be, and have been this past ten years."

"Don't you want to marry me then?" he asked in mock hurt.

Jo realised what a long way they had travelled together and was proud that he felt so sure of her that he had not needed to ask.

"Oh yes, Rob. But in truth I've never felt anything but married to you," she said seriously.

"I know that, love. But this isn't for us. This is for your father and our children."

"But Father doesn't know about Liz."

"Did you think he couldn't put two and two together then?"

Jo blushed. "Do you think he has known all along?"

Rob nodded. "But of course he has been too much of a gentleman to admit it."

They continued the journey in silence until a thought suddenly struck Jo.

"But Rob; what about Liz? If you have arranged this it can only mean that ..." Her voice trailed away.

"I'm afraid so, love. Do you remember that letter I had about a month ago that you were so inquisitive about?"

Jo nodded. "Yes. For a moment I thought that you had acquired a lady friend. But you said it was from Liz."

Rob sighed. "I lied. It was from a girl called Emma who was apparently a friend of Liz's. She had promised Liz that she would write to me when the end came, and she was fulfilling that promise. Liz, it seems, had some kind of tumour, and she knew that she was dying. I gather that she had specifically asked Emma to write to me, thus clearing the way ahead for us."

"Oh, I'm sorry!" cried Jo.

"Are you? Well, yes, I suppose you would be. However I'm glad that I have been given the opportunity to put right a wrong, and to regularise our union, so to speak. Although it will make no difference to you or me, your father will I know feel happier, and it is bound to make the children's path in life easier."

Jo burst out laughing. "Really, Rob! You sound so pompous! Regularise our union, indeed!"

"Well if you must insist on trying to turn me into a gentleman farmer, you must expect me to sound pompous now and again," he grinned.

A flicker of doubt crossed Jo's face. "Rob, you don't mind moving in with Father, do you?" she asked uncertainly.

Rob pulled on the reins and held her close again.

"No, I don't mind. I can see that your father is becoming lonely in his old age and it will do him good to have his grandchildren about him. Besides, our house is too small for our growing family, and if I don't move us in with your father I shall have to do some more building! In any case, I've worked hard on that farm for the last nine years, I almost feel like a farmer already!"

They kissed, a long tender kiss. Rob pulled apart with a grin.

"Mrs Berrow! If you continue to do that I shall never get you to the church!"

****

The children were in bed; Jenny had cleared away the supper dishes and was sitting by the fire opposite Peter, who gazed absently into the flames.

"I wonder where they are," murmured Jenny.

Peter grinned. "I don't know, but I think they are probably somewhere they should have been ten years ago."

Jenny frowned. "On their honeymoon?"

"Yes. On their honeymoon," agreed Peter, nodding contentedly to himself.

Appendix

The Lion of Freedom (Northern Star 1841)
A Chartist song written by William Cuffay to celebrate the
release of Feargus O'Connor from prison.

The lion of freedom comes from his den,
We'll rally around him again and again,
We'll crown him with laurels our champion to be,
O'Connor, the patriot of sweet liberty.

The pride of the nation, he's noble and brave
He's the terror of tyrants, the friend of the slave,
The bright star of freedom, the noblest of men,
We'll rally around him again and again.

Though proud daring tyrants his body confined,
They never could alter his generous mind;
We'll hail our caged lion, now free from his den,
And we'll rally around him again and again.

Who strove for the patriots? was up night and day?
And saved them from falling to tyrants a prey?
It was Feargus O'Connor was diligent then!
We'll rally around him again and again.

Further information about the Chartist movement and
the Chartist Land Plan can be found on the following
website: www.chartistancestors.co.uk

The following article was written by Mark Crail and provides an interesting and colourful description of the final years of Feargus O'Connor.

The tragic death and magnificent funeral of Feargus O'Connor by Mark Crail

Feargus O'Connor had a powerful presence. Standing 6ft tall in an era when the average man was less than 5ft 6inches, he towered over his contemporaries. Powerfully built, with a voice and speaking style to match, an exuberant personality and an unshakable sense of self belief, he could hardly do otherwise than dominate any public gathering.

For many, O'Connor did more than just lead the Chartist movement; he personified it. Though he rarely held any elected office of importance within Chartism, his opinion carried a weight afforded to no other individual. By turns eloquent and blustering, hard headed and sentimental, he imposed his views on the Chartist movement for nearly 15 years, brooking no rivals and little criticism.

But by the early 1850s, O'Connor's erratic behaviour was exciting concern among his friends and comrades. For years he had worked unrelentingly for the cause under great personal pressure, and he drank heavily, but his behaviour has subsequently been ascribed to the late stages of syphilis. As time went on, his ebullience began to seem increasingly bizarre, manic and even violent.

With hindsight, it has been suggested that the early symptoms of his condition were becoming apparent years earlier – possibly even during the mid-1840s when the failures of the Chartist Land Plan conceivably owed something to O'Connor's intricate and, by his own admission, largely incomprehensible and inexplicably complex structure and operations.

By 1852, however, when he caused such a scene at a London theatre that he was dragged before a magistrates court, his friends were becoming increasingly concerned.

O'Connor took himself off to the United States, where he shocked his hosts with his inappropriate behaviour, asking young women why they did not grow beards, insisting fellow restaurant diners share their wine with him, and telling rambling stories to all who would listen (Reynolds's Newspaper, 30 May 1852). "He sometimes takes a fancy to dishes not to be found in the bill of fare, and fights with the waiters for not attending to his orders."

Smuggled on board a steamer home from New York after its captain proved reluctant to offer him passage, O'Connor's "eccentricities were so offensive that the honourable gentleman was frequently expelled the cabin" (Reynolds's Newspaper, 6 June 1852). Neither did a return to familiar surroundings appear to help.

Making his way to Westminster the day after his return only to find that the House was not sitting, he pushed his way through a crowd watching proceedings in the Court of Exchequer and sat down at the attorneys' table facing the judges, where he interrupted proceedings by "waving and kissing his hand to bench" and began to laugh "in a very hearty style (Reynolds's Newspaper, 6 June 1852).

When the usher was called, O'Connor "hurriedly snatched up his hat, and laughing, and bowing to the bench, took his departure".

His interruptions continued, first in the Court of Common Pleas, then to the Court of Appeal and finally to a court where the Lord Chancellor was sitting, where he again disrupted proceedings by laughing, making loud remarks on the cases in hand, and telling incoherent stories about his trip to America.

Matters came to a head later in the week when O'Connor took his seat in the House of Commons. At one point, Sir Benjamin Hall, Tory MP for Marylebone rose to complain to the Speaker that while he was speaking, O'Connor had "turned round and struck me in the side". O'Connor responded that Hall was his "greatest enemy" and began to offer a garbled defence of the Chartist land company before being ordered by the Speaker to apologise. This O'Connor did. But this time he had gone too far.

Feargus O'Connor's final days

The following day, after a short debate MPs directed the sergeant-at-arms to take O'Connor into custody. Within 24 hours he had been examined by two doctors, declared insane, and at the urging of his sister committed to the Manor House Asylum in Chiswick run by Dr Thomas Harrington Tuke.

O'Connor was by all accounts well cared for at Chiswick, but over time he continued to deteriorate, and by 1855 he had largely lapsed into an unconscious state. However, his sister became alarmed at his physical condition and, overruling objections from O'Connor's nephew Roger, had him moved to her house at 18 Albert-terrace, Notting Hill.

Less than a fortnight later, Feargus O'Connor was dead.

The inquest that followed was acrimonious. O'Connor's sister asserted that he had been stupefied by drink while in Dr Tuke's care; his nephew complained that the state of his uncle's body suggested he had not been cared for since his discharge from the asylum. Both allegations were disputed by medical men called as expert witnesses.

The coroner, Thomas Wakley, diplomatically steered the jury to a verdict of natural death and no blame was attached to either party. In addition to his duties as coroner, Wakley was MP for the strongly radical borough of Finsbury and must have been well acquainted with O'Connor.

It became clear that nothing remained of O'Connor's money. What little there had been had gone on three years of medical care. Indeed, at the close of the inquest, Dr Tuke offered to advance the cost of his funeral "as a mark of respect". A member of the jury added that he too would contribute a sovereign towards the cost (Reynolds's Newspaper, 9 September 1855).

Feargus O'Connor's funeral

The public funeral was set for Monday 4 September. That morning, large numbers met at Finsbury-square and Smithfield, where they formed a procession with banners and flags (Reynolds's Newspaper, 9 September) before moving on to Russell-square and merging with a second contingent and heading for Notting Hill, where O'Connor's body rested at his sister's house.

No doubt through chance rather than political design, the funeral arrangements had been entrusted to a Mr Lovett.

According to Reynolds's Newspaper...

"the cortege consisted of a hearse and four horses, profusely loaded with feathers, two mourning coaches with four horses each, conveying the immediate personal friends of the deceased, and preceded by a board of feathers, borne by porters. A dozen men with wands in their hands walked at the sides of the hearse.

"The procession was formed at the Prince Albert public-house, Notting Hill, and several foreigners carrying a banner which is said to have been present at the Parisian barricades in February, 1848, bearing the inscription 'Liberte, Egalite, Fraternite! Republic Democratique et Sociale!' and another red one, with 'The alliance of the peoples!' conspicuously inscribed thereon."

Reynolds's reporter put the size of the procession itself at around 10,000, "walking four and six abreast", with the whole line of the procession from Russell-square to Notting-hill also "thronged with people". The Times, no friend of O'Connor, put the crowd at 30,000 to 40,000, while some later commentators have suggested as many as 50,000 may have been present.

When the body was brought out, there was a loud cheer. It was followed by O'Connor's nephew Roger, his long-standing friend and lawyer William Prowting Roberts and two other men as chief mourners.

"They started shortly after two o'clock, proceeding through Wesbourne-grove and Harrow-road. An enormous number of people lined the Harrow-road, the crowd becoming denser as the cemetery was approached. At ten minutes past four o'clock the cortege reached the cemetery, and the hearse, with the carriages that followed it, were admitted. The gates were then most injudiciously closed against the vast mass of persons who sought admission, but the crowd, who were greatly irritated, unceremoniously broke them open."

Not all had come to pay their last respects. The following week's paper (Reynolds's Newspaper, 16 September 1855) reported that Thomas Downs of Nelson-street, Shoreditch, had been brought before Hammersmith magistrates for trying to steal a watch from William Murphy as he watched the funeral procession pass along Notting Hill. A second man, George Stichtery "aged 28, a tall, dark, respectably dressed man" was accused of a similar crime at the chapel door. Thomas Scudder, a 14-year-old boy, had stolen a silver watch from a man on the Harrow-road and passed it to another boy who ran off. And James Sullivan, also charged with picking pockets at the cemetery, exacerbated his offence by fighting with the police constable who took him into custody.

Those who had made it in to the chapel, however, were able to take part in a service according to the rites of the Church of England before O'Connor's body was taken to the grave, where thousands had already assembled.

There "Mr W Jones, formerly of Liverpool" delivered an oration in which he lauded O'Connor as "one who had given his life to the cause of liberty and humanity, to the cause of the poor and the oppressed". O'Connor had been the champion of democracy, and now it was for the representatives of the working class who formed that democracy to offer a tribute of gratitude in return.

"Tyrants might call him a demagogue – slaves might call him a madman – the rich might term him a fool, while the indifferent multitude left him to his poverty – yet liberty and humanity would moisten his grave with their tears, and his memory would be enshrined in the hearts of thousands."

As his oration came to an end, a hymn was sung, "and the people quietly dispersed". And so ended the very public life and times of Feargus O'Connor.

Feargus O'Connor. Photograph with kind permission from the University of Nottingham Manuscripts and Special Collections. Reference (Not 1.W8 HOW/W vol. VII, p.421).

Printed in Great Britain
by Amazon